The Cole Hard Truth

By
Eric Dwyer

To Dawn,
I hope you enjoy.
1/18/23

Copyright © 2012 by Eric Dwyer
All rights reserved. No part of this
Document may be reproduced or
transmitted in any form or by any means,
electronic, or otherwise, without prior
Written permission of Eric Dwyer.

This is a work of fiction. Names, characters, businesses, organizations, places and incidents either are the product of the author's imagination or are used fictitiously. Any resemblance to actual persons, living or dead, events, or locales is entirely coincidental.

Editing by Clear Copy Editing
www.clearcopyediting.com

Cover Design by Michael Weber
www.mweberdesign.com

Photo Credit by Eric Dwyer
www.ericdwyer.com
IBSN-13: 978-0-9856273-0-0
ISBN-10: 978-0-985627301
Printed in the United States of America

Available in e-book format

Dedication

This book is dedicated to my wife Marell. Without her encouragement, guidance, and confidence I could never have done it.

For my children Melissa and David.

Acknowledgements

I would like to thank Janice McVety for her support and hard work toward making this book possible.

Wayne Culp for showing me you can never be too kind.

Don Butine for teaching me anything is possible if you put your mind to it.

And the memory of Bill King "Lucky" for being a friend.

Chapter 1

Monday, 9:10 AM

There were two distinct but opposing sounds punctuating the morning silence that August morning. The more prominent sound was the constant ticking of the second hand on the clock, a few feet away. The slow endless rhythm of forward lurch, pause, tick, forward lurch, had already moved the small hand past the nine. The other sound, much more soothing, was the timeless lapping of waves against the sand on the shore of his Englewood Beach home.

Just as he was pouring himself a second cup of the gourmet coffee he only got to enjoy on his few and far between days at home, the doorbell rang.

The doorbell was something he had promised himself would be replaced, ever since he'd moved into the house three years ago. Unfortunately, he hadn't yet had the opportunity to replace the irritating device.

Because of his job and its location, his house in Florida was only used as a vacation getaway. His brief stays were for relaxation and keeping a low profile, but time seemed to fly by. He had gone to great lengths to keep his vacation home a secret, from all but the closest of friends and relatives.

When he moved here permanently, he would have time to do all the small chores he had been putting off, though the doorbell would have to go before then. Once he retired to the house, his first undertaking would be to beef up the security system that was almost nonexistent.

The peacefulness of his morning shattered, he made his way out of the kitchen and down the short hallway toward the front foyer. He intentionally made sure his shoes were clacking loudly on the tile floor in the hallway and entrance foyer. He hoped the person responsible for setting off that intrusive noise would hear him coming, and not push the button again.

As he walked past the innocent-looking box camouflaging the doorbell on the wall, his face twisted in disgust and he shook his fist at it.

Looking ahead he could see a blurred silhouette through the opaque glass of the front entrance. Normally it was his habit to look out the sidelight panel next to the door, to see who was there before opening the house to the outside. For some unknown reason, he didn't this morning — it never even crossed his mind.

He turned the dead bolt and the sound of metal sliding against metal echoed across the hard surfaces of the foyer. He pulled the massive door open to reveal the person standing before him. With the bright morning sun shining in his eyes, there was just an outline of a human figure until he shifted, to position the sun behind the person's head. With the sun blocked, he could see a tall, thin man standing on the welcome mat. He was wearing a brown uniform and holding a package. He had small beads of sweat on his forehead.

"Good morning sir. I have one package for you today," the man said with a small smile as he passed a box to him.

With an apologetic look, the delivery man hesitated, then said, "I'm sorry sir; this package was supposed to be a Saturday delivery. On my way here Saturday, my truck broke down and it was too late to bring another truck. My supervisor has assured me the sender will automatically be refunded the full shipping cost."

"No problem, I wasn't even expecting a package."

The delivery man held his electronic pad out for a signature. The front door was facing directly east, so the bright morning sun was glaring off the plastic surface of the pad. He looked down at the reflective screen trying to see where to sign, but because of the glare on the LCD, it looked blank. So he signed where the screen appeared to be scratched. He had a good-looking signature, but on the electronic display it looked like a child had signed his name.

"Thank you, have a good day," he said as he handed the pad back to the delivery man and stepped back into the house. The door closed with a loud, solid thump. He turned the package around so he could read the label among the half-dozen barcodes that camouflaged the address.

"Senator Irwin Cole" was the addressee.

Senator Cole then looked at the fine print at the top of the address label.

"Last Chance Publishing" was the sender.

The senator carried the package back to the kitchen, giving it a single shake, before laying it on the small counter in the center of the room.

First things first, he thought as he went back to the coffeepot to finish pouring his second cup of coffee. In his mind, nothing could be more important this wonderful morning than having another cup of his favorite morning brew.

As he brought the cup up to his lips he could smell the aroma of the gourmet blend. The steam rising from the cup tickled his nose. He couldn't help himself; he drew in a second round of the pleasing smell. It wasn't often he had time for such simple indulgences, and he was treasuring every moment of it. When working, he was forced to drink the burned blend served in the Capitol building; it was more a chore than a comfort.

The pleasure he felt was apparent in the reflection of his face in the glass door he sat next to. His smile widened. He thought he looked more like a child with a bowl of ice cream than a United States senator.

He took another sip from his cup, and let out a long sigh, as he looked through the huge glass doors across the blue waters of the Gulf of Mexico. He was glad to be separated by at least a thousand miles from Washington D.C. Since last Friday, he and all the other senators were on their summer recess.

He watched his reflection as he approached the sliding glass doors that opened onto the huge covered patio at the back of the house. He slid the door open and stepped through the frame onto the brick pavers that made up the main area of the floor. The outer edges of the patio were wood decking, so the beach sand could fall back home through the cracks between the boards.

The morning sea breeze was blowing lightly against his face as he neared the table next to the ornate, wooden railing of the elevated deck. He peered over the railing at the white sand that was about eight feet below. It was called "sugar sand." Because it was so white, it reflected almost all the heat from the sun, and could be walked on with bare feet in the middle of the day without burning them.

The hot morning sun was on his back, and he could feel the heat burrowing through his shirt. He didn't mind though, because it meant there was no glare. In the afternoon, the sun's blaze across the water and the sand was too strong for the naked eye. He needed sunglasses to look at the sand and surf in the afternoons, but he didn't like the unnatural tint that they added to the sea and sky. Another reason he loved the mornings—no need to distort the true colors nature had chosen to paint itself.

He marveled at how the light was brighter and clearer than usual. It seemed this phenomenon only occurred on vacation days.

He slid a chair from under the table, and then sat with his cup of coffee in hand, gazing across the Gulf. He could barely determine the horizon because the water and sky were almost the same shade of blue. A flock of gulls was skimming effortlessly across the top of the water, grabbing the small minnows that made the surface of the water boil. It looked like invisible raindrops were pelting the smooth, placid water.

The lapping waves and the sound of gulls screeching were the only noises in the morning air. The mechanical ticking of the clock was contained securely inside the walls of the house. He took in a deep breath. The air was heavy, damp, and had the strong scent of sea salt. He could smell the sweetness of blooming flowers blending with the salty air, completing his sense of wellbeing.

The senator had been looking forward to this vacation more than he could ever remember in his life. The press in Washington had been relentless for the last two and a half months. Since the oil spill in the Gulf, his life had been under a magnifying glass. He couldn't step outside his office or his D.C. home without being mobbed by reporters. All the talk shows were competing for his attendance.

For years, he had been an outspoken opponent of opening the Gulf to offshore drilling. Just as he was about to lose this battle to a poor economy and rising oil prices, the disaster happened: a huge oil spill.

Now his fellow senators were stepping forward to denounce the big oil companies. It didn't matter that most of them had been proponents for offshore drilling a few months earlier. His party had pushed him into the spotlight of their newest cause, touting him as "the man who warned of the disaster." It seemed every speech in Washington included a mention of how people should have listened to Senator Cole.

Cole had grown up on the Gulf as the son of a commercial fisherman. As a child, during the summer months, he would help his father on his fishing boat. He regretted not being on the boat with his father the day he was killed. His father had found an abandoned cargo container floating in the water. Knowing it was a hazard to navigation, he tried towing it to shore by himself. The line broke and the container slammed into his father knocking him unconscious into the water. The senator always felt if he had been there that day, he might have been able to do something to save him.

He loved the water and beaches of the west coast of Florida. For him, protecting the waters of the Gulf had come naturally. It wasn't anything political; it was the life he had grown up with that mattered to him. He wanted to make sure that tomorrow's children had the same opportunity to enjoy the clean, clear waters of his childhood.

Now the battle was more about power, greed, and politics rather than preserving nature for the next generation. He knew this was a formula that would spell disaster.

He reached for his cup and raised it to his lips, anticipating his next swallow, only to find his cup empty. He slid back in his chair and headed for the kitchen to get one last cup of coffee before starting his busy day. The instant he opened the sliding glass door the enticing aroma hit his nose and he smiled. *It's the small things in life that give us the most pleasure,* he thought.

The small smile remained on his face as he poured his final cup of brew into the clear glass mug. He raised the mug in the air looking through the glass at the rich dark liquid.

Looking past the cup at the island counter, he noticed the package he had set there a little while earlier. His fantasy morning was over; time to get back to real life. He walked to the counter, grabbed the parcel and shook it, trying to divine the contents. He tilted it on end to rip the packing tape loose, and could feel something heavy slide inside the box. He tugged at the cardboard, but the tape was winning the battle. He opened a drawer and grabbed a sharp knife to slice the tape. It gave way and the flap at the end of the box popped open.

He dumped the box upside down and the contents began sliding toward the open end. A gob of white packing paper fell on the granite surface of the counter. He reached down, removed the paper and inside was a new hardcover book with a red dust jacket. He smiled briefly. He loved reading. Finding time for it though was always a challenge.

He held the new book up and read the title on the shiny jacket:

The Cole Hard Truth
By
Irwin S. Cole

He swallowed hard, shocked, as he stared at the book. His face was frozen in confusion and bewilderment.

"Is this some kind of a joke?" he asked himself in a low whisper.

He pulled the shiny red book jacket back from the front cover of the book and looked at the printing on the book itself. He found a replica of the text on the jacket.

He then looked at the back of the jacket. He was startled when he saw a picture of himself taking up three-quarters of the cover. The picture was definitely him, but he couldn't remember ever being in such a state, let alone posing for a photograph. Not a flattering picture by any means. His usual attractive smile, well-groomed light brown hair, and Hollywood image were all absent. The eyes in the picture were projecting violent rage, instead of the normal warm welcome his bright blue eyes displayed. It depicted a man about to go off the deep end, with several days of whisker growth and unkempt hair. He couldn't remember the last time he hadn't shaved first thing in the morning.

He spun away from the counter and looked out the big sliding glass doors as if the view was going to offer him the answers he needed. The sound of the ticking clock on the wall assaulted his ears louder than usual. He looked up at the clock and thought, "*You're going to follow the path of that damn doorbell.*"

He turned the book back over and opened the cover. The first page was blank. He let out a huge sigh of relief, and thought to himself, *Thank God.*

He wondered who would play a joke like this on him. Then a thought came to him, and he chuckled. He was part of a small group of senators, who constantly played gags on one another. The game was innocent fun to help pass the stress of some of the more demanding days at the Capitol. However, this gag seemed a bit extreme compared to their usual fare. He relaxed slightly as a small grin came to his face.

"Those guys outdid themselves this time," he laughed.

Turning back to the counter, he touched his index finger to his tongue, wetting it, then touched the next page of the book and flipped it over. The next two pages were covered with printed text and looked like any other book he had ever read.

Last Chance Publishing
August 2010

It had an ISBN and a copyright notice. The last line of the page was in bold print.

This is a true story!

He reluctantly turned to the next page of the book, and it was the dedication page.

Dedicated to the memory of my wife, Barbara

His brief smile quickly faded and became a frown. "What kind of sick son-of-a-bitch would do something like that?" he exclaimed out loud.

He moved his thumb to the edge of the pages and let them fan back. He watched as pages of text flipped past his eyes. In his hand was a complete book, cover to cover. He went back to the beginning and turned one more page past the dedication, and in the center of the page was a brief review.

> *Never has a true confession been so compelling. A murderer's mind is opened for all to see, as he reveals the very thoughts that drove him to commit this hideous crime!*
> *--John R. Telling*

The reality of what he was seeing was now starting to sink in. He turned another page and scanned the Table of Contents. His eyes immediately focused on a particular chapter title.

Chapter Four: Today She Dies, page 146

He quickly turned the book to page 146 and began reading.

> *Today is Wednesday, the day I have been working towards for such a long time. The grueling hours and hours of painstaking planning will all come to an end today. Today I kill my wife, Barbara.*

Cole dropped the book on the counter and ran for his bedroom. He rushed into the room and headed for the nightstand beside the bed. He bent, picked up his cell phone and started pressing buttons looking for his contact screen. His shaking hands caused him to hit the wrong buttons.

He stopped, took a deep breath and slowly exhaled, trying to relax. Holding the phone in front of his body until his hands stopped shaking. With his thumb, he hit the cursor and paged down to Barbara's cell number and hit the send button.

It immediately went to her voice mail. "Hello, this is Barbara Cole. I'm unable to answer your call, please leave a message at the tone" — *beep.*

"Barbara, it's me, please call me on my private cell the second you get this message."

It's all right, he thought. She was visiting her mother in New York for a few days. She wasn't due to head down here until tomorrow. They were probably out and about the town. Maybe she didn't have her phone with her, or she had turned it off while they had lunch at some posh restaurant. He had called her yesterday and got her voice mail also, but he left a message saying he was going to be tied up the rest of the day and he would call her Monday. She was good at returning her calls. He shouldn't have to wait long for her to call back and set his mind at ease.

Last week, it had come as a surprise to him when Barbara informed him she was going to spend some time with her mother before coming to Florida for summer recess. He didn't question her about it, but as far as he knew, she hadn't visited her mother in years.

With the recent loss of Barbara's father a few months ago, he was glad to see that she was finally getting back together with her mother. After all, he and her mother were now the only family that Barbara had left.

He scrolled through the contact numbers in his phone again, stopping on "Helen," Barbara's mother.

"Helen, it's Irwin, how are you doing today?"

"Irwin, well hello, I'm fine. It's been so long since we talked. I enjoyed my visit with Barbara. I can't remember ever having such a wonderful time."

"I'm sure Barbara feels the same. I know it has been a while since you two have spent time together. Is she close by? I need to speak to her if you don't mind."

"Well, no Irwin, she left Saturday as planned. Is there anything wrong?"

Cole fell silent, then finally spoke. "No, I was under the impression she was staying until Tuesday — tomorrow — then flying straight to Florida."

"Irwin, try the town house in Tyson Corner. She's probably there getting ready for her trip to Florida. As far as I know her plan had always been to leave here on Saturday."

"Ok Helen, I'll call her there. Take care of yourself. Bye."

He watched as the text scrolled down the small screen. When he came to the entry for "Home," he stopped and stared at the word, his mind working. His stomach felt sick. Finally, he pressed the send button and put the phone up to his ear with his trembling hand, trying to hold it steady.

He heard the ring once, twice, three times, and then the recorder came on: "Hello; you have reached the Coles. We cannot answer your call so please leave a message at the tone" — *beep*.

"Barbara, it's me, please call me on my private cell the second you get this message."

Under normal circumstances, he wouldn't have been concerned because Barbara led a full life of her own, aside from being a senator's wife. Her schedule was usually teeming with appointments as much as his. She was involved in numerous charities and volunteered three times a week at a shelter for single mothers. Between his and her busy schedules, it wasn't unusual for them to be apart for several days, or even a week at a time.

This time though, he was worried. The damn book that he supposedly wrote but knew nothing about made him uneasy, and for the first time ever, he feared for the safety of his wife.

He decided to call his assistant, Miles, in Washington. Miles had been with him since he had volunteered as an intern during his college years.

Miles was a detail man, and in fact he had a photographic memory. Unfortunately, he also had a stutter. This caused him to be slow at answering questions and providing verbal information. His social skills were almost non-existent as from an early age he had retreated from people who laughed at his stutter. Miles was twenty-six, but looked and acted more like a teenager to anyone who met him for the first time. All this combined to make him appear slow-witted, which wasn't the case.

He had felt sorry for him and gave him a chance to work in his office and prove himself. It was a decision he never regretted. Miles had proved to be extremely loyal as well as efficient and highly competent.

As always, Miles answered on the second ring. "Yes Senator Cole, this is Miles. How's your vacation going?"

"Miles, I need your help locating Mrs. Cole. I haven't been able to reach her this morning."

"I-I-I think she is in N-New York City visiting her mother, s-s-sir."

"That's what I thought also, but according to her mother, she left there on Saturday. I called both her private cell and the town house phone. There's no answer at either one. You know Miles, she never goes anywhere without her phone. I thought for sure she said she was coming to Florida from New York on Tuesday."

"Y-Y-Yes sir, that's my understanding. She's probably at one of her f-fund raising events. You know how she hates to m-miss any of those f-f-functions."

"I thought of that, but you know she would have let us know if she changed her plans. She never changes her schedule without informing us."

"Yes sir, y-y-you're right, but maybe she is having pho-phone problems. These new phones haven't been tested thoroughly yet."

"That still wouldn't explain why she left New York on Saturday. I'm concerned for her safety. I received a disturbing package here in Florida today.

"P-p-package? I'm con-confused. Wha-what kind of package? What can I do here senator to h-help you?"

"Don't worry about the package. I need you to check at the three places she volunteers and ask whether anyone has seen her. If you don't locate her, contact Doug Mackey and see whether he can help you find her. Be sure to tell him to keep this under wraps. With all the publicity lately, I don't need this getting out to the press."

"I understand Senator; we will find her before you know it. B-By the way, we received a shipment of six boxes in the o-o-office today. I haven't had a chance to open them yet, but they are from a pub-publishing company. Were you expecting them?"

Cole froze. *No, this can't be happening!* Then he asked quietly, "Last Chance Publishing Company?"

"Y-Y-Yes, Senator, I believe that's what the labels said. Should I open them?"

"No, under no circumstances should they be opened. Lock the boxes in the back closet right away. Do you understand me, Miles?"

"Yes sir, I-I-I will move them right now, then I'll try to locate Mrs. Cole."

"Good job Miles. Contact me immediately if you have any news about Mrs. Cole. I will be waiting to hear from you."

The senator tapped his left hand against the top of the nightstand. *Six more boxes from Last Chance Publishing? What the hell is going on here?*

He looked at the picture standing upright on the nightstand and his mouth turned up at the corners. Their wedding picture was taken at the island home of Barbara's father. They were married there nine years ago after a brief courtship. He picked up the framed picture and brought it closer to his eyes. He smiled at how beautiful she was in her wedding gown. Her long brown hair fanned out behind her in the breeze. She was a slender, elegant young woman standing next to her adoring new husband. He whispered, "You haven't changed at all, my love."

He went back out to the kitchen and grabbed the book off the counter. He stared at the cover as he carried it out in front of him on his way to his study. Sitting at his desk, he opened the book to begin reading. But his mind was full of questions and he gazed out the window toward the beach, wondering why Barbara had told him she wasn't leaving New York until tomorrow.

He tried to remember everything that had happened over the last couple of weeks, anything that might help, but the only thing that came to mind was that work had been hell lately. He realized that he had hardly seen or talked to Barbara in the last month. He had been so busy with the press frenzy that he had ignored her. When he did see her, she seemed fine and understood what he was going through. She had commented on how glad she would be when the recess started, and they could spend some time together alone in Florida.

Maybe she had left New York early because she was having problems with her mother. It had been a long time since they had spent any time together. All he knew about the situation was that since her parents divorced years ago, Barbara and her mother had been at odds with each other. He had asked her what the problem was shortly after they were married, but she refused to discuss the details. He had never asked her about it again. He supposed someday she would be ready to talk about it.

He picked up the book from his desk and began reading at page one. He was determined to figure out what was going on. His wife's life might depend on it.

* * *

Barbara Cole was pacing in a small room. She was beginning to think she had made the biggest mistake of her life.

Chapter 2

Monday, 12:15 PM

Lieutenant Doug Mackey was sitting behind his desk at the Capitol Police building, which was where he spent most of his time at work. He'd been working for the last five years as a coordinator and liaison for the Capitol police, FBI, and Secret Service. His primary responsibility was to keep information flowing back and forth amongst the various organizations. The idea was to allow the three organizations to operate as one. Everyone involved knew it would never happen, but after 9/11 it was the plan and no one was prepared to voice a negative comment. One good thing that came out of the collaboration was that each agency had a contact person like Mackey. The different agency liaisons had become close friends, despite their agency's various philosophies, policies and procedures. Their friendship was what kept the information flowing.

Today, like most days, he wondered whether leaving his job as a detective with the D. C. police had been a smart decision. The money was good, and his wife liked the idea of him not being in harm's way, but he missed not being a detective. He had been good at it. By most peoples' estimates, he was the best. Now, he was as far from police work as he could get and still carry a badge. Hell, he hadn't carried a gun in three years.

Mackey and Cole had become good friends after the senator won his election and moved to Washington several years ago. Mackey first met Cole after an official business lunch the new junior senator had attended. He was with several senior senators in a restaurant down the street from the Capitol building.

Midway through their lunch, a man approached their table and began screaming obscenities at the startled group. The man then reached inside his jacket and began fumbling for something. Young Cole jumped up, wrestled the man to the floor, and pinned his arms behind his back until the police arrived a few minutes later.

Mackey was the head detective and interviewed all the witnesses. The only thing they found in the man's jacket was a picture of his son, who had been killed in Iraq.

The police wanted to press charges against the man, but Cole insisted that he be let go. Mackey had worked with many politicians, but this new senator from Florida impressed him. He was nothing like the type he was used to. The two of them became very close, having lunch together and stopping in the evenings for a cocktail to vent about their days. Their wives, who had many common interests, also became close friends.

The phone rang. He picked it up and barked his usual greeting. "Mackey."

"Lieutenant Mackey, this is Miles Connor in S-S-Senator Cole's office."

"Yes, Miles how are you doing today? Is your boss lying on some white-sand beach in Florida getting sunburned?"

"Y-Y-Yes sir, he is in Florida at the beach house."

"Well, he deserves a break what with everything he has been through lately. What can I do for you, Miles?"

"We've been u-u-unable to locate Mrs. Cole."

"Barbara? I'm not sure I understand what you mean, Miles."

"The senator called me this morning and said he had tried calling M-M-Mrs. Cole and he couldn't get hold of her. She was supposed to be at her mother's in New York City u-u-until Tuesday and then she was flying to Florida to join him there. I-I-I just got off the phone with h-h-her mother, and she said Mrs. Cole left Saturday morning. There's n-n-no answer on her cell phone or at the town house."

"You know Miles, Barbara's an independent woman with a life of her own."

"I know sir, but she always lets us know where she's going. The senator is worried for her safety and asked me to contact you, to see whether you could help locate her. H-H-He asked that you keep a low profile so the press doesn't find out."

"I'll start right away. No one will know anything about it."

"Thank you M-M-Mr. Mackey."

He hung up the phone, and dialed his home number.

"Hi honey, do you have any idea where Barbara Cole is now?"

"Yes, she's at her mother's apartment in New York and then she's flying to Florida tomorrow morning to join Irwin. Why?"

"She left her mother's on Saturday, and no one has heard from her."

"Oh my, that doesn't sound like Barbara. I hope everything is all right."

"I'm sure it will all be fine, honey. Don't worry. I'm going to track her down and I'll call you when I find her."

"Doug, I'm worried. This isn't like Barbara at all. Please try to call me soon. I don't know what I'd do if anything happened to her."

"It will probably end up as just a miscommunication of plans. Don't worry, honey. I love you, bye."

Mackey began tapping keys on his computer. One thing about this job was he had almost unlimited access to the national databases. He would first check the airline flights out of New York.

Bingo. Barbara Cole, Delta flight 1141 from LaGuardia to Southwest Florida Regional. She had a direct flight booked for Saturday August 7th at 11:45 AM, arriving at 3:15 PM. He dialed Delta to verify if she had been on the flight. After several minutes the person on the other end said, "Yes sir, she was definitely on the flight."

"Thank you." Mackey hung up the phone. He leaned back in his chair and looked up at the ceiling in his office. He knew every little yellow stain in the plaster by heart. He had spent a lot of time staring at this ceiling. Usually, it helped him find the answers he needed, but this time the ceiling wasn't giving up any information.

He punched more keys on his computer keyboard and got the telephone number for security at Southwest Florida Regional Airport. He dialed the number and explained who he was, and that he needed information about a flight on Saturday. The person at the other end assured him he would find the information and call him right back.

A few minutes later his phone rang. It was the head of security from the airport. "Lieutenant Mackey, we checked all the video we had for that period on Saturday, and nothing seemed unusual. If you send us a picture, we can review the videos and see if we can identify your person."

"So, no disturbances anywhere in the airport?"

"No, everything seemed normal. I was on duty myself, and it was a quiet day for a change."

"I bet you don't get too many of those. Thanks for your help. I'll let you know about the picture; it's a sensitive concern right now."

"I understand."

Mackey looked up the number for the Lee County Sheriff's office and called them next. The duty desk officer informed him nothing unusual was reported in the area around the airport on Saturday.

It wasn't looking good at all. Mackey had been in the business a long time, and his gut was telling him something was awry. He knew from this point on, every step was going to get more and more difficult. Mackey's mind was spinning as he dreaded his next call, to Cole's cell phone.

* * *

The senator looked up from the book with a small glimmer of hope as he checked which of his phones was ringing. He was disappointed when he saw that it was his regular cell phone.

"Hello."

"Irwin. It's Mackey."

"Hi Mackey, I assume Miles called you. Have you located Barbara?"

"I'm sorry Irwin. She did leave New York on Saturday morning and arrived at Southwest Florida Regional that afternoon. Then we don't know what happened. There wasn't any kind of disturbance at the airport or in the surrounding area. Is there anything you can tell me that might help?"

"Saturday? I wasn't expecting her here until tomorrow. She was going to call me today and give me her flight information so I could pick her up at the airport."

"Irwin, do you have any idea why she would leave early and not tell you?"

That's the question I've been asking myself all morning. "No, that's not like her at all. You know Barbara; she wouldn't do anything like that. Not without letting me know first."

"When's the last time you talked to her?"

"She left me a message Friday night saying she had arrived at her mother's that afternoon. She said she would call me either Saturday or Sunday and let me know how it was going. I didn't hear from her on Saturday so I called her yesterday and got her voice mail. I was on my way to see an old friend so I told her I would talk to her today and get her flight information. I was trying to give her as much time alone with her mother as possible."

Mackey cleared his throat. "Irwin, we have to get the FBI involved with this right away. In cases like this just minutes can create a difference in the outcome, never mind days."

Cole looked down at the book on the desk in front of him, and his stomach did a flip flop. The book outlined the planning and killing of his wife and it was supposedly written as a confession by him. How would he ever explain this to the FBI? That was the last bunch he needed probing his life right now!

He remained silent as he thought about the consequences.

"Irwin, did you hear me? We have to contact the FBI."

Finally, he said, "Yes, whatever you think is best, Mackey. I just want to find Barbara."

"I'll call a friend at the FBI and ask him to try to keep a lid on it, just in case it's a miscommunication, but I can't promise anything. The more people involved the greater chance for a leak, but the important thing is to find Barbara. Listen buddy, before I place the call I need to ask you if there were any kind of problems between you and Barbara."

"What problems, Mackey? What do you mean?"

"Are you and Barbara having any kind of marital concerns?"

"No, you know how happy we are."

"Are there any, um—any affairs going on?"

"No! That's ridiculous. We're happy with one another and our marriage. You know that better than anyone, you're my best friend."

"I know Irwin, but these, and many more questions like them are going to be asked. You need to understand that."

"Please, just find Barbara, Mackey."

"I will do everything I can. In the meantime, why don't you check around the house. Look through Barbara's things for any clues that may help."

"I will, but as you know, we don't keep much down here yet."

"Anything you can find may help. With your permission, I'll do a search on her cell phone signal to see whether we can locate her that way."

"Okay. Anything that will help find her."

As Cole ended the call, he wondered whether she even had her old cell phone with her; the one that could be traced.

* * *

Mackey hung up the phone and again looked up to the ceiling for answers. As before, there were none; just the same yellow stains on the plaster. He moved his attention to the harsh fluorescent lights hanging from the ceiling. He noticed idly how the ends of the bulbs were all turning dark, and he could see the cycling of the gas in the tubes.

He tapped his shoe against the leg of his desk as he planned his next conversation. This was the first police work he had been involved with in several years, and he could feel the adrenaline pumping through his system. For a moment, he was enjoying the feeling until he reminded himself it was his best friend's wife at the center of it all. He stared at the telephone for several moments and finally reached over and pulled it closer.

Pausing again, he thought about his friends' marriage. They did seem happy, as Irwin had stated. The only thing Mackey wondered about was . . . something he had thought about several times in the past. The time they were separated always seemed excessive. Mackey couldn't remember the last time he was away from his wife for more than a day or so. Finally, he came to the same conclusion that he had before. He assumed it came with being in politics and Irwin and Barbara were okay with it.

He dialed the number of his good friend at the FBI, and the phone was answered on the second ring.

"Good morning, Mr. Anderson's office. How may I help you?"

"Hello, Mrs. Blake. It's Mackey. Is he available?"

"Yes, Lieutenant Mackey, I'll put you right through."

"Mackey, what's up? Are you buying lunch? I believe it's your turn."

"Not today, William. We have a situation. Senator Irwin Cole's wife is missing."

"Damn. Missing? What do you mean? How? When?"

"She was in New York City visiting her mother and was supposed to be there until tomorrow. Instead, she left Saturday on a Delta flight for Florida to join the senator at their beach home. She arrived at the airport, and that's the last place I've been able to trace her."

"Why did she leave early?"

"That's the million-dollar question, and I don't have the answer. William, I know I don't need to remind you that Senator Cole is in the fast lane now. Rumor has it he is the party favorite for their next presidential hopeful. We need to try to keep this under wraps. The press will have a field day with this. Plus, we're not sure whether the situation is serious at this point or not."

"Mackey, I understand, but you and I know these wife things always get messy. The dirty laundry just pours out of the closet."

"I've known them for almost a decade, and they are the perfect couple — if there is such a thing."

"I hope for everyone's sake you're right, Mackey. Don't worry. I'll pick the people for the case myself, but we both know the longer this drags on, the harder it will be to keep it under wraps."

"I'll send you everything I have so far."

Mackey hung up the phone and sat back in his chair. He forced himself not to look up at the ceiling. He sent an e-mail and attached all the information he had collected. Next, he called Miles at Senator Cole's office, to bring him up to date on what he had discovered so far. Plus, he had a few more questions.

"Miles, one last thing I need to ask you. You are probably the person closest to the senator and his wife. Have you noticed anything lately that might have instigated this situation?"

Miles began stuttering; "W-W-What do you mean Li-Lieutenant Mackey?"

"You know, anything unusual. Like mood swings or little subtle changes in the senator's or Barbara's habits maybe?"

"N-No, they s-s-seem the s-s-same as always. As you know, the s-s-senator is under a lot of pressure lately with this oil s-s-spill."

"How has he reacted to all the pressure?"

"I-I-I think probably better than most. He's been m-more to himself. M-M-Maybe a little short-tempered, but how can you b-b-blame him, with the press after him night and day."

"What about others in their lives? Maybe a new person or someone from their past who has shown up lately?"

A long silence on the phone and finally Miles said, "N-n-no sir, n-n-no one new in their lives."

"Thanks Miles, I'll let you know when I hear anything else."

Miles hung up the phone and removed one of the new books from the box that he had opened and scanned the pages.

Chapter 3

Monday, 6:05 PM

Cole had been reading for hours and couldn't believe what was printed on the pages in front of him. Every detail of the planning process had been meticulously presented. However, it seemed the more he read, the more confusing the book became.

The details of his life were flawless. How could anyone know such personal things? Even his most private moments were revealed. A shiver ran through his body as he glanced around the room. Was he being watched now?

Many of the occurrences on the pages in front of him happened when Barbara and he were alone. How could anyone else possibly know what had transpired between them? Still, it wasn't quite right. The thoughts and feelings in the narration weren't his. He was sure of that. No one was capable of reading his thoughts. He turned the page to arrive at that hateful page 146. He read the first lines again.

Today is Wednesday, the day I have been working towards for such a long time. The grueling hours and hours of painstaking planning will all come to an end today. Today, I kill my wife Barbara!

Cole felt a lump in his throat, and his stomach churned. Tears formed in his eyes, fogging his vision, as he faced the prospect of reading the chapter. The words in front of him were going to be horrid, but he knew there had to be clues to what was happening to him hidden in these pages.

He was interrupted once again by the obnoxious doorbell. So far, answering that damn door today had not been a good thing. He reluctantly slid back his chair and glanced at the desk clock. It was 6:10 PM and he wondered who could be at the door. As he entered the hall, the bell rang again, assaulting his ears like clanging cymbals.

"I'm coming!" he yelled down the hall, hoping they wouldn't push that damn button again before he could reach the door. As he approached the front entrance, he saw a distorted shadow of a woman through the opaque glass. He pulled the door open. "May I help you?" He didn't recognize her, and she wasn't wearing a brown uniform.

"Good afternoon, Senator Cole."

He looked at her wordlessly with a small guarded smile.

She was an attractive young woman in a dark business suit. Her face betrayed no emotion. He couldn't believe the press had found him at his vacation home, especially now. *Enough,* he thought. He was sure he was going to have to get rude with this young woman.

She reached into her pocket, pulled out a folded wallet, and opened it in front of him. "My name is Melissa Martin. I'm an agent with the FBI. May I come in please?"

It took a few seconds for her words to register. Surprised at how quickly things were occurring, he found himself speechless. He was going to have to change his demeanor to handle these new circumstances.

He cleared his throat, making a welcoming gesture with his arm. "Yes, I'm sorry. Please come in."

The moment was awkwardly quiet as he tried to recover from the surprise visit. Mackey had said minutes count, but he wasn't expecting someone at his door this quickly.

He led her down the long, tiled hallway toward his study, where it was customary for him to receive guests. As he approached the doorway to the room, he saw the book lying on his desk. He came to an abrupt stop, causing agent Martin to run into him.

When he turned he was startled to find her face about six inches from his. "Actually, we'll be more comfortable in here." He raised his arm and led her into the living room. She followed him in with a quizzical expression.

"Please sit down—Miss Martin, is it?" he asked after glancing down at her left hand.

"Yes," she replied with a small smile as she sat on the sofa, "but Agent Martin will do."

Cole sat opposite her in a big leather chair. "May I get you something Miss, uh, Agent Martin?"

"No, thank you, sir. I'm fine. I'm sorry that you have to go through all of this, and I can assure you the FBI is doing everything possible to locate your wife. I also want to let you know we understand how sensitive the situation is. We will do everything possible to keep this as low-key as we can, but I think we agree that locating your wife is our first priority."

Cole nodded his head.

"To make that happen, I will need to ask you some personal questions that might be uncomfortable," she continued.

"I understand and I am willing to do whatever it takes to locate Barbara." His voice sounded anxious as he ran his hand through his hair.

He studied Agent Martin as she glanced around the room, apparently trying to evaluate the situation. She didn't look like any FBI agent he had ever seen in Washington.

"I'm sorry Agent Martin, but you seem so young to be an agent working on a case like this."

Her face visibly reddened as she said, "I've been a field agent for four years now. I am a well-seasoned professional. My friends are always saying how fortunate I am to still look like a young college girl. Someday, I'm sure I'll be glad, but currently it is a liability on the job."

He nodded his head, and a slight grin formed on his face.

"I know exactly how you feel. I was quite young when I became a senator. I was thirty, the minimum age when I ran for my first term. I was the improbable upstart running against a longtime incumbent. He used my youth to discredit me as a serious candidate. His constituents felt otherwise though, because I won the election by a huge margin." He smiled broadly.

That made her smile, and her face became more relaxed.

"When you first opened the door, I wasn't sure it was you. I have seen you on the news, but never in person. I knew you had been a senator for about ten years, but you don't look any older than my brother."

As she removed her notebook from the inside pocket of her jacket, he continued to study her. Hell, she looked as if she should be wearing a cheerleader's outfit, but she assuredly had gone to great lengths to look older and professional.

Her long blonde hair was pulled back and clipped into a pony tail, and it didn't look as if she was wearing any makeup. She didn't need any; her complexion was flawless. Her black business suit looked like it was specifically picked out to hide her feminine body. When she smiled, her teeth were as white as ivory soap. Nature had planned for this young woman to be on the cover of a fashion magazine, not carrying a gun under a bulky business suit.

He took note of her professional manner and could tell she was confident, and he assumed, deservedly so. *Okay, this young gal is going to be all right.*

"What can I answer for you, Agent Martin?"

"We're assuming no one has tried to contact you about the disappearance of your wife, is that correct?"

He could feel the lump in his throat again. He was sure there had to be a slight change in his expression as he tried not to swallow, afraid it would reveal a huge bulge in his throat. He shifted in his chair to buy a few seconds. "No — no one has communicated with me."

He watched her face for a change in her expression as she made notes in her book, but there wasn't any. Either she was good or his response hadn't been as awkward as he had thought.

"Why do think your wife decided to leave her mother's home in New York earlier than she originally told you she was leaving?"

Good, something I don't have to lie about.

"I have no idea; it's not like her at all. She always follows her plans. If she makes any changes to her schedule she always lets us know — to the point of being obsessive about it."

"Us? Who else would she notify, Senator Cole?"

"Miles Conner, he's my assistant in Washington."

She nodded and continued writing notes in her book without any discernible expression.

"Senator Cole, I'm sorry, but do you think that your wife could be having an affair with another man?"

He wetted his lips with his tongue as he pondered the question. "I'm sure I would be the last to know. But, to answer your question, no, I do not believe that my wife is having an affair. We are very much in love with each other. From the first day we met, neither of us had any doubts that we belonged together."

"Nothing in her recent behavior has indicated to you any change in the way she felt about your marriage?"

He began thinking about the way he had selfishly ignored her lately, because of his own problems with the politics and press in Washington. Then he snapped back from his thoughts, aware that Agent Martin was watching him. "No, nothing that I have noticed."

They sat in silence as she wrote in her notebook, and he began to wonder. Was it possible he had been so self-centered that he hadn't noticed something different occurring with his wife?

Martin broke the silence. "Your wife is a wealthy woman, is she not?"

He paused briefly, looking at her face for indications as to the intent of the question, and again, her expression was neutral.

"Yes, she inherited a large sum of money recently from her father."

"Senator, you are her sole beneficiary. So you would inherit her entire estate, is that correct?"

Cole's pleasant expression disappeared as he sat up straight in his chair and said, "Yes, Agent Martin, I'm sure that's the first thing on the mind of the FBI. I have no need of her money. I can assure you I am not involved in my wife's disappearance."

Again, there was an awkward silence; just the background sound of the waves breaking against the sand. Martin's cell phone interrupted the uneasy interlude.

"Excuse me." She nodded her head as she listened to the voice coming through the small speaker. Then he noticed her eyes getting big as she glanced over at him and quickly looked away. *No poker face this time.* He knew something was wrong.

She quickly turned sideways in her seat, so she wouldn't be facing his stare. She stood up from the sofa and slowly walked to the other side of the room with the phone against her ear. After a long delay, she began talking, but she was facing away from him, and her voice was so low he couldn't hear what she was saying. After the short conversation she turned back around and said, "I understand," closed her phone and put it back in her pocket.

She walked back to the sofa, her expression markedly changed. It seemed the temperature of the room had dropped twenty degrees.

She spoke quietly. "That call was from my supervisor, Bill Hansen, in Tampa. He was just on the telephone with the Washington office. They went to the Capitol building to check your office for any clues that might help locate Mrs. Cole."

She paused for what seemed an extraordinary amount of time.

His mind was racing as he ran all the possible sequences through his head. His throat was getting dry, and it was getting harder to swallow.

"Sir, have you ever done any book publishing?"

His face went slack as he tried to move his lips. "No."

"Inside a back closet of your office were six boxes full of newly published books. All the books were the same title. *The Cole Hard Truth,* by Irwin S. Cole. It's a complete account of the planning, execution and confession of the murder of your wife."

Cole's skin was as white as Martin's teeth. His body sank deeper into the big leather chair. His eyes wandered across the room and then fixated on the windows that looked out over the Gulf.

She said, "My supervisor is on his way down from Tampa, and will be here in about an hour. He has questions he needs to ask you about this book."

Cole didn't respond. The straight posture and youthful looks he had borne when he had ushered her into the room had all but disappeared. He sat wordlessly, his eyes empty.

Eventually he raised his head and looked back at her. Slowly his body regained life as he pulled himself upright in the chair. In a sudden motion, he moved toward the edge of the chair, and sat up tall.

She said quickly, "Please Senator; I need you to stay seated in the chair until my supervisor arrives, and we can discuss this new development."

Without realizing, Martin had moved her hand to the inside of her suit jacket, and her hand was inches from her weapon in the shoulder harness.

"This is crazy!" he exclaimed sharply. "I didn't write that terrible book."

He continued earnestly. "Earlier this morning I received a package here at the house, and when I later opened it, I found the book inside. After examining the cover and first few pages I was terrified. I immediately tried to call my wife. When I found out she wasn't at her mother's or the town house I called Doug Mackey with the Capitol police. If I were guilty, why would I call the police myself? And I certainly wouldn't write a book about it and have it published. Someone is setting me up."

"Senator Cole, I understand what you're saying. It is bizarre, but it's not our job to judge guilt or innocence. We follow the evidence. I'm sorry to say, all the evidence is currently pointing in your direction."

Their eyes locked, neither wanting to blink or show any sign of weakness. Cole struggled to contain his emotions, taking long deep breaths to steady himself.

"Agent Martin, do you believe," he paused, "that I hurt my wife," he paused again with anguish etched across his face, "and then wrote a book about it for all to read?"

"Senator Cole, as I said before, it's not my place to make that judgment."

He leaned forward in the chair again and spoke firmly. "I believe it is your place. You're the one sitting in my home, in front of me, looking me in the eyes. I believe at this moment, you're the only person in the world that can make that kind of judgment."

Martin glanced away, and he saw that she was stressed by his question. She seemed to be struggling with how to respond. He knew that as an FBI agent she was trained to stay uninvolved. He felt a tiny glimmer of hope.

Finally she met his eyes. "If you are responsible for this, I think you're the dumbest-ass person I ever met in my life."

"Thank you, Agent Martin. I think. I assure you your confidence in me is well founded."

She smiled almost imperceptibly. *Round one Cole*, he thought. He had defused a confrontational situation and hopefully garnered some sympathy. His debating experience had served him well.

"Please, follow me, and I'll show you the book in my study, and see what you think."

"I think we should probably wait here for my supervisor to arrive."

"No, please Agent Martin, I need you to see this so you believe what I'm saying. It's important to me, because I can hardly believe it myself."

He stood and began walking without waiting for her acknowledgment. He could hear her shoes gracefully ticking against the tile floor as she followed him across the hall to his study. He wondered if he had an ally walking behind him.

The study was decorated with a man's taste. The teak desk was in front of a wall of white bookshelves filled with books. The opposite wall was covered in pictures and military plaques, including two large pictures of Cole with two Presidents. To the right were sliding glass doors that opened out to a back patio. The Gulf of Mexico sparkled beyond the sand. On a credenza was a huge model of a three mast sailing ship and in front of the massive glass window was a free-standing globe of the earth. The room had a comfortable, warm feeling about it,

"I've always dreamed of living at the beach since I was a little girl, though I hate the water." Martin's comment eased the tension. "Well, not the water so much as being on boats in the water. I think it would be wonderful living in a house like this, sitting in a swing on the back patio, watching the waves roll onto the sandy beach."

"Indeed, it is lovely." Cole walked to the desk, picked up the book, and handed it to her. She looked at the cover then flipped it over. A small smile came to her face, and he thought he heard a small chuckle, but he wasn't sure. She looked at the picture again, then back up at Cole. "Bad day?"

He looked back at her, shaking his head. "I don't know when or where that picture came from."

Her eyes twinkled. "I don't think there's a jury in the world that would believe you put a picture like that on the book yourself."

"Again, thanks for your confidence in me, Agent Martin. Can't you find who ordered the book through Last Chance Publishing? Then we would know who's behind this."

"They're researching it now. We should know something soon. I wouldn't expect too much to come out of it, though. It's probably going to come back that Irwin S. Cole ordered the book online. The publishing houses can receive it as a file upload, print it, and ship it without ever talking to a person—modern technology. The only break we might get is if we find the computer used to send the file. Do you have a computer in the house, Senator?"

"No, not here in Florida. I intentionally left my laptop at home in Washington, so I wouldn't be tempted to work. Agent Martin, that's not the news I was hoping for about the publisher. Tell me some good news."

"The only good news I can think of is the press hasn't gotten hold of that photograph of you on the back of your book yet. Other than that I'm afraid I'm out of good news."

He simply nodded his head at her words.

"Have you read the book yet? Did you find any clues about who might be doing this?"

Cole noticed her demeanor had changed back to what it was before her telephone call.

"I've read about halfway through the book and I'm afraid it's as if I wrote the damn thing. There are items on those pages that only Barbara and I would know. How is it possible, how could someone know so much about me and what I did?"

She shook her head. "That tells me whoever is behind this knows you well. Possibly a close friend; how else would they know so much personal information about you? Please forgive me sir, but at this point you can't rule anyone out. Possibly it could be the closest person in the world to you."

He fell backward against the desk, catching himself on the edge with his hands. Then he stared vacantly across the room out the window at the beach. A long silence settled in the room.

"I will never believe Barbara would do something like this. It's impossible."

There was another long pause as they each avoided looking at the other.

"Do you have any enemies that you're aware of, Senator?"

He was slow to respond but finally turned and looked at her. "I'm a senator. Half the country hates me. In my party, only about 60% of the people approve of my performance, at any time. I have been a strong opponent of offshore drilling all my life, and that alone creates many enemies. Now with the spill, people are blaming me as if I willed it to happen, to prove my point. Officials said one oil worker was accusing my office of sabotage, so the drilling would stop."

She nodded. "I do realize that being a senator places you in so many difficult situations. It's like no matter what you do someone isn't going to like it."

He looked her straight in the eyes. "Welcome to my life."

"Senator Cole, I hope I haven't given you the wrong idea here. You need to understand that no matter what I think about the case, when my supervisor arrives, he will follow protocol. He will ask for my opinion based on the time I have spent with you, but it will be his call how we proceed. He's a good man, but he follows the book and right now it's not looking too good for you. I'm sure, if it wasn't for you being a United States senator, they probably would have already had me read you your rights."

"I have confidence you people will help me find my wife."

"I suggest you use the remaining time until my supervisor gets here to read that book, and try to find something that will help us with this case."

Cole picked up the book and said, "Let's go to the kitchen and get something to drink, and I'll start back on this book again."

Chapter 4

Monday, 6:35 PM

Mackey was at home trying to comfort his wife in her distress over Barbara's disappearance. His churning gut told him it was going to be a long night. Just as he was about to suggest they go out to dinner to help take the situation off her mind, the phone rang.

They looked at each other as he picked up the phone.

"Mackey."

He listened without saying a word. "I'll be right there," he said finally, and hung up the telephone. He saw his wife waiting with her hands pressed on the sides of her face, as if to cover her eyes if necessary.

"It's the FBI. They want me to come down to their office right away."

"Is there some news about Barbara?"

"They didn't say, they just asked whether I could attend a meeting. I'll be home as soon as I can."

Mackey put his arms around his wife and gave her a hug. "Don't worry Doris, if they had found anything wrong, they would have told me."

It only took Mackey twenty minutes to reach William Anderson's office at the FBI building. Traffic was light this time of the evening. He had been to Anderson's office many times on business and pleasure, but never in the evening after hours. He was surprised to find the receptionist was still there.

"They're expecting you, Lieutenant Mackey. You can go right in."

From the tone of the call he had received at home, he didn't have a good feeling about this meeting, but he had kept those thoughts from Doris. He cleared his throat as he opened the door and walked into the office.

The room was large for an office, but it doubled as a conference room and a tactical operations center during a crisis. The office was furnished in the typical government fashion, no frills, strictly business, but it was much nicer than his office. There were four people sitting at the conference table on the opposite side of the room.

William Anderson looked up from the book he was reading. *What a time to be catching up on your reading,* Mackey thought.

"Mackey, come on in and join us. You already know Tom and Raphael, and I would like to introduce Dr. Moiré."

Dr. Moiré was a short, frail-looking man in his early forties. His suit was wrinkled, and his long out-of-date tie was crooked in his collar. His glasses were thick and heavy, and made his eyes look large. Despite his odd looks, his precise, deliberate movements as he sorted and arranged his notes, bespoke competency and organization.

Mackey had worked with Agents Tom Wilson and Raphael Martinez several times in the past, and was comfortable with them. They were both about thirty and were good at their jobs. They were dressed in suits, and Mackey thought they looked exactly like what FBI agents should look like.

The two agents' similarity ended with the suits as their ethnic backgrounds were very different. Tom had grown up on Long Island in an affluent neighborhood with the best education money could buy. Raphael had spent his childhood on the streets of Los Angeles, but unlike most of his friends, he had managed to stay out of trouble with the authorities. Despite this disparity, they worked together as one of the best teams in Washington.

Tom was tall, thin, with blond hair and a fair complexion. His good looks and boyish grin were always attracting women. Raphael was a foot shorter with black hair and dark skin tones. His face displayed the old battle scars he had earned on the streets before making changes in his life. They did not, however, hide the kindness that was evident in his eyes. Anderson had surrounded himself with the best talent available.

William Anderson was about fifty, but didn't look a day over forty. He had worked his way up through the ranks, starting as a field agent twenty-four years earlier. He knew the score, but his career hadn't advanced as much as it should have. He wasn't into the office politics that were required to climb to the top. Had he been more politically motivated, he might have been the director by now. He had the experience, but that wasn't the only prerequisite for the job.

Mackey, with his short, stocky physique, appeared to labor as he walked over and shook hands with each of the four men. He pulled out one of the chairs and joined them at the table.

Anderson began to speak. "Mackey; I want to thank you for coming over here this time of night. For most of the day, we have been approaching this case with the theory that Barbara Cole has been kidnapped, either for financial gain, or for the pressure that could be placed on her husband, Senator Cole. He has top-secret clearance on matters that could be of interest to terrorist groups."

Mackey looked around the room, and nodded his head in acknowledgment of the statement. Then he noticed that no one was returning his nod.

Anderson continued. "Then late today, we uncovered a development that has led us in a different direction. That's why I asked Dr. Moiré to join us.

"Dr. Moiré is a psychologist at the Bureau. He heads the department that develops psychological profiles for most of the cases we investigate. He has been studying this book for the last couple of hours, trying to determine a profile for the author."

Mackey frowned in confusion. What could a book have to do with Barbara's disappearance? Anderson slid the book across the polished table to Mackey. He looked down at the shiny cover and his forehead wrinkled as he read the title.

He turned the book over and looked at the back, his head shaking in denial. He thumbed the first few pages, and read the brief review of the book. He felt four sets of eyes watching his every move. He shook his head again, as he read the table of contents. He let the book fall to the table and looked over at Anderson in silence.

Anderson said, "We found six cases of these in Senator Cole's office at the Capitol Building. Mackey, I don't need to tell you how damaging these books look for the senator. From first impression, it seems to go through the crime from conception to confession in explicit detail."

Mackey twisted in his chair slightly before sliding it away from the table. He tugged at his collar as if it was choking him. His massive neck strained for space in his shirt.

"I can't believe this, William. It's not possible that Irwin could be responsible for something like this. It has to be a setup of some sort. It's too damn easy. You know it's never that simple. A book. Christ! Come on!"

"That's why I asked Dr. Moiré to join us, and give his initial opinion about the book. Doctor, if you would please?"

Dr. Moiré slid out of his chair and stood next to the table. He reached down and picked up his notebook, and held it out in front of his body. His head moved around the table making eye contact with each person in the room, one at a time.

"First let me preface my remarks by saying that this book is possibly the most complex writing I have ever had to review. I've only had a few hours with it, so I can't say much at this point. It could take months before we begin to unravel the true thought process behind this work. My preliminary finding is that it's brilliant."

Mackey and someone else grunted in disapproval.

"What I mean is, the book seems to offer details and insight into the murder of the author's wife. But the reality is, there's so much conflicting detail, it's like there is no meaningful insight."

Anderson slammed his hand on the table. "I don't understand, Doctor! The damn book is nothing but details and accounts of what he did."

"Yes, Mr. Anderson, at first glance that's what it seems. Once my team and I began studying each chapter more closely, however, we began to realize that's not necessarily the case. I have only read two chapters thoroughly. I can say, whoever wrote this book is highly intelligent, and understands the power of words used in the right subtext. For instance, at first we told you we thought the crime was to happen in Naples, Florida. After further examination, I believe we were wrong. I studied that chapter repeatedly, and now I believe it could happen anywhere. We were duped. We were taking the words literally instead of understanding the underlying message the words were carrying."

The doctor opened his copy of the book to where he had it marked and began to read.

*The words behind her came into focus:
"Welcome to Naples." I raised the gun until
she was in my sights. The shrill of her
scream ripped through my ears as I
squeezed the trigger. Instantly, her scream
was lost to the explosion of gunpowder. She
fell backward against the railing, and her
body flipped over it as she fell helplessly to
the ground far below.*

Dr. Moiré let the book fall to the table with a thump as he paused a few seconds.

"Based on that passage, we assumed the author was in Naples when he killed her. Or at least he was planning to be in Naples if we are to believe the timeline of the book. According to the schedule in the book, no crime has taken place yet. The crime is supposed to occur this Wednesday at 6:00 PM.

"After further study and discussions with my team, I'm fairly sure the crime won't take place in Naples. The statement was a diversion, a ruse, like everything else in the book. All the details about the crime are so contrary to one another that we have no idea what facts are real and what aren't. For that matter, we don't know whether any of it's true at this point. I'm sorry, Mr. Anderson. I sent your men on a wasted trip to Naples. In the future, we will be much more diligent in our advice about this book."

"You couldn't have known, Doctor," said Anderson. "Tom, get on the phone and get those men back up to Ft. Myers. Doctor, what I need from you now is your opinion on who wrote the damn thing. Do you think Senator Cole is capable of writing a book like this or not?"

Dr. Moiré looked down at the book on the table, then around the room at the other men. "I have never met the senator."

He continued, "As I said before, the person who wrote this book is highly intelligent. The true motive somehow seems buried in its content, and I think it's a diversion. Can a normally functioning person of society and possibly a US senator be capable of this? My answer would have to be, yes.

"I must also say, I would have thought the author of this book would have disappeared once the news of its existence surfaced. I understand Senator Cole is at his home with an agent. That doesn't follow the course we would normally see from a case like this, so I would suggest proceeding with caution until we know more."

"Thank you, Doctor. You and your team continue your analysis and let me know if you find anything else. We need some solid information we can use to find Mrs. Cole."

Mackey spoke up. "This is bullshit," he exclaimed as he looked at the other men. "I have known Irwin Cole for almost ten years. Our wives are best friends, and we have all gone on vacations together. It's impossible for me to believe this garbage. I would have noticed something.

"Before I got this job with the Capitol Police, I was a detective for ten years and a damn good one. I was trained to notice things that were off kilter. I never saw anything in their relationship, or the senator's personality, that would indicate there was anything wrong. I think we are all being taken for a ride, and we are allowing it to happen. Instead we should be spending our resources finding Barbara."

An eerie silence hung in the room as they sat at the table trying not to look at one another. Anderson stood.

"Mackey, we understand how you feel. That's why I asked you here tonight. I need your opinion. I want to make sure we are looking at all sides of this. This is not a case with which we can afford to make a mistake.

"You and I both know, in cases like this, 90% of the time it's the spouse. Plus, we can't forget Barbara Cole's affluence. She has become very wealthy and her husband is her sole beneficiary — not to mention that damn book. If it were anyone else other than a senator, we would have already arrested them."

Anderson leaned over the table. "Mackey, maybe you were too close to the senator to notice the warning signs."

Mackey abruptly stood and his chair fell backward on the floor. "As a senator you make a lot of enemies, especially when you are an outspoken senator, on a controversial issue like drilling in the Gulf. I'm no expert on this stuff, but I suspect that offshore drilling is worth billions and billions of dollars. That means there are many people who would like to see him out of the picture. I think we need to start focusing on some of those possibilities, not to mention that top-secret information you were talking about earlier."

Anderson let out a sigh, tossed his folder on the table and said, "We have to follow the evidence and right now it's pointing toward the senator. Mackey, if I had any other lead to follow, you know I would be on it like flies on shit."

Mackey and Anderson stared at one another across the table. Mackey broke the stare to bend and pick up the chair he had knocked over. Tom and Raphael were looking at each other with cocked eyebrows. Anderson's demeanor and language were usually unimpassioned and proper. His lack of emotion during a crisis had earned him the nickname "Iceman" behind his back.

The moment of silence was interrupted by the telephone on Anderson's desk. He strode over and picked it up. He listened and then said, "Good work, follow up the number and let me know whether you find anything else."

He continued to listen, turned and looked at Mackey before he said, "No, just check out his story. Don't do anything without checking with me first, and make sure we keep an agent with him at all times."

He hung up the phone and said, "We finally got our first break—but it's a small one."

Everyone sat forward in anticipation. "They found a few frames of video of Mrs. Cole getting off the plane in Ft. Myers. Now we have visual confirmation she made it to Florida. We also have a camera outside the airport that caught her from behind getting into a limousine. They say it looked like it was a prearranged pickup. We got one and a half digit of the license plate. The team upstairs is working on cleaning up the video as we speak. They'll send it down when they're done."

Mackey and Anderson looked at one another. Neither of them wanted to speculate whether this new information was going to be good news or bad news.

Anderson said, "We have an agent at the senator's house with him now. Bill Hansen, the Tampa director is on his way and should be there in a few minutes to handle the interview with the senator personally."

There was a knock at the door, and it opened slowly as a man stepped in and said, "Sir, it's ready on your monitor."

"Thanks Jim," Anderson replied.

Anderson walked to his desk and picked up the remote control for the huge wall monitor. The three other men eagerly gathered in front of the screen as he pushed the power button and a still video image appeared on the screen. The scene was at an airport gate, and the door to the ramp was closed. Anderson pushed the play button.

The picture on the screen changed and the door at the gate swung open and people began coming out from the plane. The four men all watched intently as people from the flight filed by the camera lens and headed down the corridor.

Mackey raised his arm and pointed at the screen, "That's her now. That's Barbara Cole." Anderson hit the pause button and froze the image on the screen and asked, "Are you positive?"

"Yes, it's definitely Barbara Cole. It looks like she's by herself. I don't recognize any of the people around her."

The men were looking at the image of the beautiful woman on the screen. Her long dark hair flowed down to the middle of her back. With her tall, sleek, frame she could have easily been mistaken for a model. Her face carried no signs of distress, only a pleasant smile.

Anderson said, "We're working the passenger manifest to see if anyone on the flight looks a little too coincidental, but we haven't had any luck yet. We are also contacting and questioning passengers that sat in the seats surrounding her. We are hoping maybe someone saw or heard something that can help."

Anderson hit the play button, and the video advanced while they watched the rest of the passengers disembark. No one in the room noticed anything unusual.

The video changed to a view from an outside camera. They were looking at the sidewalk and pick-up zone in front of baggage claim. They all leaned closer to the screen as they watched several people stepping down off the curb and walking out of view of the camera.

A woman was walking down the sidewalk away from the camera with a small carry-on bag.

"That's her again," said Mackey. "Same outfit as before at the gate." She stopped next to a dark luxury car parked at the curb and set her bag on end at her side. The view of the car was partly blocked by a huge support column for the roof canopy. They watched a man enter the scene and open the rear passenger door for Mrs. Cole to climb into the back seat of the car. The man closed the door behind her.

The same man picked up her carry-on bag and started walking toward the back of the car. Just as he was turning toward the camera, he went behind the column and disappeared out of the picture. He apparently loaded the bag in the trunk and walked down the other side of the car. A few seconds later, the car pulled away from the curb. At the same time, the taxicab parked behind the black limousine pulled up and blocked the license plate from view.

"Shit! Can't we get a break here?"

Tom and Raphael looked over at the Iceman, then at one another, once again with cocked eyebrows.

Anderson reversed the video and played it again. When the video showed the man opening the door, he slowed it and began advancing frame by frame. Just as the man's face was about to turn for a profile shot, he moved behind the column.

He slowed the video again as the car started to pull away. For one second, the edge of the license plate was visible, and Anderson hit the pause button. They all agreed the last number was a 7, but the next number could have been an 8, 3, or possibly even a letter B.

The time stamped on the video was 15:50 8/07/10. Tom looked at his watch and said, "It's been 54 hours since we last saw Mrs. Cole. We all know the statistics. If it was a kidnapping, we would have heard something by now."

Anderson said, "The video doesn't look like she's being kidnapped. It looked more like a prearranged pickup to me. This case is starting to make even less sense than before. We need to get an agent up to New York to talk to the mother. She was the last person we know of who talked to her. Raphael, get all the phone records for all numbers associated with the Cole family. I want to know every person they talked to for the last month. I also want to know both of their most recent week's schedules right down to when they used the bathroom."

"Will do boss," said Raphael. "By the way, we still haven't been able pick up a signal from Mrs. Cole's cell phone. Apparently it's turned off, but I instructed the lab to keep watching for it in case it gets turned back on."

Mackey asked, "What's your plan William?"

"My plan is to handle this like I would any disappearance. I'm going to turn over every rock, look in every hole, and follow the evidence where it takes me."

"Thanks, William," Mackey nodded his head in affirmation.

Anderson underscored his next statement with a quick slash of his hand. "Mackey, please understand, the second I get something that's conclusive against the senator I'm going to bring him in."

"I understand, William. I would expect nothing less."

"Mackey, now that you've seen the video, what are your thoughts?"

"I agree Barbara wasn't under any duress. She had no concerns about getting into the limo. In my mind, it's looking less and less like the senator has any involvement despite that—that fucking book. I also think we agree that we are not dealing with some street punks here. Whatever is occurring, or whoever concocted this plan, had to know we would have this video from the airport. The placement of the limo was too good to be true. You know how I feel about too good to be true scenarios. I'm beginning to think the airport scene was staged for our benefit."

"What benefit would that be?"

"The only thing I can think of is they wanted to make sure we knew she was in Florida and not elsewhere. Why? I have no idea."

The phone rang again. Anderson quickly picked up the receiver and listened. Anger spread across his face.

"Bill! What the hell happened? Is the agent gone too?"

He listened again as he shook his head and looked around the room.

"Damn Bill, call me when you learn anything."

He hung up the phone and let his head fall down toward his desk. He drummed his fingers on the desk in a nervous beat then looked back up at the others in the room. They were staring at him silently, waiting for the news.

"That was Bill Hansen on the phone. As I said earlier, he is Director of the Tampa office. He arrived at Senator Cole's residence a few minutes ago and found the place empty. It looked like there had been a struggle, and shots had been fired. There's no sign of the senator or the agent we sent to interview him."

They stood in silent shock, processing the news. Was the senator now a victim, or a criminal?

The phone sounded yet again. "Yes," said Anderson. He listened for several seconds then dropped the receiver back in the cradle.

"They identified the license plate on the luxury car at the airport. It's a rental car. The car was rented by Irwin S. Cole."

Chapter 5

Monday, 7:40 PM

"Well, that was fun," muttered Bill Hansen as he ended his phone call with Anderson.

He dialed Agent Martin's cell phone again, but once again it went straight to her voice mail. He should have sent a second agent with Martin, but at the time, it was a simple missing person case. And if most of his team hadn't been sent on that wild goose chase to Naples, he would have had another agent available.

He turned to Jerry Moore, the agent who had driven him down from Tampa. "I never should have sent Martin alone. She's a good agent, but her four years of field time hasn't included any kind of situation like this. If something has happened to her, I don't think I will ever be able to forgive myself."

"Martin is one of the brightest agents I know," Moore replied. "I think she can handle about anything." Agent Moore was an analyst, usually working white-collar crime and while he was good at his job, he hadn't done any crime scene work in the field. Tonight he would learn, because there weren't any other agents available.

"I hope you're right, Jerry. We need to start looking for some clues to determine what happened, but make sure you don't disturb anything until forensics arrives. The lab boys won't get here for another hour. In the meantime, grab the kit, we can't afford to waste time. Martin's life could be at stake."

They were standing in the front foyer of the house. "It looks like they weren't alone," observed Hansen. The front door had been hanging open and they could see several dusty footprints on the tile.

Hansen headed back to the kitchen where it appeared a struggle had taken place. Moore went in the other direction through the hallway door into the garage.

The sliding glass door in the kitchen was shattered, and little pieces of safety glass were sprayed across the kitchen. Mixed with the glass, which looked like chips of ice on the floor, he saw small drops of blood. In the center of the glass chips was an area of mostly bare floor. By the pattern surrounding the area, he surmised that someone had been lying on the floor in that spot. He walked around the edge of the glass fragments as best he could, so nothing would be disturbed.

Removing a pair of latex gloves from his pocket and hastily pulling them on, he flipped the light switch on the wall next to the sliding glass doors. The first switch turned on a single light over a small table. The second switch turned on several lights outside and illuminated the back patio with a flood of light.

Now he could see that it looked as if the struggle had started on the patio and someone had been thrown through the glass door into the kitchen. Furniture and potted plants were knocked over and scattered. Dirt from the pots was strewn across the pavers. He stopped in his tracks when he heard a crunching noise coming from behind him in the kitchen. He turned around and saw Moore making his way through the obstacle course of glass on the kitchen floor.

"Geez, Jerry, what the hell are you doing? Don't disturb the glass. Walk along that far edge by the pantry. We need to treat this as a crime scene."

As he jumped off to the side of the glass fragments, Moore said, "Boss, there are two cars in the garage and the registrations in the glove boxes indicate they belong to the senator and his wife."

Hansen said, "Martin's car is still in the driveway, so how did they leave, why did they leave, and most important, how many left?" He looked down on the brick pavers and saw a small puddle of blood reflecting the light from the overhead fixtures.

"Look, fresh blood, it's still bright red. Whatever happened, it was just before we got here. I also found two bullet holes in the kitchen wall. We need to inspect this area carefully for additional clues."

Hansen walked to the side of the deck, leaned over the rail and stretched as far as possible to look at the adjacent property.

"With the distance between this house and the next, not to mention the offshore winds, I doubt whether anyone heard anything, but we need to check with both neighbors. First go out to the car and get a couple of flashlights, so we can check the patio area closer. And Jerry," he added sarcastically, "how about you go this way so you don't track back through the glass?" He pointed to the rear steps leading from the patio.

Moore headed down the steps and around the side of the house. The lights that flooded the patio area didn't illuminate the path. As he reached the corner of the house on the dark brick path, he tripped over something.

"Shit!" He fell forward, catching himself with his hands and landing on his knees.

"Jerry, what the hell's going on, you all right?" called Hansen.

"Yes, I'm okay. I tripped on something here in the middle of the path."

Moore picked himself up from the brick path, and saw that he had tripped over a small carry-on bag and an attaché case. He still had his gloves on, so he grabbed them and headed back to the patio and set them on the steps. He then turned back down the path to get the flashlights. A minute later Moore was handing his boss a flashlight as he pointed at the steps and said, "There's what I tripped on in the path."

Hansen spun around to look at the bags, his eyes opened wide. "You moved those up here?"

"Yeah, I was wearing my gloves," he said defensively.

"You never move anything at a crime scene until the lab boys have it photographed every way from Sunday."

"Sorry boss, I thought because it moved when I tripped over it that it wouldn't matter."

Moore headed down the steps as Hansen held the light on the identification tag on the carry-on bag. "Barbara Cole." He lifted the attaché case, and the gold-plated plaque attached above the handle had the initials I. S. C. on it. He silently mouthed, Irwin S. Cole.

He tried the latch on the attaché, and it was unlocked. He lifted the lid and saw a laptop computer and a manila folder. He picked up the folder and opened it. Inside was a rental agreement for a 2010 Cadillac DTS. *The car from the airport.* The document was made out to Irwin S. Cole.

Moore called out from the beach. "Boss, down here, hurry."

Hansen rushed down the steps. "What do you have?"

"Look, there in the sand." Moore pointed the light toward the water. Two parallel marks in the sand could be seen leading all the way down to the water's edge.

Hansen knelt to examine the curious furrows. They were about fourteen inches apart, and continued to the water's edge.

Moore squatted beside him. "Looks like someone's been dragged through the sand to the water. These marks look like they were made by something narrow; maybe like the heel of a woman's shoe."

Hansen said, "Very good Jerry, I think you're right."

Moore's voice waivered a bit as he asked, "Do you suppose someone dumped Martin's body in the water?"

"I don't know." Worry etched Hansen's face. Mist from the water swirled in the flashlight beams. The waves foamed and sparkled in the light as they scoured smooth the scars in the sand. The ends of the two furrows were filling with water and disappearing into the Gulf. They searched back and forth across the surface of the water and down the beach, but saw nothing.

Hansen said, "We're going to need more people. Call it in and have them get the local Sheriff's office down here. We're going to have to comb the beach and the Gulf. Have them notify the Coast Guard. The tide is coming in so evidence is disappearing fast."

They walked back to the light of the patio, and Moore got out his cell phone and called the Tampa office. He gave them the information he had, while Hansen scanned the area surrounding the patio. At the edge of the deck, there were several large sea grape trees growing over the railing from the ground below. One was leaning slightly and had a couple of broken branches. He walked to the rail and shone his light down into the growth. He turned to Moore and said, "We're going to need the coroner too."

Moore interrupted the person he was talking with on the phone. "Hold on a minute; we have something else."

He walked to the rail where Hansen was shining his light into the bushes. Moore followed Hansen down the deck stairs and around to the sea grapes. He bent over the rail and saw a bloody body lying twisted in the brush. They squirmed their way through the dense bushes and found the body jammed between two small tree trunks. Hansen put his hand on the neck, checking for a pulse. He couldn't feel one, so he lifted and turned the head of the lifeless body so he could see the face.

Hansen and Moore exchanged blank looks.

Moore said into his phone, "We have one dead, unidentified male here also."

They worked their way back out of the brush, and Hansen shined his light at the water to see where the tide was. The water was another foot farther up the beach. He noticed something tumbling in the surf. He took off running toward the water. Sixty feet later he reached down and picked up a woman's shoe. He carried it back to the patio and held it up for Moore to see.

Moore said, "Hold on again," as he put his hand over the microphone and asked Hansen, "Martin's?"

Hansen shrugged. "I don't know. It could be hers. All women's shoes look the same to me."

Hansen pulled out his cell phone and scrolled to William Anderson's number. After the third ring a voice greeted him with, "You'd better damn well have some good news for me."

"Hold the line one second, William." Hansen rushed over to the brush, reached in, and delicately retrieved a gun about to fall from the swaying branches.

Hansen cleared his throat and said, "William, we've found the body of an unidentified male in his early thirties outside the Cole home with an apparent gunshot wound to the chest. We also discovered Mrs. Cole's carry-on from the airport video and a rental agreement for the Cadillac in Senator Cole's name. We still haven't found any signs of Agent Martin, but her car is still here. We found marks in the sand that possibly were made by someone dragging a body to the edge of the Gulf. The only thing we've found on the beach is a female's shoe washing in the surf. As we speak, I've recovered the probable murder weapon. It's not looking good down here, William."

Hansen was shining his light along the railing as he talked on the phone. At the bottom of the hand rail of the steps leading up to the deck, he noticed a flicker of light on the wooden rail. He inspected it and found stuck to the railing a long blonde hair fluttering in the breeze.

He finished with sorrow in his voice. "I shouldn't have sent Martin alone, William. Maybe she'd still be alive."

Chapter 6

Monday, 7:50 PM

Miles Conner was still frantically pacing Senator Cole's office in the Capitol, even though the FBI had finally left two hours earlier. The two agents had treated him well, but their presence in the office had made him nervous. All the questions they were asking made his stuttering worse than he'd experienced in a long time. At one point, he had to stop answering their questions and walk outside to calm his nerves.

The worst part of the visit was when they took the boxes of books from the back closet that Senator Cole had instructed him to lock away. If only he had remembered to lock the door before the FBI showed up, maybe they wouldn't have found them. He hoped he hadn't let the senator down. That would be the last thing he would want.

Miles continued to pace like an animal trapped in a cage. He mumbled aloud to himself. "This is getting way out of hand, what have I done here? I should have suspected that what Father asked me to do wasn't right. My instincts were telling me no, but I trusted him. After all, he is my father."

The sound of the office door opening caught his attention. He turned with surprise.

"Miles, is that you?"

"Yes, h-hello Annie," he said with a small forced smile.

"Who were you talking to, Miles?"

"No one, it's just m-me."

Miles's smile quickly changed to embarrassment, and he began to fidget. He liked Annie and didn't want her to think he was some kind of idiot talking to himself. Annie was a few years younger, with short dark hair and an ever-present smile. She was the only person working in the Capitol, other than Senator Cole, who treated him with respect. He secretly had a crush on her, but he knew all the single guys did, because she was so cute and bubbly.

Annie worked as an aide for Senator Kappleman, but Miles had never cared much for him. Kappleman was rude to him when Senator Cole wasn't around. He and Annie enjoyed spending time together talking during breaks. Annie said, "Wow, what a day. The FBI was searching the place all afternoon. Are you all right? I know they were questioning you for a long time."

"Y-Y-Yes I-I'm f-f-fine. Were y-you a-able to get the information I n-needed on that S-Sullivan guy?"

Annie looked at Miles with her head slightly cocked and her hands on her hips.

"Yes, I got your information. Is that all you want me for, to get your information? I had to promise that creep Shawn that I would go to a Redskins game with him this season in exchange for the address. You owe me big time, and you can start by buying me a drink at Mulligan's. If we leave now, we can still catch the rest of the gang there."

"You g-go Annie, I have a l-lot of things I-I need to take care of t-t-tonight. B-Besides none of those people like me joining them anyway."

"That's not true, Miles. They're jealous of you being the personal assistant for Senator Cole. After all, he's the most popular senator in the Capitol and he's always making such a fuss about the good job you do for him."

Miles smiled and said, "Next time I p-promise; I'll g-go with you and b-buy you that drink."

"Okay, but the least you can do is walk with me, so I don't have to walk down the street alone after dark."

Miles nodded his head in agreement as Annie reached into her pocket and handed him a slip of paper with the address of Alan Sullivan on it.

They locked the office and left the Capitol through the security checkpoint. As they were walking down the sidewalk toward Mulligan's, Annie cuffed her arm under his. Miles was shocked and his heart began racing. Annie smiled at him and leaned her head against his shoulder.

As they reached the front door of Mulligan's, Miles could hear the music blasting through the glass.

Annie asked, "Sure you won't come in for one quick drink?"

Miles looked at the huge smile on Annie's face, and as usual, he was having a difficult time saying no to her. His heart was still practically pounding out of his chest from her leaning her head on his shoulder. He took a deep breath and could still smell her perfume on his shirt. Trying to decide, he looked through the glass doors and saw the other aides inside laughing and having a good time. One of them pointed outside, and the rest of the table turned to look at them.

"N-N-No, I-I have t-t-to g-go."

He reddened with embarrassment from not being able to talk without stuttering after Annie had been so close. He turned and headed down the sidewalk toward his apartment as quickly as he could without actually running. His mind was going crazy. He had enough to think about tonight without Annie doing that.

He unlocked his apartment door and rushed inside. He settled down in his chair and breathed deeply, to calm himself. Then he removed the paper from his pocket to check the address. He smiled. The address was only a few blocks away. He opened the door of his locked spare room and a few moments later came back out with a black gym bag in his hand. It contained all the equipment that his father had provided him.

"Okay, Mr. S-Sullivan lets s-see what you are u-up to, I-I know it's no good."

Alan Sullivan was a lobbyist well known in Washington's political arena. He had no passion or interest aside from making money. He would sell his services to whoever was willing to pay his exorbitant prices. He was the "go-to guy" for things that needed doing, but were questionable. He had been investigated several times for some of his inappropriate lobbying tactics, but there was never enough evidence to prosecute him. It seemed most politicians he worked with were reluctant to get involved in the investigations.

Miles also knew from the office gossip that most senators didn't want to be seen talking to him, much less associating with him. A few days ago Miles had discovered Sullivan's name in a secure file on his father's server. He was reluctant to say anything to his father about what he had stumbled across because he had been accessing files he shouldn't have been. His father thought nobody else could access these files, but Miles had a way with computers.

The information about Sullivan was vague, but his name was listed in several different locations and just seeing it on the computer caused Miles to be concerned. He wanted to warn his father about Sullivan, but how could he without admitting he had been in his private files. He was sure his father had no idea about Sullivan's reputation in Washington.

Miles knew that his father would never do anything to harm him or the senator, but with Sullivan involved, who knew what could happen next. Miles was sure Sullivan was the person behind those terrible books that were sent to the senator's office.

He needed to learn what Sullivan was up to, and then he would warn his father. Finally, he would be a shining star in his father's eyes and be treated with the same respect as his brother.

Miles changed into jeans and a dark shirt before leaving his apartment. His mind was focused, and nothing was going to get in his way. He headed down the dark street that ran in front of his apartment with a new sense of confidence. He was on a mission of his own initiative. No one was giving him orders this time.

Ten minutes later he approached the block where Sullivan's house was located. The street was ominous looking, darkened further by the huge trees that lined both sides of the pavement, forming a solid canopy of leaves. He didn't mind the darkness—except for the closet where as a child he was often forced to stay. He hated that dark confined room.

As he approached the address on the paper, he slowed to inspect the brick house. The lights were on inside. *Sullivan is home*, he thought.

He ducked behind a row of hedges that ran along the side of the house, staying in the shadows as he made his way closer. He felt his heart beating in his chest in response to the danger, and he was beginning to enjoy this adventure. Squeezing behind a bush next to a lighted window, he rested his body against the wall of the house. Slowly, he moved his head and peered through the glass into the empty living room. He waited eagerly, but no one was in this section of the house.

He bent low as he moved toward the back of the house. His heart and mind had both settled down, and he was completely focused on the task at hand. When he rounded the corner, he saw light beaming out of a back window. He needed to get closer to that window, but there was an open area at the back door that he would have to cross to get to it.

He knelt low in the bushes as he surveyed the area, looking for a better approach. Luck wasn't on his side tonight; a street light from the alley that ran behind the property was illuminating the area he needed to cross. Either he would have to go all the way around the front of the house and come down the other side, or take his chances crossing the open space.

He watched and listened from the protection of the shadows as he made his decision. *Do it.* He jumped up and ran for the window, crossing the open area in one quick sprint. He dove behind the trash cans as he slid on the ground, stopping just under the window. As he landed, he hit one of the cans with the gym bag, knocking it over with a loud clatter. He heard a chair scoot across the floor inside the house, and footsteps coming toward the window. The neighbor's dog began barking.

The window over his head began to slide up, and he pulled himself as close to the house as he could; trying to hold his breath in silence. A voice came from the open window.

"Just some animal trying to get in the trash cans."

The window slammed shut and Miles recognized the voice. Sullivan. He lay quiet on the ground for a few minutes to regain his composure. Finally, he grabbed his gym bag and removed the portable listening device. He slid the headphones on and pointed the directional microphone toward the window glass. He could hear two voices inside.

Sullivan was speaking. "I'm sure it was all part of the plan. The man I'm working with doesn't make mistakes."

"I hope for everyone's sake you're right," said another male voice. "The damn FBI was in the Capitol all afternoon. That's too close for my comfort."

The phone rang and the noise blasted his ears through the headset. He pulled the microphone back from the glass.

Sullivan answered it before it rang a second time. "Hello, we were just talking about you—No, not you personally, our arrangement. My other client is concerned about the FBI showing up at the Capitol today. I assured him it was all going as planned."

There was a long silence, and Miles assumed Sullivan was listening to the person on the other end of the call. He thought it would be a good chance to look in the window and see who the other voice belonged to. It was a distinctive voice that he had heard before—many times, in fact—but he couldn't put a face to it.

He raised his head until he could see the ceiling of the room. Slowly, he rose higher until he could see the back of the head of the man he was trying to recognize. Without seeing his face, he couldn't identify the man, but the shape of his head was familiar. He waited and hoped the man would turn his head sideways, and he could catch a profile. Looking farther into the room, he saw Sullivan sitting behind a desk with the phone to his ear. He had a smirk on his face as he began to turn his head toward the window.

Miles dropped and fell to the ground in a stance that would allow him to take off running if he needed to. He listened intently and didn't hear any footsteps or noises coming from inside in the house. After waiting for a few moments, he put the headphones back on and positioned the microphone at the window again.

Sullivan said, "Yes, I have written it down and will call my contact with the information tomorrow. Bye."

The phone's handset clattered into the cradle. Sullivan spoke again. "Everything is going as planned. You have nothing to worry about. He assured me."

"I hope you're right because you know our friends don't tolerate failure."

"I know our friends all too well, and I'm completely comfortable with how everything is proceeding. In fact, I have a small task to handle for him tomorrow to make sure everything is going as planned. I'm going to call my contact at the Journal and leak some information to him."

The other man's voice was loud and sharp. "What kind of information are you leaking? I'm never comfortable when the press is involved with anything."

"I'll be leaking a story that the FBI is searching for Senator Irwin Cole in connection with the disappearance of his wife Barbara. Also, there's evidence that suggests they have a confession written by the senator admitting to the murder of his wife."

"I hope your man has everything—"

Miles grabbed the headphones off his head. Behind him in the yard was the next-door neighbor with a dog on a leash growling at him. The man was pulling back on the leash as the dog tried to get closer to where Miles was lying on the ground in the bushes. The dog was barking fiercely and the man hollered at Miles. "Hey! What are you doing over there?"

The dog was about to pull loose when the back door of the house flew open and Sullivan stepped out and yelled, "What the hell's going on out here?"

Miles grabbed his bag and dashed off through the bushes on the other side of the house. He ran as quickly as he could through the neighbor's yard and cut back across the alley. He kept running for another block and finally slowed to a fast walk as he headed down the street for his apartment. As frightening as the moment had been, Miles found he liked the excitement, he had never done anything like that before. He could feel the adrenaline rushing through his body, and he couldn't remember ever feeling better. His mind was as clear as it had ever been and he began congratulating himself for getting away unscathed.

By the time he was back at his apartment, the adrenaline high had disappeared. He flopped down in his chair in the dark room. His head was spinning and began to hurt from all the thoughts running through it. He yelled, "S-S-Sullivan, you b-bastard."

He needed to find a way to let his father know that Sullivan was interfering with the plan. He couldn't just call and tell him; he would never believe him. Miles already knew deep down his father was disappointed in him and thought he was a dimwit, though he at least had the decency to treat him otherwise.

His adrenaline high a distant memory, he again paced back and forth in the dark of his house. All the confidence he had gained earlier was gone, but he needed to make the call.

He picked up his cell phone and hit the speed dial for one of the three numbers programmed into his phone, and he noticed his hand was shaking. The call was answered on the second ring.

A slow, deep voice said, "Hello, Miles."

"T-T-There's a m-man n-named S-Sullivan that's t-trying to i-interfere with y-your p-plans."

"Miles, you need to calm down and relax. I know about this guy Sullivan and it's all right. I will handle him when the time comes. How did you learn about him anyway?"

"I-I-I …H-He wants to harm S-Senator C-Cole."

"Miles, listen to me. There are many things about this plan that you don't understand. I need you to get yourself together. You have to act like everything is normal until Wednesday, as we discussed. I've waited a long time for this day. Can you do that for me, son?"

"Y-Yes s-sir."

"Good boy Miles, now get some rest, and I will talk to you later."

Miles hung up the phone. He was furious and hated his father when he treated him like that. "If Father hadn't been the one to get me this job with the senator, I would tell him to go to hell," he muttered angrily. He resumed his pacing hitting the wall with his fist every time he got close to it. "Why can't my father be more like Senator Cole? I wish the senator had been my father," he cried out in anguish.

At that moment it hit him and he stopped in his tracks. "Senator Kappleman! That's who was with Sullivan. Father will never believe me, but I know who will, and I'll teach Father a lesson. I need to tell Senator Cole everything. He'll know what to do."

Chapter 7

Monday, 8:00 PM

Senator Cole was out of breath and covered in sweat when he found the small ceramic frog in the garden next to the back door, just where he remembered it to be. He picked up the smiling green frog and retrieved the key hidden under it in the dirt. He was at Ross's beach house, three houses down from his own. Ross lived in North Carolina most of the time and used his beach house as a vacation getaway, much the same as the Coles. They had become good friends and checked on one another's houses when they were in town.

He wiped the dirt off the key and put it in the lock of the back door. Anxiously, he turned the key until he heard the lock click, and he let out a small sigh of relief. With a grunt, he turned the knob and gave the door a push. The door didn't move, and he couldn't remember whether there was a second lock. He then remembered the door always had a habit of swelling during the summer and was difficult to open and close. He gave the bottom corner a light kick with his foot, and it popped open.

Reaching his arm inside the door frame, he felt for the light switch. He flipped the light on and heard a steady beeping coming from the panel on the wall. In the excitement of the moment, he had forgotten the alarm. He rushed in and over to the corkboard hanging on the wall, looking first in the left corner, then the right. Two sets of numbers had been posted in each corner in case he couldn't remember the code. Hurrying to the panel, he entered the digits, and it made one final loud beep, and the green light came on. He looked around the kitchen, and everything looked just as it had the last time he was here at Easter.

He leaned against the sink, still trying to catch his breath, and dropped the canvas bag with the book in it on the counter. The vision of what had happened flashed back in his mind. Clarity returned to his brain, and he rushed back across the kitchen floor to the back door.

He fought with the door again and rushed back outside onto the beach behind the patio. He bent down and put his arms under the shoulders and legs of Agent Martin, who was lying on the ground. He lifted her up and carried her through the doorway into the bright light of the kitchen. She was unconscious and had several wounds that were still leaking blood. Blood was running down the side of her head and staining her blouse at the shoulder.

He gently placed her on the kitchen floor and went to the guest bathroom across the hall. He came back with several towels and some antibacterial ointment. He rolled one of the towels up and placed it under her head. He took another towel to the sink and soaked the end of it with water. He knelt next to her and started wiping the blood from her face with the wet towel.

He carefully dabbed the towel against her skull until he found the source of the blood. He examined the small cut on the side of her head. He thought it must have been a piece of safety glass that caught her just right. The cut wasn't long or deep, but there was blood everywhere.

He grabbed the ointment and dabbed a big gob on the small gash trying to seal it to slow the seeping of blood through her hair.

The ointment slowed the flow from her head but her right ear was covered in blood. He tried to clean off her ear and neck with the wet towel. As he worked he noticed her ear was small and delicate next to his big clumsy hands. He pulled back the collar of her blouse and found more blood running down her chest. Her jacket was torn below her shoulder on the right side and blood had soaked through the material in about a six-inch radius.

He was far from being a doctor, but he had learned rudimentary first aid in the military. He had been assigned to a Special Forces group that had trained at the Navy SEAL facility in Pensacola, Florida. His training had prepared him to handle a medical emergency such as this without much thought.

He opened the buttons of her jacket, pulled it open and saw her white blouse was torn in the same place as the jacket. He lifted her blouse at the collar to look at the wound. The best he could tell it was about two inches long, but he didn't know how deep it was. He unbuttoned her blouse and folded it back to get a better look at the cut, to determine how deep it was. The wound ran almost parallel to the bra strap running over her shoulder. Most of the bottom of the cut was under her blood-soaked bra strap.

He leaned her forward and unhooked her holster so he could slip the jacket off her shoulder, and then pulled her arm through the sleeve. He did the same thing with the blouse and slowly lowered her back on the towel. He then slid her strap off her shoulder and took the towel and lightly dabbed the area. The cut was still bleeding but now he could see it wasn't that deep, and as he applied pressure, it readily stopped bleeding. The gash was probably caused by a sharp edge on the patio door.

He rose to his knees and checked the cut at the top of her head again. It had stopped bleeding altogether. He hurried to the bathroom across the hall and came back with a bottle of rubbing alcohol and some bandages that he found in the cabinet. He unscrewed the cap and poured it over the cut on her chest. She flinched, and let out a quiet groan as she began to regain consciousness. She swung her arms in the air and mumbled something he couldn't understand.

He grabbed her arms to hold her still so she wouldn't aggravate her wounds and restart the bleeding. "It's okay. It's me, Irwin Cole."

She looked at him with bewildered eyes. He said, "It's all right; you have some cuts from going through the glass door. I'm trying to bandage them for you."

He could feel her begin to relax, so he released his grip on her. She reached across her face with her left arm and felt her head. He said, "Careful, you have an open cut on your head. It's small and I've stopped the bleeding, so I think it will be okay. Just try not to move around too much."

She still seemed confused as she looked down and saw her blouse was half off, and her bra was covered in blood. She reached down with her right arm to cover herself and groaned from the pain. He noticed her eyes looking down, and quickly said, "I'm sorry. I had to open your blouse to see how deep that cut was. I poured some alcohol on the wound, and that's when you woke."

"It felt like someone held a red hot poker against my skin and it still burns like hell."

"Sorry, that would be the alcohol, but you don't want an infection, do you?"

He picked up the roll of gauze and a pair of scissors and said, "I need to put some pressure on that cut with a bandage to stop the bleeding."

He cut a length and folded it over twice to make it thicker. He tore off several pieces of tape, and laid them upside down on the pile of towels. He placed the gauze over the cut and told her to hold it in place with her left hand. Very carefully he put the first piece of tape securely across the top of the bandage. When he tried to put the second piece across the bottom, it wouldn't stick because the area had become wet with blood.

"I need to wipe this area dry again."

She looked at him. "Are you sure you know what you're doing?"

He began dabbing the blood off the top of her breast. He pulled down on her bra cup slightly to try and dry the area thoroughly. He looked at her and she returned his look with raised eyebrows and a slight frown.

He said, "It's okay; I was trained as a medic in the military."

"Yeah, like I've never heard that one before."

He switched to the other end of the towel and dried the area, and then placed a new piece of tape across the bandage.

"Good, it's sticking now," he said without expression.

"It better be Mister, after that," she replied with a small turn of her lips.

He returned her slight smile. "All in the call of duty, ma'am."

He covered her chest with a fresh towel. "Good as new."

"Thank you. Where are we, anyway?"

"We're at my friend Ross's place, a few houses down the beach. We try to check one another's places when we are here."

She reached into her jacket pocket and pulled out her cell phone. "Crap, the display is shattered. I need to call in and let them know where we are "

He shook his head and said, "For so many reasons, I'd really like it if you wouldn't do that. For one, I shot and killed a man at my home. Second, the FBI thinks I killed my wife for her money, and oh, don't forget that pesky little book detailing the crime and including my so-called confession. I need to get some answers before I talk to the FBI. Whoever is doing this to me, I think that's exactly what they want, for me to be arrested. "Now with a shooting at my house the press is going to have a feast. My opponents in Washington will have me convicted and headed for the gallows before you can blink an eye."

"What shooting are you talking about?" she asked with a puzzled look.

"Don't you remember what happened at the house?"

"No, it happened so fast. I remember seeing something moving on your back patio while you were reading the book. I thought it might be my boss from Tampa, so I opened the glass door and went out to see. The next thing I knew I was wrestling with some guy on the patio. He shoved me hard toward the house and the last thing I remember was hitting the glass door in the kitchen headfirst. Now here I am on the floor of this kitchen half naked. I need to tell you, Senator; your alibis are starting to wear a little thin."

"I was sitting there minding my business, reading the book in the kitchen, when suddenly you came crashing through my glass door," he replied indignantly. "That door was expensive, by the way.

"I jumped up and saw the man outside, and I ran out after him. By the time I caught up to him, he had already pulled out a gun. We wrestled a bit with the gun and the next thing I knew. two shots fired. I think they hit somewhere inside the house. I had a hold of the hand that his gun was in and twisted it backward far enough to make him either drop the gun or end up with a broken wrist.

"That's when the gun went off again, and he was shot in the chest. We both fell sideways against the deck railing and he flipped over the top rail. I looked down and saw him lodged in the bushes. He looked like he was dead. When I went down to check, he was definitely dead."

"My God!" she exclaimed. "Why didn't you call the local police instead of bringing us down here? It was obviously a case of self-defense."

"I'll tell you why. Just before you came crashing through the glass I heard the front door open and footsteps in the foyer. I assumed it was your boss from Tampa. After the struggle and the gun went off, I heard two car doors closing in front of the house. That's when I suspected this guy I fought with wasn't by himself. I snuck around the side of the house, just as a car's engine started. I wasn't sure of their intent and you were lying on the kitchen floor out cold. I assumed they had guns also, so the first thing I could think of was grabbing you, the book, and heading down the beach to get away."

"Running after a man with a gun is a stupid thing to do, Mr. Senator. It's not like arguing some point on the floor of the house. You could have been killed, and my ass would have been in serious trouble."

"I was special ops in the Navy long before I became a senator, thank you. It's like riding a bike. Once you learn that stuff it just comes naturally."

"If I don't call my office and let them know where I am I will lose my job. Is that what you want?"

"No, Agent Martin, that's the last thing I want. But remember earlier you said that finding my wife was your number one priority? I need some time to figure out what's going on here. I believe the secret has to be in this damn book. Let me finish reading the book, and then you can contact your office and have them pick you up. I love my wife, and I need to find her. Also, your phone is dead so you have a legitimate excuse for not calling. I'll back up your story."

She looked at the broken cell phone in her hand then glanced to the wall phone in the kitchen. She tried to stand but her legs wouldn't hold her.

"Easy there, let me help you up." He bent and put his hand under her left arm and pulled her up in front of him. As he did, the towel covering her fell to the floor. He picked it up and she grabbed it out of his hand.

"Thanks." Her face was red.

He looked in her eyes pleadingly. "Please, Agent Martin, can you give me some time to figure this out, an hour or two at the most?"

She sat down in a kitchen chair and stared down at her feet. He knew she was weighing the situation, and he waited patiently.

Finally she spoke. "I know I'm going to regret this but, yes, I will give you more time, until you finish reading the book and maybe figure out what's going on. You know I can't take sides. On the other hand, you're right about how the FBI will handle this. It would take days to sort through the bureaucracy—especially a high-profile case like this one. And I am going to give you the benefit of the doubt, since you helped me to safety. And why don't you just call me Melissa."

He smiled with relief. "Thank you, Melissa. There's a bathroom in the master bedroom, you can use it to get cleaned up. I'm going to finish reading the book while you're in there."

She disappeared through the bedroom door, and he took the book out of the canvas bag he had brought with him from the house. As he leaned back on the sofa and began to read, he could hear the water begin to run in the room behind him.

He found his place, about three-quarters of the way though the book, where he had stopped when Agent Martin came flying through the glass door. It gave him a sick feeling in his stomach, but he forced himself to continue reading.

* * *

Agent Martin found some shampoo in the cabinet and began gingerly washing her hair in the sink. She very carefully cleaned off the matted dried blood on the right side of her head, working slowly so she wouldn't aggravate her wound and cause it to begin bleeding again. After rinsing all the blood down the drain she mused about how long it had been since she had soaked in a bath. She closed the drain stopper and let the tub fill with hot soapy water. She positioned herself against the edge of the tub, being careful that her bandage on her chest didn't get wet. She had forgotten how relaxing it was as she leaned back and soaked. She allowed her lower body to float, and before long she felt as if she could have stayed in there all night.

She closed her eyes and allowed herself to drift, far from the tub in Ross's house . . .

She was alone, lying on her back, floating in a small boat. The sun above her head was bright, and the waves were lapping against the hull. The boat rocked gently with the movement of the waves, and she felt as one with the lolling movement. She felt disconnected from her arms and legs, as though she couldn't move them even if she wanted to.

Without warning, the waves began splashing over the sides of the small boat. She let out a scream as her fear of drowning suddenly gripped her.

She tried to sit up to stop the water from splashing her face, but she couldn't. She was being held down. She struggled and twisted but couldn't break loose, her arms and legs wouldn't respond to her needs. The bright light was blinding her view of the force that had her pinned to the bottom of the boat.

She screamed again, and with one final, sudden burst of energy, she raised her upper body, pushing her captive back away from her.

She opened her eyes. She was face to face with Senator Cole. She screamed, "Let me go!"

He grabbed her swinging arms and held them. She twisted in the water, splashing it everywhere.

"Melissa! Melissa, it's just a dream. It's okay, you're having a dream."

She looked up at him in terror. Then she finally stopped struggling, realizing she was still in Ross's tub and not on a tiny boat.

He said, "Its all right, you must have fallen asleep. You were screaming, and I came in to see what was wrong."

She looked at him uncomprehendingly. "That dream was so real. I was in a little boat, and the waves were splashing over the sides of the boat. I tried to get up, but my arms and legs wouldn't move."

He grabbed the towel and wiped the soapy water from her eyes. "Are you going to be all right?"

She looked up at his soaked clothes. "Yes. I'm sorry."

"Fortunate for you that the tub is full of bubbles."

Then she realized she was lying naked in the tub and quickly covered herself with her arms, flushing.

"I'm going to go find some dry clothes." He jumped up and left her in the tub and headed to the closet.

She let out a huge breath. *How embarrassing is that? He must think I'm a nut case. I haven't done something like that since I was a little girl.* Her mind switched back to the tub, and she started thinking about the predicament she was in. Her stomach was churning, and she knew the right thing to do was call in and let her office know where she was. She put her hands on her face and whispered, "I have to do it."

She stepped out of the tub, and wrapped the towel around her as she walked out to the bedroom. There was a telephone on the nightstand. She turned and looked at the closed bedroom door, and picked up the receiver. Her head was hurting, and she couldn't remember the direct number for her dispatcher, so she dialed the main number. A few seconds later a voice said, "FBI. How may I assist you?"

She opened her mouth to speak, but nothing came out.

"Hello, you have reached the Tampa office of the FBI. How may I assist you, please?"

Finally, she said, "I'm so sorry; I have the wrong number." She hung up the telephone and put her hand on her forehead. Then she turned and saw Cole standing in the doorway. They looked at each other silently.

"Damn you, what the hell am I doing?" she blurted. "I'm going to lose my job. I'm breaking every rule there is."

"Melissa, I need some time to find Barbara."

She stared back at him and sighed resignedly, and he gave her a single approving nod.

"My clothes are a mess. I can't put them back on."

"I'm sure Ross's wife Jeanie has some clothes that will fit you. She might be a tad bit heavier than you. I'm sure under the circumstances, she wouldn't mind if you borrow some of her things."

He went out to continue reading while Martin got dressed.

"Have you seen my shoes?" she asked when she emerged from the bedroom.

"Yeah, they came off in the sand when I was dragging you down the beach. I'm sorry. I was trying to get as close to the water as I could so we wouldn't leave tracks in the sand. I thought about stopping and picking them up, but with trying to carry you and the bag my hands were full. Maybe Jeanie has some shoes that would fit you."

"Those were Manolo Blahnik pumps." She sighed deeply. *There's several hundred dollars out to sea.*

"Mana—what?"

"Never mind. That must be why my feet have all these scratches on the bottom. I noticed them in the tub and was wondering how I got them. Look."

She walked to the chair beside him and raised her foot to the arm and let it rest there for him to see. He could see tiny slices all over the bottom of her heel and toes.

"I never realized the sand and shells would do that, but then again I've never dragged anyone across the beach."

She disappeared again into the bedroom, mumbling something, and returned a few minutes later. "I found some sneakers and with a couple pair of socks, I think they'll work. I'm going to go find a bag to put all these bloody clothes in."

She went to the kitchen and he could smell the fresh scent of shampoo as she walked past him. She bagged her old clothes and then went to the guest bathroom to pick up his wet clothes from the floor. She heard the senator let out a gasp, and the sound of the book dropping on the coffee table.

She rushed out and found the senator holding his head in his hands. "What happened, did you find something in the book that can help?"

He lifted his head. "It says Barbara dies Wednesday at 6:00 PM. I've got less than two days left to find her. I finished reading the confession, where I'm presumably confessing to the murder. The last chapter is the only one I could to connect with in the book. It's hard to explain, but it's as if I did write the book. The voice of the book, it's me talking, but when I try to imagine writing such terrible things, I can't. Those kinds of thoughts aren't in my mind. It's written as I would write it, but I could never think of those awful thoughts. I know it sounds crazy."

She put her hand on his arm. "It's important that you keep trying. After all, I'm risking everything here."

He patted the top of her hand. "I know."

"The last chapter differs from the rest of the book," he continued. "I can't make any sense out of most of the book. However, the last chapter is about feeling regret and remorse. I can, and I have, felt those feelings before, though I never wrote about them. But the style would be the same."

A sound like a Big Ben chime suddenly came from the hallway. She looked at him with surprise. "It's the doorbell," she whispered.

"Who do you think it is?" she whispered again as she followed him to the foyer.

"I don't know, but I'm not answering it, that's for sure," he answered quietly.

All the blinds were closed at the front of the house. He looked through the peep hole on the door, and saw two uniformed police officers standing outside under the porch light.

The bell rang again, and she jumped slightly. He held his index finger to his lips, then made a hand signal indicating that there were two people outside.

A voice came out of the speaker on the wall behind them, and both of them jumped. He quickly placed his hand over her mouth, thinking she was going to let out an involuntary noise. The sound was coming from an intercom system connected to the outside.

"Hello, is anyone home? We are with the Sheriff's office, and we need to ask you a few questions please. It will just take a moment."

Cole whispered in her ear. "I helped Ross install this new intercom last time we were both in town. We got the wires mixed up and it stays active all the time on the outside."

"Don't any of these people ever stay home in these big fancy houses out here?"

"Should I go around back to see whether I can find anyone?"

"No, this place is too far away for them to have heard or seen anything anyway. The Feds wanted us to go way down here, it was their idea to go this far out."

"Who's this guy they're looking for anyway? I heard he was some big-wheel politician?"

"Yeah, that's what I heard too. The one agent said they found his fingerprints on the murder weapon."

"If he's a politician, I'm sure he'll be able to talk his way out."

"I don't think so. I heard them say he's being taken into custody and sent straight to Tampa to the FBI office up there. Come on, let's get out of here, nobody's home, and my feet are killing me with these new shoes."

They listened to the sound of footsteps moving away from the entrance. Agent Martin looked through the peep hole and saw the officers walking to their car. She then turned and looked at the senator, who was leaning against the wall staring at the dark entrance. She knew this changed everything. Now he was a wanted man.

"You touched that guy's gun at your house?"

"When the gun went off, he lost his grip, and I pulled it out of his hands. I tossed it over the rail before something else happened. How would they be able to get my prints off the gun that quickly? I thought it took days."

"Like most people, you've been watching too much television."

"I have to get out of here before they find me. Give me an hour, and then you can notify them of your whereabouts. Just say you woke from the hit on your head and have no idea how you got here."

"No way. I'm not letting you out of my sight. I'm in enough trouble without telling my boss I let you go and have no idea where you are. I realize the game has changed, but where you go, I go, from now on. Do you understand?"

"I need to go to the bathroom."

She had to smile, and some of the tension of the day lifted. "Very funny, Senator. I'll be right outside the door."

Cole found the keys to Ross's Ford Explorer hanging on the bulletin board in the kitchen. He grabbed a few bottles of water out of the refrigerator and slipped them into his bag. He found a pad of paper next to the telephone and left Ross a note on the bulletin board saying he had borrowed his car and a few personal items, and that he would call him when he could to explain everything. He didn't think Ross was planning to come home until Labor Day anyway and by then he would have everything back where it should be.

He turned off all the lights, and they walked out into the garage and got in the black Explorer. He pushed the button on the opener clipped to the visor, and the overhead door began to rise. The drive was a long winding path leading through dense growth to the road.

They headed down the dark drive with the headlights turned off. As they rounded the last curve before the road, a faint light could be seen shimmering through the bushes. He stopped the car with the emergency brake so the brake lights wouldn't come on, and turned off the ignition.

They looked out the window at the car parked on the road with its interior and parking lights on. In the dim light they could see the reflective tape running down the side of a Sheriff's cruiser.

Chapter 8

Monday, 8:40 PM

Barbara Cole sat staring out the small window at the marina. It was dark, and the dock lights glimmered across the water, transforming the brightly colored boats she had gazed on earlier in the day to dark outlines. *Here I am*, she thought, *near the water again, where I spent most of my life. It seems so unreal.*

The memory of her father came to mind, and his love of the water and of boating, and of all the times they had spent time together when she was a child, swimming and boating at the beach house.

Her mind drifted to her wedding day. It seemed like yesterday . . .

She stood in her wedding gown on the white sand in front of the beach house. It was the happiest day of her life.

She was marrying a US senator, whom she adored. Although she had only known him for a few months, it had been love at first sight. She was twenty-two and out of college with a business degree. He was thirty and had just won the senate election.

Before she met him her plan had been to work at her father's company. He would teach her the business, and someday she would take over the reins when he retired. She and her father had talked about it since she was a little girl.

But that began to change once she met Irwin. After graduation, she delayed her start at the company in order to spend the summer in Washington near her newfound love. And now, she was getting married.

Barbara looked across the glare of the white beach sand and saw her father standing on the back porch. Shoeless, she lifted her gown a few inches as she headed across the sand to talk to him.

When she reached him she wrapped her arms around the parent who had raised her on his own. They squeezed each other hard as she whispered, "Daddy, I love you, and I always will."

She looked in his eyes and could see them beginning to well up. Her father had never made her feel guilty about the choice she had made.

Roger Morrison forced a smile. "I remember the day when your mother and I were married. It was the happiest day of my life, too. We were so much in love, dedicated to each other. We were so happy and looking forward to our lives together, like you and Irwin are now. Then you came along, making our lives complete."

"Daddy, I know you've never wanted to talk about it, but what happened between Mother and you?"

He looked into her eyes for a few moments and finally began to speak. "I still love your mother as much as I did the day we were married. I'm not sure how she feels, because we have never discussed it.

"After the divorce, I was hoping she would be more involved in your life, but that never happened. I tried not to force the issue. She was having a difficult struggle and I thought I was protecting you by shielding you from the truth. I suppose I was trying to protect her as well. But now you're a grown woman, so you deserve to know the truth."

He hesitated for a few seconds as he collected his thoughts. "Back when the company was in its early days, your mother worked there too, as you know, because we couldn't afford a secretary. We would bring you to work and put you in the playpen we had set up in the office. Your mother had a best friend –her name was Susan—who would watch you when things at the office got too hectic.

"Susan and your mother had been friends for years. I suppose it was inevitable that your mother would introduce her to Mark Kraus, since he was my business partner. You know that Mark, as brilliant as he is, isn't a social person, but he and Susan hit it off right away. The next thing we knew Susan was pregnant. She and Mark were married and two years later they had another child."

He paused, and his expression darkened. "I came home early one day from an out-of-town business meeting. When I went to the bedroom to put my suitcase away, I found your mother and Susan together in our bed. She told me she couldn't help it; she and Susan had been lovers since they met in college. She had hoped that once they were both married it would change the feelings they had for each other. But it didn't.

"Susan Kraus killed herself in front of her family a few days later. Her death devastated both Mark and your mother. Neither of them were quite the same after that dreadful day. Mark seemed more distant and even weirder than before, if that's possible. Our business relationship remained fine but we never again socialized away from work. Your mother started drinking excessively, and she became harder to live with. I tried to get her to go to therapy, but she wouldn't have any part of it. Eventually, it led to our separation and divorce."

Barbara stared at her father in disbelief as she tried to take in what he had just told her. Eventually her gaze shifted out over the water as she leaned back against the porch railing. Her father put his hand on her arm.

"I'm sorry for burdening you with all of this today. I should have explained it to you a long time ago. It's just that after those terrible events, you and the company were all I had left. Now today in a sense I am losing you too. At least I will always have the company. I made sure of that."

"Daddy, that's crazy. You'll always have me. Being married to Irwin won't affect my relationship with you."

"I know, sweetie. I'm sorry; I want you and Irwin to enjoy your lives together. He's a great guy, and I wish you nothing but happiness."

"Thank you, Daddy."

A thumping noise on the outside wall brought Barbara back to the present. As the sound faded, she continued staring out at the water with tears in her eyes.

She reflected back to when she was a small girl. She could never understand why her mother wouldn't come to see her. She would often lie in bed at night and cry herself to sleep, wanting her mother. Later, as a teenager, her feelings turned bitter: she felt abandoned, and hated her mother. When she finally found out the truth on her wedding day, she had felt sorry for her mother, realizing what she must have gone through all those years.

Two weeks ago she had been caught off guard when her mother had called. She couldn't even remember the last time they had spoken, other than when they had both been at her father's funeral a couple of months earlier, but their conversation had been brief.

"Is everything all right?"

"Yes, I am fine. I was wondering whether you would like to come to New York and pay me a visit."

"You want to see me after all of these years? Why? Why are you doing this?"

"I know how you must feel, Barbara. You probably despise me, and I couldn't blame you for that. However, it's extremely important that I speak to you in person as soon as possible. Will you grant me that one request?"

"I don't think that would be a good idea, Mother."

"Barbara, someone's life is at risk here."

"What are you talking about?"

"Barbara . . . honey . . . it's your life that's at risk."

Chapter 9

Monday 10:50 PM

Senator Cole and Agent Martin had waited several minutes in the drive until the Sheriff's cruiser finally pulled away. They headed south on the beach road in the borrowed Explorer. The road was narrow and winding as it snaked its way through the residential area, and with the dense brush on both sides it was barely wide enough for two automobiles to pass each other. Usually one car would pull to the side as far as possible and stop while the other passed. Cole had cautiously rounded the last bend before it widened to a normal county-maintained road when he saw the flashing blue and red lights.

He hit his hand against the steering wheel in frustration. "Damn, a roadblock." They were too close to stop and turn around without being obvious.

"What are we going to do? They're going to recognize their senator."

"Don't be too sure of that. A fellow senator once told me that fewer than 10% of my constituency would recognize me out in public. At the time, I thought he was full of crap, but now I hope he's right."

"You know they're going to ask for identification."

He didn't respond, as they slowly approached the flashing lights and were the second car in line waiting to pass through the checkpoint.

"Maybe I can use my FBI credentials to get us through? I'll tell them I'm taking you into headquarters."

"I don't think that will work. I'm driving, for one thing, and we're heading in the wrong direction for your office."

"It's the only choice we have. Hurry and change places with me."

They unbuckled their seatbelts and just as they began to slide in their seats the car ahead of them pulled away. The officer began waving for them to pull forward with his flashlight.

"Shit, it's too late, we have to pull forward."

He reached behind and grabbed a hat from the back seat and put it on.

She smiled. "Cute."

The officer continued to wave his flashlight indicating for the Ford to pull forward. Cole pulled ahead and rolled the window down as he stopped next to the officer. "Good evening officer, is there some kind of a problem?"

"No sir, I need to see your license and registration please."

Cole looked over at her and swallowed.

"One moment, officer."

Just then he heard the short blast of a siren, and saw more red and blue lights in his rearview mirror. The radio on the officer's belt started screaming, and the deputy grabbed his microphone from his chest. Cole couldn't understand what was said over the radio, but he heard the officer say, "Affirmative."

His heart was about to beat out of his chest. The officer bent over and put his head at the open window.

"Sir, I need you to pull ahead and park off the side of the road and let the patrol car behind you get by. Once he has safely passed, you can continue on your way. We appreciate your patience."

They pulled ahead and the patrol shot around them with a loud squeal of tires as it sped down the road. Cole let out a sigh. "That was close."

Martin shook her hands and rubbed her arms. "Wow; that was intense. I can't believe how calm and collected you were. Maybe you should have been a criminal instead of a senator."

"Some will argue they are one and the same," he laughed and then added, "Remember, I am a criminal in the eyes of the FBI."

They continued south on the beach road and followed it over the bridge and off the island to the mainland. As they approached Highway 776, the primary north-south thoroughfare through Englewood, he noticed two patrol cars parked in the parking lot of a fast-food restaurant. They were facing the beach road, watching the cars coming off the bridge from the island. He glanced down at the speedometer without thinking about it then glanced at her.

She said, "Don't worry, we're just another car on the road," as they passed them by and headed south on 776. According to the clock in the Explorer, the time was 11:16 PM. The traffic on a Monday night was light, almost nonexistent. He was concerned about being one of the few vehicles on the road while they were still so close to his house. He felt the chances of being stopped randomly were too high. He turned right again on Placida Road and headed toward the Cape Haze peninsula.

"Where are we going now?"

"Some obscure thing I read in the book has given me a hunch, and I need to follow up on it. It's probably nothing, but I need to check it out to be sure."

"What obscure thing are you talking about? Senator Cole, I need to know what's on your mind."

"I don't think I can explain it to you. It's something I'll have to show you for you to understand. Trust me, you'll see what I mean."

The road was deserted, no cars in either direction. He watched his speed closely, thinking it would be stupid to get pulled over for speeding after all he had already been through. He could feel a new tension in the air as he drove down the dark deserted road. He had put her in a terrible position, and decided to try to lighten the mood.

"Melissa, where are you from? What made you decide to join the FBI"?

"I'm a local girl. I was born in Port Charlotte. I live in Tampa now, near the office, which makes it convenient. I was fortunate to get my first assignment so close to my hometown. I think it helped that I was the only agent in my class that didn't request a big city like Washington, New York, or Chicago. Everyone in the class wanted to be close to where the action is.

"I was attending USF, studying for my law degree. I was planning to become a lawyer, against my father's wishes. He's been a cop all his life and he used to say the cops would spend months getting enough evidence together to arrest someone, and then some high-paid lawyer would come along and get them off in a few hours. He never told me not to be a lawyer, but I could tell it wasn't his first choice for me."

"From a lawyer to an FBI agent is quite a change of direction. How did that happen?"

"No, most agents in the FBI have some sort of a law degree. I met this guy in my last year of law school. He had already applied to the FBI and had been accepted at the Academy when he graduated from school. The FBI was all he ever talked about. I had never met anyone so committed to anything in my life. He told me that he had lived and breathed the bureau day and night since he was ten.

"I was so impressed by his dedication that I began to think maybe it was something I should check into. I was beginning to teeter with the lawyer career. The other students in the law classes weren't the type of people I enjoyed being around. The more I thought about practicing as an attorney, the less attractive it became.

"I talked to Josh—that's his name—and he thought it was a great plan. He helped me apply, and the FBI informed me that when I passed the bar exam I would be accepted into their program. He began coaching me every day on what I needed to know to get through the Academy. He taught me how to shoot a gun, and we would work out at the gym at school."

"Well, it sounds as though you were fortunate to have your own personal trainer for the FBI."

"I was. I don't think I could have done it without Josh's help. He taught me everything, like he knew what the entire written and oral exam would cover. When I went to Quantico it was a breeze. I was number one in my class. I assume that helped me get the Tampa assignment also."

"I'm sure that had a lot to do with it. You earned it. What about Josh? Is he in Tampa also?"

Martin looked out her window and became quiet. Then she looked ahead, avoiding his eyes as she spoke.

"No, he's not in Tampa. He was removed from the program right before graduation. I was so distraught for him, and offered to try to help him. He kept saying he had a backup plan, and everything would work out."

"I'm sorry Melissa. That must have been very difficult for both of you. Did you two continue to see each other? What did he end up doing, if I may ask?"

"No, it wasn't like that, we weren't a couple or anything, just good friends. He left Virginia . . . and disappeared. He called me a few times right after graduation at Quantico, and then he vanished. That was four years ago, and I haven't talked to him since. I used the FBI computers to try to locate him once, and it's as if he vanished off the face of the earth."

They rode in silence for the next several miles until he slowed and turned into a marina parking lot. He drove toward the last covered building in the complex, pulled up next to a shed and turned the engine off. The place was deserted and quiet except for the sound of water lapping against the seawall.

Martin asked, "Where are we? What are we doing here?"

"We're in Cape Haze at a marina, and we're going for a boat ride."

"Senator Cole, I think I have been more than accommodating with you thus far. But unless you can give me a specific reason for us being here, I'm going to contact my office immediately."

"As I told you on the way…"

They both noticed a man approaching the Explorer with a cell phone to his ear. When the man was about five feet away from the front bumper he stopped and stared at them through the windshield. He spoke into his phone, turned and walked toward the other end of the parking lot.

Cole asked, "What do you suppose that was all about?"

"It looked as if he thought he knew us. That seemed odd. Do you come here often?"

"Not anymore."

"Hmmm, well, tell me more about this boat ride,"

He began explaining his theory as they got out of the Explorer and headed for the boat shed.

Once inside, they were walking on rickety docks over the water in the pitch dark. Then she tripped on one of the uneven boards, making a loud scuffing noise as she caught herself before falling. He turned. "Are you okay back there?"

"Yes I'm fine. When I was a child, my brother and I had been on a small sailboat that had capsized. I almost drowned when I was pinned in the boat, under the rigging. My brother was finally able to pull me loose, and I haven't been on a boat since."

He climbed on Ross's 31-foot Whaler and lifted the cover of the small compartment at the stern. He reached down inside. "One thing about old Ross is he's predictable. The keys are right where he said they would be if I ever wanted to borrow his boat."

"Remind me to thank old Ross someday," she whispered.

He held his hand out to help her climb on board. As she took the first step, he could feel her arm quivering as he pulled her across the open space between the dock and the boat. She immediately moved to the center of the boat, and held the handrail next to the companionway door. He put the key in the ignition, and the engine fired up with a loud echo under the shed's tin roof.

He undid the bow and stern lines and then put the boat in forward gear, as they began moving slowly out of the slip. She came toward him. "How can you see to drive the boat? It's pitch dark; we could run into something or another boat."

"First, I know the way to where we're going. If I didn't, I could always turn on the chart plotter, and it would show me the way. Second, that's what running lights are for; so you can see other boats, and they can see you."

She climbed into the chair next to him as they made their way out of the marina toward the Intracoastal Waterway. She asked, "Aren't we supposed to be wearing life jackets?"

"The life jackets are in the cabin if you would like to put one on, but the law doesn't require you to wear one."

He could tell that she did want one, but she didn't say anything.

At the channel marker, he headed south and increased the speed of the boat slightly. He used the spotlight to find the next red marker, then the green one. Martin began to see how they were following the channel markers like highway road signs. He handed her the spotlight, and they made their way through the maze, staying in the channel headed for Little Gasparilla Island.

Suddenly they heard a roar coming from in front of them. Out of nowhere, another boat shot across in front of their bow and passed them about fifteen feet from their side. It was headed in the opposite direction, coming out of the same channel they were planning to turn into. The other boat didn't have any running lights on and was traveling at top speed.

"Asshole!" Senator Cole hollered, but the boat was already long gone in the dark. Its wake hit them, causing their boat to roll violently from side to side. Martin grabbed the railing, trying to hold on, and dropped the spotlight.

"Are you all right over there, Popeye?"

She had no reply as she glared into the dark.

A few minutes later the dock was in view. "So much for your running lights philosophy."

"That's the kind of idiot who gets people killed out here on the water."

They tied the boat to the dock and began walking down the wobbly pier toward the island. He looked back and asked her, "Did you bring your weapon with you?"

"Now you're playing my game," she said, as she reached into the small canvas bag with the book and water inside and brought out her pistol. "Why…do you think we're going to need it?"

"I have no idea what we are going to run into out here. I hope nothing and that it's a wasted boat ride."

"Great, a wasted boat ride. What is this place anyway? Where are we?"

"It's called Little Gasperilla Island. It's only accessible by boat since the Intracoastal Waterway went through back in the sixties. Before the wooden bridge was removed for the Waterway, residents could drive to the island from the mainland. Most people still keep old Jeeps and golf carts on the island for hauling supplies between the docks and their homes. My father-in-law owned a house over here on the island that he used as a vacation getaway. Before Barbara and I bought the house on Englewood beach, we would use this place for vacations also. We thought it was the perfect retreat, isolated from the public."

They walked up the sandy path that led from the docks to the crumbling road that ran the full length of the island. When they reached the broken asphalt road, they walked south toward the house. The island at this end became narrow; it was about five-hundred yards from the Gulf to the bay side. The pavement narrowed into an easement for access down the bay side of the properties.

The easement was overgrown and the moonlight that had been showing them the way was almost blocked by the dense overgrowth. The path was barely wide enough for a golf cart to pass through.

"The house hasn't been used in some time. After Barbara's father died three months ago, I suggested to Barbara that she should sell the place, but she has so many childhood memories here that she couldn't bring herself to do it. She remembers spending most of her summers at the house before she moved away for college."

Cole shined the flashlight at a trellis, and they could see a small opening in the overgrown vines. "Here we are." He led the way through the gate. Once they were inside the fence, the area was open and spacious. They felt the breeze blowing in from the Gulf on their sweaty faces and the sound of the surf could be heard on the other side of the house.

They walked up a brick path that was almost covered with sand as they headed toward the steep stairway on the front of the house. The house was up on stilts like all the other houses they had passed on the path. Under the house was an open-air Jeep parked under a makeshift plywood cover. Overhead, a covered porch went completely around the perimeter of the house. The house was covered in lapboard siding, and the roof was made of galvanized tin. The many windows were covered with vertical wooden shutters.

He was ahead as they started up the stairs, and Martin said, "Let me go first." Cole followed close behind her. On the porch she said, "Wait here Senator, while I check it out."

The wooden floor creaked with every step they took as they approached the front door. He bent and lifted the floor mat and picked up the key. When he started to put the key in the lock, the door pushed open. It wasn't latched.

"Now might be a good time to have your gun handy."

He pushed the door farther open and there was a strained screech from the door hinges. She removed the gun from her bag and held it out in front of her body. She grabbed his arm, indicating for him to wait and let her go first. She slid past him and went into the center of the room. He whispered, "Ready," as he flipped the light switch on. Martin spun in all directions pointing her gun as she scanned the visible areas.

She said, "I don't think anyone is here, but we should check the rest of the house to be sure."

She checked the kitchen and the utility room, and all seemed clear. Then she went back to the living room and waited at the foot of the stairs.

Finally she called out. "Senator Cole, is everything okay?"

When she didn't receive an answer, she headed up the stairs with the gun ready. There were two doors at the top of the landing, and the one on the right had a light on. She slowly walked to the open door and peeked around, keeping her body behind the wall. She saw Cole standing next to the bed, staring at something in his hand.

"Senator Cole, are you all right? What's wrong?"

He slowly turned to face her and his face was as white as a ghost. He held out his hand, holding a picture. It was a photo of him and his wife behind the glass of a gold frame. A large X, drawn with a red marker, was covering Barbara's face.

Chapter 10

Tuesday, 5:50 AM

The meeting was set for 6:00AM in William Anderson's office at the FBI building. The attendees were the same as the previous evening. Mackey walked into room feeling tired; he had been awake most of the night reading the book. Everybody was already in the room except Anderson.

Tom and Raphael had been laughing about something when Mackey entered the room. They were the jokesters of the office and could always be counted on to lighten the mood.

In reply to Mackey's inquiry as to Anderson's whereabouts, Raphael spoke up. "He's in the Director's office, getting himself torn a new asshole, I imagine."

Tom and Dr. Moiré exchanged smiles. Mackey looked down at the table because he knew Anderson had bent a few rules with the case as a personal favor to him.

The door flew open with a loud thump, and Anderson hustled into the room and joined them at the conference table. Despite his businesslike manner they saw disgust written on his face. Tom and Raphael looked over at each other and winked.

Anderson said, "Good morning. Mackey, thanks for coming in this morning."

Mackey nodded his head in acknowledgment. "Morning, William."

"Dr. Moiré, why don't you go first? Has your team discovered anything new since last night?"

"Thank you Mr. Anderson. We have compared the writing of the book to that of several papers that Senator Cole has written. The sentence structure, syntax and grammar were all identical. We feel certain that all the documents were by the same person. So, based on those discoveries, it is our conclusion that Senator Cole did indeed write this book."

The room was silent. Anderson watched Mackey as he rose from his seat, walked to the credenza, and poured himself a cup of coffee.

"Doctor, are you saying that you and your team are confident enough about your conclusions that I can issue an arrest warrant for Senator Irwin Cole?"

"What I'm saying is that it is what it is. We are comfortable stating that the book and all the documents we studied were written by the same person."

Anderson asked, "Mackey, did you finish the book last night?"

"Actually I just finished it this morning."

"What do you think? Do you think Senator Cole wrote the book?"

Mackey walked to the table with his coffee cup and set it down in front of him. He looked over at Dr. Moiré, then at Anderson.

"I'm no scholar, but that book was one mass of confusion as far as I'm concerned. The thoughts and feelings in the book made no sense to me whatsoever. To answer your question, yes, everything about the book, the voice, the word structure, and the details, sounds like Irwin Cole. I lay in bed this morning trying to think of any possible reason he would write a book like this and there's nothing, no reason in hell why he would do it. He's the hottest man in Washington right now. For him it would be political suicide, not to mention heaven forbid, that if he did murder Barbara, he would be the first US senator to die of lethal injection."

"I know what you're saying, Mackey. I paced the floor for hours last night myself trying to make some sense of it. We have to remember that this wouldn't be the first time that a perpetrator has introduced evidence himself. Remember the stockbroker who killed his wife and left that evidence trail for us to find. Later, he argued that he was set up by her lover. He kept insisting that no one would be stupid enough to leave that kind of evidence. He almost got away with it, too. If the woman he was having the affair with hadn't come forward, he would probably be a free man right now. Doctor, can you shed any more light on a motive for the book?"

"As I said last night, the book is both confusing and brilliant. It's like the words were written by opposing personalities. One personality feels remorse and confesses to the crime, while the other personality is deceitful and blocks everything that the first personality is confessing to. As to a motive for the book, I would suggest that it was to create mass confusion, which it has achieved. The motive for the crime, on the other hand, I believe is hidden in one sentence. Let me see, page 212; yes, this is the line."

The time has come for me to make restitution for all the injustices I have inflicted on others and to deliver revenge for the injustices that have been inflicted on me.

"This is one of the few statements in the book that's not later rescinded by misdirection. Clearly, the author of the book has deep psychological issues, perhaps multiple personalities, and the feeling he has been treated wrongly and needs to make it right through revenge."

Raphael said, "He sounds like he's a nut to me."

Anderson leaned forward. "Okay gentlemen, let's stay focused. Doctor, do you know if the crime has taken place yet or when it will?"

"I believe it will happen Wednesday night at 6:00 PM unless of course the book is one huge farce and Mrs. Cole is already dead, and the killer is using this time for his escape."

The men sat silently as they processed the new information.

Anderson let out a small sigh. "Assuming Dr. Moiré's prediction is correct, that gives us less than two days to resolve this. Tom, why don't you bring us up to date with the information we received from the field so far."

"Well boss, unfortunately there's not much. The gunshot victim found at the Cole residence in Florida has been identified as a Billy Parker. He's a small-time criminal with a long record and was recently released from Raeford Prison. Most convictions were for burglary and extortion. He's a local punk for hire.

"We're still checking his known acquaintances for connections to anyone else. The gun that killed him was stolen and had his prints and Irwin Cole's fingerprints on it. The gun was fired at a point-blank range. The bullet went through his chest next to his heart, and death was probably less than a minute later. The lab boys are saying there may have been a struggle because of the acute upward angle of the bullet and the gunpowder residue on the victim's hand. However, he could have been the one who fired the other shots found in the kitchen wall and that would explain the residue on his hands. The bullets recovered were from the same gun. A bottle of chloroform was found in his pocket wrapped in a cloth. The cloth tested negative for chloroform. Our thinking is that the chloroform was for Mrs. Cole if she tried to resist, but wasn't needed.

"Agent Melissa Martin's body has not been found. The Coast Guard is still searching, but they believe based on the tides last night if her body was in the Gulf, they would have recovered it by now unless the body was weighted or consumed by marine life."

Tom stopped speaking and looked at Anderson with a puzzled look. "I never worked with her, but I recognize the name Melissa Martin."

Anderson said, "You should; she is the only person in the history of the Academy at Quantico to pass with a perfect score."

"Yeah, I remember now. Everybody assumed she cheated somehow."

Anderson shook his head. "She didn't cheat. I can assure you of that. In fact, I was the supervisor responsible for the training program at the Academy at the time, and she is one intelligent young lady. I can remember it like it was yesterday because of what happened. Another person in the class also aced the entire program, but I had to make the decision to remove him before graduation because he couldn't pass the psychological examination."

Tom nodded and continued. "It doesn't look good for Agent Martin. It's been twelve hours since we had any contact with her. Her shoe was the only thing we found in the water at the end of the tracks where she was apparently dragged. Her cell phone trace has been negative also and as you know our phones continue to generate a signal when they are turned off. The blood type found on the kitchen floor was a match for hers, and the DNA results will be back soon.

"Mrs. Cole's carry-on was found at the house. They say it was the same bag that we saw in the video from the airport. The bag didn't reveal anything that could help us with her whereabouts. The fingerprints we could identify on the bag were from Mrs. Cole, Senator Cole, and Billy Parker.

"We talked to several passengers on the plane, and no one noticed anything unusual occurring with Mrs. Cole. The woman sitting next to her couldn't remember Mrs. Cole saying a single word the entire flight."

Tom paused and glanced at Mackey for a moment. Mackey said, "That's unusual for Barbara. She has a very outgoing personality."

Tom looked at Anderson. "The Tampa office is working on the theory that Parker was employed by Senator Cole, and that's how his fingerprints got on the bag. He fits the description of the man driving the rental car that picked up Mrs. Cole. Tom looked down at his notes as he made his next statement. "The senator's laptop was the computer used to upload the file to the book publisher." Mackey sat stock still.

"Several sets of footprints were found at the front foyer and we are speculating there may have been other people in the house. The front door was discovered open when they arrived at the home."

"Maybe they were grabbed by these other people," Mackey suggested.

"We don't have a clue. So far, nothing else has been discovered at the house that would indicate that's what happened. Both Cole vehicles are still in the garage and Martin's car is parked in the drive. The senator has also vanished. Roadblocks were set that night, but apparently he slipped through before we were in place. The rental car that picked up Mrs. Cole at the airport was abandoned about five miles from the Cole's home. The car had been wiped clean, but we have it at the lab looking for traces. That's all we have from the South. Raphael has the Northern stuff."

"Tom, what would be the reason for abandoning the car five miles from the house?" asked Mackey. "That doesn't make any sense to me."

"I asked the same question. We can only hypothesize that it was part of the falling out between Senator Cole and Billy Parker which then resulted in the gunshot."

Mackey looked skeptical as he then directed his attention toward Raphael.

Raphael opened his notebook and began. "We talked to the mother in New York but didn't get any new information. She said that her daughter and the senator were the perfect couple and were very much in love."

"I agree," Mackey said quickly. "There was never the slightest indication of friction in their marriage."

"Mackey, I know what you're saying, but we've seen this before in multiple personality cases," Anderson said gently. "Everybody who knows the person can't believe he could be responsible for such horrible crimes. The person can function normally in society, and no one suspects his dark side."

Raphael continued. "The mother admitted that the relationship with her daughter had been strained for a long time. She confirmed that this visit was the first time in many years that she and her daughter had spent time together. She kept repeating how happy she was that they had finally gotten together. She also said that Senator Cole had called her looking for his wife on Monday at 10:00 AM. She said he seemed confused about which day she was going to fly back to Florida. One odd thing was that the telephone records for the mother's phone confirmed a phone call that morning, but the number for the phone that placed the call wasn't captured."

Anderson asked, "What do you mean it wasn't captured?"

"The telephone company couldn't tell me what the originating number was for the phone call. They said there's no record of the number." Anderson shook his head. "How can there be no record? Check that out further, it doesn't make any sense."

Raphael said, "The other odd thing is that we could find no record of Mr. and Mrs. Cole calling each other on their cell phones for the past two months. Before that time there were regular calls between the two phones. That seems strange for a husband and wife to stop communicating like that." He raised his head and looked around the room. "Apparently they never run out of bread or milk. Nothing else in the phone records seemed unusual.

"The mother did say that her daughter received a call Saturday morning on her cell phone and after that she was packed and ready to go. That call didn't show up on her cell phone records either. I'm going to call the mother back and verify the time.

The agent who visited the house said the mother seemed confused and unsure of the details. She begins her day with a cocktail. At one point, she insisted that she had already talked to the FBI, and it was our fault. That was puzzling. The senator's aide Miles Connor confirmed when we talked to him, that the mother does have a drinking problem."

Anderson asked, "Have we learned anything else about the senator from this aide? He would be the one to see him at his best and worst times."

"He's coming down today to talk to us at the office. He seemed cooperative and willing to help when we questioned him at the Capitol office, but he seemed nervous."

Mackey nodded his head. "I know Miles. He's very dedicated to the Cole family and yes, because of his stutter he gets nervous around people he doesn't know. But Irwin has said several times how fortunate he is to have him as an aide. Miles was the one who notified me about Mrs. Cole's disappearance in the beginning."

Raphael turned to Anderson. "We will be interviewing the Coles' acquaintances today to set up a timeline. We have people going through his office files as we speak. By the end of the day, I should be able to tell you what he had to eat last week."

"Good job Raphael." Anderson stood.

"Well, here's where we are as I see it at this point. First, we all seem to agree that the indications are that the book was written by Irwin Cole. As to why, only he and his God knows.

"Next I think we agree that the victim in Florida, Billy Parker, was killed by Senator Cole for whatever reason. Possibly Agent Martin has also fallen victim to the senator. Without a body, we won't know. Mrs. Cole has been missing for sixty-seven hours now, and we have to face the possibility that we may never find her. That makes one positive and two potential victims at this point. Generally, with this much evidence we would have issued an arrest warrant by now.

"I came from a long discussion with the director about the situation. He's about to shit himself over the mess. He says that we're damned if we do, and damned if we don't, and this time I agree with him. Remember it was the FBI that did the background check on the senator and he passed with no problems.

"So far, I don't think the press has found out about any of this mess, and that's the way I want to keep it. If this gets out, it'll be like a circus around here.

"Our job, men, is to find the senator and hold him for questioning, and that's it. The director was specific on this. The senator is not being accused of any crime as of yet. He doesn't want us throwing a US senator in jail to find later that it was all some big mix-up. On the other hand, he doesn't want us sitting around doing nothing when we have bodies, missing people, and a book confessing to it. The director said, and I quote, 'The line we must walk is very fine. If anyone steps off it, I will have their ass.'"

Anderson sighed. "Somehow I have a feeling we're going to be wrong no matter what we do. Just make sure you cross all the "T's" and dot all the "I's". Does anyone have any questions? Excellent, let's get to it."

They all grabbed their notebooks and headed out of the room. Anderson and Mackey remained behind.

"I'm sorry, Mackey. I know you are good friends with the senator. It has to be difficult accepting all of this. How is your wife handling it?"

"She was awake all night too. If something happens to Barbara, it will devastate her. William, it doesn't make any sense to me. I've been a cop all my life, like you. After a while, you develop a nose for these things. None of this makes any sense. I know he's my friend, and I may be biased as to how I'm interpreting things, but I refuse to believe he could be responsible for this. It's that fucking book that doesn't make any sense to me. It doesn't fit. It's a gut feeling I've had from the beginning."

"Mackey, it's seems wrong to me also. It's like someone has already anticipated every move I make on this case and is making me look like an incompetent fool. I know it sounds a little paranoid, but every time we get a break, something else goes wrong. Now the senator's disappearance has made the case against him much worse. At this point I have no other choice than to follow the evidence."

"I understand, William. You're doing what you have to. However, I'm going to do what I have to. I talked to my boss last night, and he's giving me some vacation time, and I'm taking the next flight to Florida."

Chapter 11

Tuesday, 7:15 AM

The early morning sun was beginning to rise above the eastern horizon. Narrow beams of light were peeking through the slats of the wooden shutters, hitting the wall above the sofa in the living room. The bars of light were slowly sliding down the wall as if they had been thrown against it and gravity was dragging them to the floor. No sound, no friction, only a gradual movement down.

They reached the top of Agent Martin's head as she lay asleep on the sofa where she had collapsed a few hours earlier. The light drifted lower, across her forehead and down to her eyelids. She turned her head slightly, as if to reject the kiss of light.

Suddenly, she flinched and her eyes popped open, as if the light had slapped her. She raised her hand to block the light and paused for a few seconds to regain her bearings. She sat up and twisted to look across the room at Cole, who was sleeping in the recliner. They both must have literally collapsed from exhaustion.

She watched him sleeping on the as yet dark side of the room. He had made the better choice of sleeping locations, she thought. She pulled her legs up toward her chest and wrapped her arms around them, resting her head on her knees.

As she cleared the sleep from her head, the previous day's events began flooding back. Yesterday morning she was one of the most promising agents the FBI had, and today she was on the run, hiding out with a man thought to be a killer. *How quickly one's fate can change,* she thought, as she rocked back and forth on the sofa.

She had known that she was on her own from the moment she had walked out of Ross's house with Cole yesterday. Nothing in the manual supported that decision, and she knew the manual from cover to cover. Josh had insisted on that. But nothing remotely resembling this situation had ever been discussed at the Academy. She wished she could call her father. He always had the right answers.

The one thing that had been discussed repeatedly at the Academy was that sometimes you had to use your gut feelings in a situation. She had done that last night, but now after a few hours' sleep, she began to question that decision.

On the other hand, her boss, Bill Hansen, had always said to her, "Make a decision and follow through to the end."

Confused as ever, she stood and looked over at Cole. He was twitching as if having a dream. In spite of the dream he seemed to be at peace, with a content expression. She found the overnight growth of whiskers to be quite attractive on his boyish face. She was amazed at how young he looked for being thirty-nine. At six foot, his feet were hanging off the foot rest of the recliner a good twelve inches. His light brown hair was still combed perfectly. It caused her to look in the mirror hanging on the wall and she noted that her own hair looked like a family of squirrels had spent the night in it.

She hurried to the bathroom to fix herself up before he woke. She stood in front of the mirror and removed the bandage from her chest. The cut was already starting to look better so she put a smaller Band-Aid on it to protect it. She took a couple of aspirin for the pain in her shoulder then she carefully arranged her hair.

She headed toward the kitchen, stretching, hoping to find the coffeepot and some coffee grounds.

The coffeepot was standing guard over in the corner on the counter. She glanced out the back window and saw the blue Gulf water sparkling. The surface of the water looked like a giant mirror lying down next to the pristine beach. The colorful sail of a boat on the horizon completed the perfect picture. *It doesn't make much sense that I love the beach so much but hate boats.*

She pulled the refrigerator door open to see what she could find. She was surprised to find the refrigerator was stocked with fresh food. For a second, she was delighted, but then the excitement came to an abrupt halt as she felt her stomach tense.

Why would a house that hasn't been used in such a long time have a refrigerator full of fresh food?

She stood stock still. Had she let her emotions get too involved in her decision-making? Had she been too quick to accept the senator's story? Maybe she should have waited and gathered more information first. She knew she was a good agent, but had overconfidence affected her judgment? She knew she had been taken in by his charisma and status as a senator, not to mention that she found him charming and attractive.

She grabbed the coffee off the door of the refrigerator and measured out five scoops into the filter. After pouring the water in the chute, she pushed the button, and instantly heard the gurgling sound of water dripping through the grounds.

A loud noise came from the living room. Without thinking she reached for her gun in the holster. But it wasn't there; it was in the canvas bag lying on the floor next to the sofa. She stepped quietly toward the living room and poked her head around the corner. In the holds of the recliner, the senator was twisting and shaking his body. His hands reached out in front him, and he was moaning. "No, no, no . . ."

She rushed to the chair and grabbed his shoulder and started shaking him. "Senator... Senator Cole, wake up, it's me, Melissa."

He leaned forward in the chair, and his eyes popped open wide, his face full of fright. He was breathing hard as if he had been running. He looked at her for a moment as if he didn't recognize her.

"It's alright. You must have been having a bad dream."

He looked at her for a few more seconds and rubbed his eyes. "Melissa." He let out a breath and relaxed back into the chair.

"That must have been one heck of a dream. I'm glad it was you this time and not me."

He looked at her, distraught "I was dreaming I killed Barbara."

Startled, she looked back at him silently. *What do I really know about him? Why is the refrigerator stocked?* For now, she decided she would act as though nothing was wrong, and let this play out further. Give him enough rope to hang himself; maybe, she could save her career after all.

"I've made some coffee. Would you like some?"

"I'd love some coffee, thanks, black."

Martin disappeared into the kitchen and found two cups in the cabinet. As she was pouring the coffee, she wished that she had remembered to get her gun out of the canvas bag. She went back to the living room with the steaming cups in her hands and the aroma following her into the room.

The recliner was empty and Cole was nowhere in sight. She set the cups down on the end table and went to the canvas bag on the floor next to the sofa and picked it up. Her stomach lurched; the bag was too light. She looked inside and found the holster but her gun was missing. The only other item in the bag was the book.

Just then the bathroom door popped open, and Cole walked out refreshed after washing his face. He watched her holding the open bag to her chest with a lost expression on her face.

"What's up? You look like you've seen a ghost. I know I'm not a morning person, but do I look that bad?"

She focused her stare at him as she slowly turned to keep him in front of her as he walked closer.

"My gun is gone."

"What do you mean it's gone?"

"I mean, I was keeping the gun in the bag. Now it's gone. You and I are the only people in the house. That's what I mean."

"Melissa, I heard a noise on the porch last night. I got up to see what it was and decided to take the gun with me. I discovered it was a raccoon on the porch. I didn't want to wake you trying to put the gun back in the bag."

"Where is it now?"

"It's over next to the door on that small table. Look."

She looked at the table then back at the senator.

"Senator Cole, you and I need to talk. Now."

"Ok, whatever you want, but can we drink our coffee while we're talking?"

They grabbed the mugs and sat down. She made a point to sit at the opposite end of the sofa.

"Senator Cole, tell me why we're at this house."

"Please, call me Irwin."

"Why are we here, Irwin?"

"As I said last night, it's because of something I read in the book. Toward the end of the book in the confession chapter, it described an area I know. Although the description was odd, I still recognized the setting. I have sat in the same chair looking out at the same view. It's at this house. Come with me, now that's it's light out I'll show you what I'm talking about."

He paused, "This coffee's good. I'm surprised you found any that wasn't stale."

She arched an eyebrow as she crossed the room and picked up her gun from the table. At that moment, there was a ringing noise and the senator reached into his pocket and took out his cell phone. "Hello Miles."

He listened to the caller without saying a word. Finally, he said, "Just relax Miles, you can tell me about it when you get here. I'm going to need you in Florida as soon as possible. I can't explain now, but it would be better if no one knows you're coming here. Call me when you arrive, and we'll go from there."

He hit the end button and put the phone back in his pocket.

"I can't believe you have your cell phone with you and turned on," said Martin. Don't you know they can trace your location through the signal? I'm amazed they aren't breaking through the door."

Cole looked at her with a smile. "It's a special phone. Miles got Barbara and me one two months ago. After the oil spill, the press hounded me day and night. I couldn't get away from them; it was as if they were tracking me everywhere I went. Miles found out that some electronics geek was tracking me by my cell phone. He had some kind of a program on his computer. Then he would sell the information to overzealous reporters looking for their first big break. Miles got us these phones, untraceable through GPS or the cell-phone towers."

"Those are illegal to use in the US."

"That must have been why Miles said, 'Don't ask,' when I asked him where they came from. Miles would run interference for me by taking my old cell phone in a different direction when I needed to get away. I don't know what I would do without him. He and Barbara are the only two people in the world that have the number. The best I can understand it is that it's all prepaid and sends an account number instead of the telephone number when you make any calls."

"So this Miles who called you — it seems you place a lot of trust in him."

"Yes, I do. He's my assistant, my right arm, you might say. He's become indispensible to me. He has been so loyal to Barbara and me for such a long time."

He led the way upstairs to the guest room. He walked to the big double-hung window next to a small desk. He raised the window, and then reached through and opened the shutters protecting the glass.

The morning breeze blew through the opening and instantly the sound and smell of the sea hit their senses. "Sit down here," he ordered as he opened the book to the last chapter and found the page he was looking for. He began to read.

As I look across the turquoise water in the distance, it stands upright and tall, as if at attention, standing its post, guarding the surrounding land, its pure white body gleaming in the sunlight and its eyes of glass watching what's occurring around it. Then it sees me looking at it, and sends out the flash of light acknowledging my presence. The flash of light is like a greeting welcoming me to its Kingdom – or maybe instead a warning to keep away. I'm not sure. It grabs me and holds me in its trance as another flash enters my mind through my obeying eyes. I want to look away, but I find I can't. I want to wait for another flash acknowledging my existence by this seemingly living being.

Finally, I break from my hypnotic state to notice beyond the tall protector. It's his charge: the mouth of the harbor. It's his job to protect it. The tops of the waves in the channel are white and furious as they fight one another for the chance to reach the Sea.

To my left, I can see the concrete ladder that stretches across the water connecting this paradise with the deceitful excessiveness of the surrounding area. We would all be better off if the connector was not there.

At my feet, the shiny metal reflects the bright sunlight as if to send the light back out to the heavens where it came from. The white desert separates me from the depths of the Sea.

Martin put her hand up to her mouth. "Oh my God. Look, there's the lighthouse and the channel to Charlotte Harbor. That island is Boca Grande. We used to go there when I was a child. The concrete ladder is the bridge."

She stood and leaned forward to look out the window. The tin roof was bright with reflection from the sun. The white sand below stretched to the water's edge. "You're right, whoever wrote that was sitting in this chair."

He stared out the window. "I know."

She looked at him steadily as she said, "The only question left is WHO wrote it from this chair?"

His expression didn't change as he continued staring distantly.

Finally, he turned to look at her. "I don't know about you, but I'm starved. I haven't eaten anything since yesterday midday. There's nothing here so we will have to take the boat to the mainland for breakfast."

She closely watched for any clues that he was trying to deceive her. She had always been good at reading faces. At the Academy they had told her she was the best. But all she saw was honest hunger. Was it possible he didn't know the kitchen was stocked, and maybe she was wrong about his motives for coming here?

She said, "Yes, I'm starved too, but first I need something cold to drink."

They walked downstairs, and she followed him into the kitchen. He said, "I'll have another cup of that coffee while we're here."

"I'll get it for you. Is there any cold water in the refrigerator?" She purposely faced away, trying to make it look as if she wasn't watching him.

"I doubt it. It's been a while since anyone has stayed in the house." He walked over and pulled the refrigerator door open.

She watched as he looked into the refrigerator. This time there was no doubt in her mind; he was shocked when he saw all the food in the refrigerator. *No one was that good an actor,* she thought.

"What the hell is going on here? How did all this food get here?" He backed away and sat down in the chair at the small round table.

"You had no idea that the refrigerator was stocked?"

"What? What do you mean?" he stammered.

"I'm so sorry, please forgive me. When I found the refrigerator full I thought you had stocked it and that coming to this island to hide had been your plan all along."

"No Melissa, you're giving me too much credit here. I could never think this far ahead. The person behind this is way smarter than me."

"Who do you think it is?" She knew he had to be at least considering the unthinkable now. He said nothing.

She patted his shoulder. "Since we have all of these groceries let me fix us something to eat, then we can figure this out on a full stomach."

While Martin was busy fixing breakfast, Cole went out on the back porch and paced. She watched him from in front of the stove, and she could see the worry on his face as he strode from one side of the porch to the other.

A few minutes later he came back inside and spoke animatedly. "Okay, listen to this, what if whoever wrote that book knew I would recognize the location of the lighthouse and knew I would come here looking for answers? That's what he wanted. He wanted me to come to this house. He was expecting me to come here. It's all part of his plan, don't you see? That's why there is food in the refrigerator—he knew I would come."

"What are the odds of that," Martin replied. "Many things had to happen in the right order at the right time for that to happen. Why would he want you here? Unless he was trying to keep you from going somewhere else he didn't want you to be. Have a seat and eat your breakfast before it gets cold, then we'll try to figure out what's happening here."

They gobbled down their scrambled eggs, sausage, and English muffins. "This is good. You're a hell of a cook, thank you for fixing it," he said.

She smiled. "Being half-starved probably makes it taste better than it is. I'm not much of a cook."

"No, it's good. These may be the best eggs I've ever eaten."

She took another bite. "You're right, they are good. So, what would you have been doing today if this hadn't happened?"

"I would be heading to Ft. Myers to pick Barbara up at the airport. Depending on the time of her flight I was planning to stop in Punta Gorda, and either have lunch or dinner at our favorite restaurant. Then we would come home and relax on the back patio."

"Well, I can't imagine anyone wanting to keep you from that schedule, unless they were trying to stop you from being bored to death."

"Let's not forget, Melissa, I am on vacation, after all."

"What about tomorrow? What kind of exciting plans did you have scheduled?"

"Tomorrow…let me see . . . that would be Wednesday. In the morning, I was going to read a couple reports that I need to familiarize myself with. In the afternoon, I had an appointment with a contractor in Sarasota about a small remodel project. The only other plan we had for Wednesday was that I was going to drop Barbara off for a meeting at her father's company, and pick her up afterward. That's about it, just another low-key day."

She shook her head. "Well, I think the idea of keeping you from your schedule is clearly the wrong approach. So unless you can think of a reason, I have no idea."

"No, I can't think of any reason. I deliberately left my schedule light, so I could unwind and spend some time with my wife."

"I think we have to go on the assumption that they wanted you out here for a reason, unless, whoever wrote the book had no idea that you would make the connection."

"No, I think the person put that in the book for a reason, otherwise it makes no sense. It kind of pops up in the middle of the confession chapter, and nothing before or after it has anything to do with it. Someone was baiting me."

"Who would know that you could pick up on it? After all, the descriptions in the book weren't clear. A person would have to sit in that chair many times to make the connection."

He said, "No one except Barbara. I used to like to read there because the light was so good in that corner of the room. She used to wave to me from the beach when I was sitting in front of the window. We would blow kisses to each other."

Martin placed her fork next to her plate, and contemplated her next statement.

"Irwin, please don't be upset with me, but I think we need to discuss some, shall we say, what-ifs, here."

He slammed his hand down on the table. "There's no way you'll ever convince me that Barbara's responsible for this. I've run this through my head a million times, and I have to follow my heart, and my heart is telling me no, it's impossible. She couldn't do something like this," he hesitated, "unless—maybe she's being forced by someone?"

"Bill Hansen said the airport video showed her freely getting into a limousine. I'm sorry Irwin; I think we need to talk about this, if for no other reason than to try to eliminate the possibility that Barbara is involved."

Cole jerked back in his chair and stared at her with a cold expression. Martin suspected that he must have had the same thoughts as she but wasn't ready to accept it.

"Let's think about this for a minute. What would Barbara have to gain by writing this book? She's the one with the money in your marriage, so I can't see it as a financial gain. If she were having an affair or wanted a divorce, would you agree to one without difficulties?"

"We're very much in love. If Barbara fell out of love with me, I wouldn't keep her trapped in a marriage she didn't want to be in. And no, I would feel no need to be compensated by her at all."

"So if the book was written by her for whatever reason, is there anyone else who would profit from its existence?"

"Trust me, I've gone over all the possibilities in my head. For the book to ruin me, Barbara would have to be dead. If she were dead, then writing the book doesn't do anything for her."

"Irwin, what if there was never any intent for Barbara to be killed as the book says? What if it's a hoax?"

"Then as far as I'm concerned the book becomes useless."

"I wouldn't say useless. A sitting US senator writing a hoax book about killing his wife would ruin your career, would it not?"

"Yes, but I can think of easier ways of ruining a politician's career without going through all of this. In fact, if you just leave him alone long enough he'll ruin his own career."

"Does your wife have any reason for wanting your career to end?"

He shook his head emphatically. "None, absolutely no reason at all. If she wanted me out of politics all she would have to do is ask. As a matter of fact, it was through politics that we met. It was a fundraiser when I was running for the Senate seat. I'm telling you, this is a dead end street. I've been through all of this in my head several times."

"Okay then, what if, as you said, someone was forcing her to do this? Maybe someone wants you out of politics or out of the way?"

"As I said before, there are much easier ways to do that. What kind of pressure could be applied to Barbara to do something like this? I'm sure she has nothing in her past that could be used against her. As far as I know, she's never harmed a soul, she's loved by all. I think we're wasting time here."

Cole stared out the back window as he thought. All of a sudden he turned to her quickly and said, "You were asking me about my schedule, and it's made me remember when I received the package yesterday morning. The delivery man said it was supposed to be delivered on Saturday, but his truck broke down.

Martin thought aloud. "A Saturday delivery would cost extra and would have to be requested. That would mean whoever did this wanted you to have the book on Saturday, the same day your wife went missing. He knew you would see the book and try to contact your wife, but it would be too late."

Cole began to nod his head. "Yes. The person knew I would read the book, find the window scene and head down to the island to figure out what was happening. That's why he wanted me down here, missing at the same time as my wife…on Saturday. He probably assumed I wouldn't call the police myself because of the book."

"Why would someone want you missing?"

Cole continued his train of thought. "Yes, it makes sense. The book was late arriving, so I was slow coming here. So those goons were sent to my house to get me and bring me down, except they weren't expecting an FBI agent to be at the house. The guy I shot on the back patio had a bottle of liquid in his pocket with a cloth wrapped around it. I didn't think about it at the time, but I bet it was chloroform to knock me out so they could bring me here."

Agent Martin jumped in. "They didn't realize the FBI had already been notified, and I surprised the guy on the back porch. They were probably going to notify the authorities themselves once they had everything in place. That way, the book would look more legitimate with you having disappeared."

"I think you're right. They were here at the house. That's why they took off when we arrived, because you were with me. That guy we saw at the marina on the phone must have been talking to the others waiting at the house. That's why that boat shot past us in such a hurry."

She nodded in affirmation. "We need to get more information about how this house figures in. I believe this house is definitely part of it. Let's go through it room by room and see whether we can find anything that might give us some insight to what's happening."

"Okay, but remember according to the book we only have until 6:00 PM Wednesday and time is flying by. I'm not willing to take the chance that the book is a hoax."

They started in the kitchen, opening every cabinet and drawer. She said, "I'm not going to be much help. I wouldn't know whether something was supposed to be there or not. You need to check behind me."

They systematically went through every drawer and cabinet, and then examined each room of the downstairs of the house. The only odd thing they found was a book of matches from a local sports bar in the cushions of the sofa. It could have been dropped by anyone at any time.

Martin inspected the matches more closely. "These are fresh and seem new. We should remember to check this out when we get back to the mainland. Sometimes, the smallest clues result in the largest finds."

They went through the master bedroom and found nothing. Cole was standing next to the bed when he spotted something shiny on the floor next to the wall. He reached down between the nightstand and wall with his arm and scooped up the item from the floor.

He stared at it. "It's Barbara's bracelet."

Martin smiled. "It's a beautiful bracelet, and I remember you saying the two of you came here often on vacation. She probably dropped it the last time you were here."

He shifted his eyes to hers. "I gave it to her for her birthday, two weeks ago in Washington."

Silently they stood looking at the bracelet hanging from his quivering hand.

Martin said gently, "That would mean she would've been here in the last two weeks."

Cole responded, "Or someone wants me to think she's been here."

He coiled up the bracelet and put it in his pocket. "Come on, we have the guest room to check yet."

Cole sat at the desk in front of the window in the guest room as he searched through the lone drawer. He slammed it shut. "This is useless!" he yelled. He threw his body back in the desk chair, causing it to hit the wall with a loud thump.

"Christ." He leaned forward and checked the wall for damage. The back of the chair had hit the white paneling below the chair rail. It left a smudge but no damage. He reached down to rub the smudge from the wall and noticed a small separation in the panel. He reopened the desk drawer and retrieved a letter opener. He used the point as a wedge in the crack of the panel. "I found something here."

She peered over his shoulder. "It looks like an access panel."

"You think?" he grinned.

She hit his shoulder with her fist. "Smart ass."

He pried the letter opener farther into the seam, but the panel wouldn't come out. She said, "It's stuck under the chair rail at the top and behind the floor baseboard at the bottom. See whether you can raise the panel and lift out the bottom."

"I wouldn't have ever thought of that," he said wryly. He slid the desk away from the wall to give himself more room.

He stuck the opener in what looked like a knothole in the paneling. He lifted, and the panel began sliding up under the chair rail. Once it cleared the baseboard on the bottom, he reached down and used his fingernails to pull it out from the wall. He pulled the entire 2'x3' panel away and tossed it on the bed behind him.

"Look; it's a laptop computer," exclaimed Martin. "Hurry, bring it out and set it up on the desk."

"Yes, boss." He reached in the cramped space and pulled out the computer and sat it on the desk.

"Watch out," she blurted as she slid into the seat in front of the computer. She opened it and pressed the power button. The lights flashed, and the hard drive began spinning with a high-pitched whine. They waited as the computer loaded, and finally a password screen came up. She asked, "Do you know who this computer belongs to?"

"No idea, I've never seen it before."

She pressed several keys in quick sequence, and the computer restarted. He watched as she continued to enter a string of commands on the keyboard. "I have no idea what you're doing, hopefully you do."

Finally, a different password screen came up, and she entered another string of keystrokes. It caused the screen to go blank and after a few seconds it came back on with a solid blue screen. The Windows operating system opened, and she was past the logon screen.

"Where did you learn to do that?"

"FBI Academy, where else?"

"It's good to know our tax dollars are well spent."

She moved the cursor to "recent documents" and clicked the mouse. The screen started to sparkle, and the image slowly disappeared until the screen was blank.

"Now what did you do? You messed it up."

"I didn't do anything," she snapped back at him.

Just then a new screen started forming from the bottom up and was requesting a password.

She said, "This computer has some major security software on it. It's looking for a password with sixteen digits. It could take the lab days to break this."

He reached over her shoulders and entered ten letters, four numbers, and two symbols with four of them being uppercase and hit the enter key. The cursor turned to an hourglass, and the sand started falling. After about thirty seconds the screen flashed several times, and a new screen appeared.

She gave him a sideways look. "I thought you said you didn't recognize this computer?"

"I don't. I haven't got a clue who owns this computer."

"How did you know that password then?"

"You said there were sixteen digits. That's the same as what my computer in the Capitol office requires. I thought I would try it."

"How many people know your password? Does your wife or your assistant know it?"

"No, I'm the only one who has the password. There's classified information on the server at the Capitol. No one is allowed access to that terminal and server except US senators and a new personal password is issued to me every three months."

She looked at him and said, "So what you're saying is the Capitol's computer system has been compromised?"

"Yes, I suppose that's what I'm saying."

They looked at each other, both realizing that this could change everything. The possibilities were becoming endless. She typed on the keyboard and brought up the documents stored on the computer. A single Word document: "*The Cole Hard Truth.*"

She clicked the file. It was indeed the manuscript of the book. She looked up at him. "This obviously must be where it was written. The file properties indicated it was last accessed a month ago. I wonder how long it's been since the computer was used?"

She began going through screens he had never seen. Then he watched as she was scrolling down what looked to him like an old DOS screen. He hadn't seen that in fifteen years.

He asked, "What are you doing now? What are you looking for? I haven't seen screens like that since I had my original IBM PC."

She didn't answer him as she continued to watch the lines scroll down the screen. Finally she said, "These are the logs that the computer keeps of its commands. Here we are. The last time the computer was used was 11:30 PM last night."

He said, "That's right before we got here. So there were people in the house last night, just as we thought."

She said, "Let's see what they were doing." She typed on the keyboard. "Here we are. They were running a program called S&D."

"What's that? Have you heard of it?"

"I'm not sure; it does seem vaguely familiar."

She backed out and opened the program's screens and began scanning for the program that had been running the previous night. She checked the list and didn't find anything. She went through the list again more slowly, but still found nothing.

"The program must be opened through a hidden file."

She started typing again, and different screens flashed on and off. Then she stopped. "Gotcha."

"Did you find the program?"

Just then several color bursts flashed. Large letters moved across the screen, then began spinning in different directions, finally settling into a logo. "Search and Discover." She stared at the screen thoughtfully. He asked, "What is it, do you know the program?"

"Not really. It seems familiar to me, like I've seen it before. I can't remember where, but I think it's been a long time."

She clicked the begin tab, and three names and telephone numbers appeared on the screen: Barbara Cole, Irwin Cole, and Miles Connor. A box was next to each name where she could place the cursor. She turned and looked up at Cole.

He said. "Click me first."

She clicked the box, and the screen started to turn in counterclockwise motion. It began to create a spiral starting from the center spinning out to the edges.

"She said, "I haven't seen anything like this since Josh and I used to watch reruns of *Secret Agent Man* back in college. He loved that show."

The screen continued to spin in a black and white hypnotic effect. Then it collapsed into a small black dot in the center. A few seconds passed and another screen popped up, and it looked like a map of southwest Florida. It had a flashing star over the island, the location of the house they were in.

She said, "Your cell phone. You're being tracked by that super duper secret phone of yours."

He said, "Quick, click Barbara and see whether we can find her."

She backed out and clicked the box next to Barbara's name, and they watched the spiral spinning again.

"Whoever created this program has some problems," he commented.

A couple of minutes passed, and the screen was still spinning. He said, "It only took thirty seconds to locate me."

Then the screen flashed a dialogue box advising that no signal was found. Last known location was 26 55.70 n. 82 3.85 w. at 19:43 8/07/10.

He raced toward the door and went downstairs. A minute later he was back at the desk with a marine chart of the area. "That location is close and will be on this chart. Let me see, that time was Saturday afternoon."

He spread the chart across the bed next to the desk. He followed with his finger as she read the coordinates from the screen, writing them down at the same time.

"That's Fisherman's Village in Punta Gorda," he announced. "We've been there a few times for dinner. They also have apartments or condos above the commercial shops and restaurants. It's all surrounded by a marina. They must be keeping her in one of the rooms. Come on, we have to get down there."

She closed the lid on the computer and followed him down the stairs with the computer under her arm. He held the canvas bag open for her to slip the computer inside. They went out the front door and started for the gate. Cole stopped. "Wait here. I'm going to see whether the Jeep will start. It will be faster than walking."

He ran back toward the house and went under the makeshift cover and removed the tarp. He then reached up in the floor joist and grabbed the key hanging on the hook. He put it in the ignition and turned it, but nothing happened. He got out and lifted the hood and could see the battery cables had been cut. "The raccoon wasn't the only company we had last night," he whispered.

He ran back to where Martin was waiting for him at the gate.

"The bastards cut the battery cables. We are going to have to do it on foot again."

He was practically running down the road. With his long legs and his mind on finding Barbara, he was about thirty feet in front of Martin before he realized she had fallen behind. He slowed almost to a stop and waited for her to catch up. He grabbed the canvas bag and slung it over his shoulder. They hurried along the broken asphalt until they reached the path leading down to the dock. They were both sweating from the midday heat. She looked down at the heavy jeans she had on and wished she had been wearing shorts for this kind of work out.

They reached the dock and Senator Cole stopped short.

"What's wrong?" she asked.

"The boat's gone."

Chapter 12

Tuesday, 12:50 PM

The plane from Washington had landed on time and had just arrived at the gate at Southwest Florida Regional Airport. Miles was seated in a window seat and watched the ramp being pulled into position at the plane's door. The passengers around him had jumped up and were retrieving their luggage from the overhead bins. Miles waited for his area to clear out, and then stood and grabbed his bag.

He wondered why people climbed all over one another to be the first to depart the plane. As far as he knew, there was no prize for the first person off the plane. He walked down the aisle and out the door into the long corridor that led to the terminal.

At 6'2" he could see over most of the crowd in front of him, and it reminded him of cattle being led down a chute for slaughter. As he looked ahead at the terminal, he saw a man holding the door for an elderly couple. He was a short, stocky, distinctive-looking man in a blue dress shirt, and Miles felt sure he recognized him.

He began walking faster. Senator Cole had told him not to let anyone know he was going to Florida. He needed to verify whether this person was who he thought he was. He followed the man through the terminal, staying back far enough to escape notice.

Miles was sure he had never let the senator down in all the years that he had worked for him. The words ran through his mind again. "Don't let anyone know where you're going."

He watched the man make a right turn into the men's room. Miles turned left to go across the aisle from the men's room door and sat in one of the chairs. He had only seen the man once, but Miles remembered faces. From this angle, he would be able to see the man full front when he came out. A few minutes later he emerged. Bingo. The man was Lieutenant Mackey with the Capitol police.

Miles pulled out his cell phone and called Senator Cole. He counted eleven rings with no answer. He hit the end button and put his phone back in his pocket. He started walking at a leisurely pace toward the terminal exit to make sure he didn't catch up to Lieutenant Mackey. He thought it unlikely that the lieutenant would recognize him since they'd only met once, and quite a while ago at that, but he didn't want to take any chances.

* * *

Mackey stopped for a cup of coffee at one of the terminal restaurants. He decided to give Irwin's cell phone another try. On the second ring, a familiar-sounding voice said, "Hello," but it wasn't Irwin. "Who is this?"

"Mackey, is that you?" said the voice. "It's Tom Wilson."

"Tom, what the hell is the FBI doing answering Senator Cole's cell phone?"

"We had his number forwarded here in case he received any calls that might help with the case. By the way, our conversation is being recorded so watch what you're saying, if you know what I mean."

"Yeah, gotcha, I know what you mean. I landed in Florida and thought I would try his phone one more time before I headed to his house. I tried to call him several times before, but got his voice mail."

"I see that; I have all his phone records in front of me now, and nothing seems unusual. Except we're still not seeing that call he made to his mother-in-law yesterday morning."

"Anything new since our meeting this morning?"

"Shit, we look like a team of monkeys trying to screw a football up here."

"Tom, didn't you say this call was recorded?"

"Shit, I'll call you later Mackey, if anything comes up."

"Bye, Tom."

Mackey snorted as he ended the call. *Poor Tom is going to catch hell for that one.* As he finished his coffee, he watched the people walking every which way, all so focused and determined as they rushed past. Mackey, on the other hand, began to wonder. *What the hell am I doing here?* Then he mumbled under his breath, "To help my friend. That's what I'm doing here."

He slid across the booth, grabbed his bag and headed for the car rental agency where he had a reservation. Thirty minutes later, he was driving north on I-75, headed for Englewood.

Mackey had been on the Interstate for an hour when he saw his exit was coming up next. He never noticed the Ford Taurus that had been following him from the airport and now was getting off at the same exit. The GPS in the rental had him taking Veterans Blvd to SR 776. According to the little screen on the dash, he would be at the senator's house in thirty-five minutes.

As he crossed the bridge to Englewood Beach, he remembered how beautiful the scenery was in this area. He and Doris had been down visiting Irwin and Barbara a couple of years ago. He understood why they came down here every chance they could.

After winding through the narrow residential road, he pulled his rental car into the drive of the beach house. Unmarked FBI cars were parked next to the house. He heard the Gulf waves behind the house as he headed toward the front door, but it wasn't as pleasant a walk as it had been when he was on vacation. Just as he reached to push the doorbell the door opened.

"Lieutenant Mackey, I presume? I'm Bill Hansen with the Tampa office of the FBI. We were expecting you."

The two men shook hands. "Come on in," said Hansen. "I heard you pull in the drive and wanted to open the door before you rang the bell. That doorbell makes the worse sound I've ever heard in my life. I don't know how the Coles stand it."

Mackey chuckled. "Yeah, Irwin is always complaining about that damn thing. I don't know why he hasn't changed it yet."

"If I stay here another day he'll have to change it because I'll rip it off the wall. May I get you anything, Lieutenant Mackey?"

"Please, just Mackey, that's what everyone calls me. I would love some water."

"Okay, here in the kitchen we have a cooler."

Hansen pulled out a bottle of water and handed it to him. Mackey took a long swallow and let out a satisfied sigh. "I appreciate you allowing me access. I don't know whether I can help with anything, but I need to do something. Irwin is my best friend."

"I understand, and the senator's fortunate to have a friend like you. I know you were in the meeting in Washington this morning, and I read the transcript. So I'll try to cover what we have found since then, which isn't much."

Mackey nodded. "How about your missing agent? Anything new?"

Hansen looked down. "You could call it good news. We haven't found a body yet. The Coast Guard has done an extensive search of the Gulf and hasn't found anything. The bad news is the blood found here on the kitchen floor is hers. The DNA match came back positive."

"I'm sorry Bill. I know it's difficult when it's one of your people. I understand she's young."

"Yes, for a field agent she is. I regret sending her down here alone. We were so stretched for agents at the time because of the Naples incident." He paused and stared outside toward the Gulf.

"Anyway, the other information we've learned this morning is about the gunshot victim. He's been working for somebody for the last month, and they've been paying him well. The people who know him say he's been dumping cash all over town. We're still questioning some of his known acquaintances, but I'm not expecting much from that. You know how that goes. The only promising lead so far is a sports bar that he frequented in the area. When I get a free agent, we'll follow up on that."

* * *

Miles drove by the senator's house slowly. Once past the house, he tried the senator's cell phone again and still got no answer. He continued on and a short distance later, he turned into a beach access and parked the car.

He was frustrated that the senator had put him off on the phone when he tried to tell him about Senator Kappleman. But he could understand him wanting to be able to talk in person. Miles also wanted to tell him about Sullivan. During the flight to Florida, Miles had decided he needed to tell the senator everything he knew. He didn't care anymore that his father wouldn't like it. He was tired of being bossed around all the time and treated like he didn't know anything.

He picked up his phone, dialed the second number on his speed dial. "Yes?"

"This is M-Miles."

"I know it's you Miles, what's up?"

"I'm d-d-down here in Florida."

"What are you doing in Florida? We told you to stay in Washington until we called you on Wednesday."

"I-I- know, b-but Senator Cole wanted me t-t-to come down here. H-He told me not t-to let anyone know where I-I was g-g-going."

"Okay Miles. Why don't you come to the house, and we'll figure out what to do next."

"The F-FBI agents were asking m-me questions all a-afternoon y-yesterday, but I d-didn't tell them a-anything. Father promised nothing bad would h-h-happen to Senator Cole."

"Yes Miles, see you at the house."

Miles closed his phone and slammed his hand on the dash of the car. He hated his brother's condescension. He hated it as much as being locked in the dark closet as a small boy every time he stuttered.

"I-I'll s-show t-t-them," he muttered.

* * *

"Mackey," said Hansen, "This is the worst case I have ever had. There isn't any clear-cut lead to go on. With that damn book, you would think we could have solved this in a few hours. My feeling, if I had my way, is that I would throw that book in the trash and work the case."

"I agree with you about the book. Between you and me, Bill, I know you were here first. What do you think happened?"

"Just between you and me?"

Mackey nodded and gave him a wink.

"I believe the local hood came here with the carry-on and briefcase. He was bringing them around the back of the house and for whatever reason he and Senator Cole began wrestling with the gun on the back patio. Two shots went off and went through the sliding glass door. Agent Martin must have been close to the glass when it shattered. The third shot went into the chest of the victim before he went over the rail. At the same time, one or more people entered the house through the front door. They overpowered Agent Martin and the senator then took them captive. They made it look like Agent Martin's body had been dumped in the Gulf and they left in their car."

Mackey said, "That makes more sense than anything else I've heard on this case so far. Do you have any ideas about a motive for taking the senator and Agent Martin?"

"None. Who knows Mackey, I could be way off."

"If you don't mind I'm going to get some fresh air, and take a walk down to the beach."

Mackey slid the unbroken door open in front of the plywood that had been temporarily installed in the empty frame where the glass had been broken. He walked down the sand toward the water's edge. The yellow tape, attached to stakes stuck in the sand, fluttered in the wind.

The breeze hitting his face felt good as it blew his hair back. He stood watching the waves rolling in against the sand, sweeping it clean as they receded, like a chalkboard being erased for a fresh start.

He took off his shoes and socks, rolled up his pant legs, and let the water run over his feet. He started walking aimlessly southward down the beach, lost in thought.

After a while he stopped and looked back to see how far he had gone. He couldn't see the house any longer and wasn't sure of the distance. He looked up at the house fronting the beach where he was, and smiled with recognition, pleased at the coincidence.

He was standing behind Ross's place. He had met Ross and his wife at a cookout while visiting the Coles. He had also helped Irwin check his house and open it to air it out before Ross had arrived. Then later in the week they got together on his back patio. Mackey had enjoyed himself and liked Ross. They had gotten on so well that Ross had invited him to use his place for a vacation whenever he wanted to.

Mackey headed to the house, relishing the fond memories of his visit. He could see that the place was closed up. He walked onto the patio where they had enjoyed hamburgers and drank beer a few years ago. He approached the back door and looked down for the ceramic frog in the garden. The key was still there.

He knew Ross wouldn't mind and maybe the memories would help him relax some. Probably, Irwin had already been down here checking the house for him. After turning the lock, he struggled to open the swollen door. After a solid kick at the bottom, it opened with a squawk, and he stepped inside. He was surprised to find the alarm wasn't set, but he knew the code was on the bulletin board.

He walked through all the rooms, and all seemed well. Then he entered the master bath. Lying on the floor was a plastic grocery bag. He looked inside, and his heart stopped momentarily. It was full of clothing…bloody clothing. He knew he shouldn't touch anything more, but peering in he could see that there were both male and female clothes in the bag. He set the bag back down carefully and backed slowly out of the bathroom, trying to step in the same places he had stepped before.

As a detective, he had hated when the person who discovered a crime scene walked around contaminating everything. He headed for the door to notify Bill Hansen of what he had discovered. As he passed the bulletin board hanging in the kitchen, he noticed a note pinned to it.

Dear Ross, I had to borrow your car, clothes, and some water. I will explain later. Thanks, Irwin.

* * *

Miles paced back and forth in the parking lot next to the Taurus. The more he thought about it the angrier he got. That last phone call with his brother had done it for him.

"Time to take matters into my own hands."

He got back in the car and headed south past Senator Cole's house again. Three houses farther down there were several Sheriff's patrol cars with their lights flashing. He wondered what was happening so close to the senator's house.

He continued on past the house. It felt good to feel so sure of himself, and he was energized, like the night he had been spying on Sullivan. They thought he didn't know anything about their plans. They were wrong. He had read through all the files on his father's computer. With that information he knew where to find Senator Cole so he could tell him everything.

Chapter 13

Tuesday, 1:55 PM

"I can't believe there isn't a single boat left at the dock!" seethed Cole. "I didn't notice that when we came in on Ross's boat last night. It's either because of the August doldrums and no one is staying out here, or else someone doesn't want me to leave the island. Why don't you wait here while I go see whether I can find something to get us to the mainland?"

Martin squinted from the bright sunlight and said, "No way. I'm not letting you out of my sight."

"Yeah, yeah, how could I forget? I thought maybe we were past all of that distrust now."

"It's not about trust. It's about me doing my job. It's about keeping you alive. If something happens to you, I'm finished. It won't matter whether you're guilty or not."

He smiled at her. "When this is all over, they will be giving you a commendation. I'll see to it."

"No thanks. All I want is my job, the way it was before I met you, Senator."

They walked back down the rickety dock, the bright afternoon sun in their eyes. When they reached the road they headed north, walking past one empty house after another. There were no boats anywhere.

I feel like we're stranded on a deserted island," remarked Martin.

"The weekends are usually busy," he replied. "Most of the owners have houses close by on the mainland and come here on the weekends."

"Great. We're stranded here until the weekend."

"No we aren't. We only have a day and a half to find Barbara. I'm getting off this island one way or another."

They continued on the narrow broken road, checking every yard for a boat.

"I wish we would have brought some water with us," she said. "I don't suppose there's anyplace around here we can get a drink, is there?"

"Nope, the island is all residential."

"Can we stop for a minute and rest? The heat is taking it out of me with these heavy jeans I'm wearing."

"Okay. We'll stop and rest in the shade at the next house."

They walked another hundred yards to the next house and followed the narrow path through the yard. When they reached the shade of the house she flopped down in the sand under the overhead structure. Cole leaned against one of the support pilings. He was exhausted himself. As he wiped the sweat from his eyes he looked up and noticed a kayak hanging from the floor joist of the house. It was tight against the floor, so they would have never seen it from the path.

"There's our transportation off the island," he said, pointing.

"I hope you're not suggesting we take that little play boat out on the water?"

"It's not a play boat. It's a kayak, and it will work fine."

He got up and untied the rope suspending the boat from the joist. He carefully lowered it to the ground and dragged it over next to her. The paddle and life jacket were stored inside.

"Too bad it's a single seat boat. I don't suppose you would allow me to go over and get another boat and come back for you?"

She didn't say a word. The look on her face said it for her.

"Yeah, I thought as much."

He picked up the kayak, and balancing it over his head, started walking toward the bay. She let out a sigh and picked herself up from her shady seat, grabbed the computer, paddle, and life jacket, and followed him down the dirt path. Once they reached the road, there was no path leading to the bay from where they were. Beyond the road the bay side of the island in this area was uninhabited. The going was difficult through the dense brush and palmettos, and she was falling behind.

When Cole reached the water, he called back to her. "If you can't make it, I'll come back for you."

"Go ahead, Popeye. I've got the paddle with me."

When she reached the boat, he said, "I'll get in first, then you squeeze in my lap." He took the canvas bag from her and placed it in the water-tight compartment at the stern of the kayak.

She put on the life jacket as he got into the boat.

"Now what?"

"Step here, with your left foot between my legs, and be careful I might add. Then slide your body down here in front of me, bringing your other leg in before you sit."

She stepped into the kayak and slowly lowered her body while sliding her legs forward. She was almost all the way in when she got stuck between him and the boat.

"Can't you slide back more?"

"No, I'm all the way back. You're going to have to take that life jacket off. It's too bulky. You can swim, can't you?"

"Yes, I grew up in Florida. I can swim."

She lifted herself high enough so she could unhook the life jacket. She threw it to the ground and slid easily into his lap.

He used the paddle to shove away from the shore, and they were afloat. The boat rocked from side to side as he brought the paddle across the front of her chest, so he could begin digging it into the water.

"You're going to tip us over!" she yelled.

"Just lean back as far as you can, so I can paddle the boat."

"Excuse me, that's my chest you just brushed with your hand."

"Hush, I'm trying to concentrate on my paddling."

She leaned back, and her head was against his shoulder. After a few minutes, he could feel her body starting to relax. Their heads were side by side as he tilted his head forward pulling the paddle back through the water.

Her hair was blowing in his eyes and mouth. "I know you're relaxed up there," he said finally, "But can you do something with your hair? It's getting in my eyes and tickling my nose.

She reached up and pulled her hair back over the other side of her head. The kayak slowly made its way out of the small bay and was headed toward the Intracoastal Waterway. The wind was picking up in the unprotected expanse, and the sun disappeared behind some dark clouds. He was heading east into the wind and he could see that a summer thunderstorm was building. He didn't say anything.

Her hair was blowing in his face again, but he let it go. He could feel her tensing. He knew there was a good chance of afternoon thunderstorms every afternoon this time of year, and he was well aware of how fast they came up and how bad some of them could be. Since she had grown up in the area, he wondered if she was thinking the same thing.

She turned her head, her mouth right next to his ear.

"It seems windy, and the waves are much rougher. Are we going to be all right?"

He could feel her breath and her lips touching his ear as she spoke. He could also hear the concern in her voice.

He tried to sound reassuring. "We'll be fine. It's an afternoon thunderstorm. They come up fast, and they're gone just as quickly. We have about a mile to go to the marina because the place we launched the kayak from is directly across from there. I promise I won't let anything happen to you."

He paddled harder and dug down deeper in the water to compensate for the headwind, and his arms were beginning to burn from the strain. On the mainland, he could see the dark curtain of rain leaving the shore and heading for them. The sky was a forbidding blue and a bolt of lightning flashed near the shore causing a sudden loud clap of thunder. They jumped, and he could feel the electricity in the air around them. The strong wind was saturated with the smell of rain and felt quite cool.

The waves hitting the bow of the boat were starting to break over the kayak. They were in a single-person boat with two people, and it was low in the water. He looked over her shoulder and could see the water starting to fill in the bottom of the boat.

There was another flash of lightning and instantly a bang of thunder that resonated through their bodies.

He dug the paddle into the water harder and faster. The wind was hitting them full force now, and the rain, driven by the wind, was unyielding from the first drop, stinging their faces. She turned her head and buried her face into his shoulder.

He could see the channel marker about twenty-five feet in front of them, and the red light was flashing through the blizzard of rain. That was the marker he was looking for and he supposed they had about seventy-five feet to cross the channel, then another hundred-fifty feet to the docks. It gave him the incentive to pull harder and reach deeper, but the boat was getting heavier by the minute.

From habit, he turned his head sideways as he crossed the channel looking for boat traffic. He knew no one would be able to see this small boat in the driving rain, and he wasn't sure what he could do anyway. He was already paddling as hard as he could. He noticed his arms had stopped burning now and were numb. He supposed it was like what runners called their second wind.

All of sudden he heard a roar from behind. Through the driving rain, he could barely see the white hull of a large pleasure yacht passing directly behind them. With his last morsel of strength, he dug the paddle deep into the water, trying to turn the kayak more to starboard because he knew a huge wave would be coming from behind the yacht. If he could keep the boat perpendicular to the wave, he might be able to surf down the front of it.

Before he had a chance to make the alignment, the wave hit the kayak on the port stern quarter. "Hold your breath!" he screamed.

The wave grabbed the boat like a toy, flipping it over, and they were upside down in the water. As a teenager, he had practiced this hundreds of times, but never with another person in a single-person kayak. He moved the paddle in a twisting motion and at the same time swung his body to the other side. The boat began to turn upward, and their heads popped on top of the water again. She let out a scream, frantically swinging her arms in the air. She tried standing as if she was going to get out of the kayak. He tightened his arms around her and held her down. "It's over. We're okay."

She struggled at first, but then pulled herself hard against his neck. He could feel her shivering against his body. He quietly whispered into her ear, "You did great. The dock is right over there."

She held her grasp for several more seconds, and then turned around and faced forward in the seat without saying a word.

He began paddling again toward the docks. The wind was subsiding but the rain was still coming down, though much more gently. Soon, the boat was bumping against the dock, and he threw the paddle on its surface. He held the kayak against the piling and said, "Okay; it's the reverse of getting in, except we're still floating, so you need to keep your weight in the center of the boat."

She slowly climbed out, and held the boat while he climbed on the dock. He opened the water-tight compartment at the stern of the kayak and removed the bag with the computer. He stepped on the dock and gave her a big hug. "You did great kiddo, but you look like a drowned rat."

"You're looking a little ratty yourself, Mr. Senator."

He dragged the kayak up on the dock, and they began walking down the rickety pier toward the parking area beyond the shed. As they got near the entrance of the docks, she suddenly looked at him and said, "There is a God."

She took off running toward the soda machine sitting next to the shed wall. She reached into her pocket, and realized all she had with her were credit cards in her badge wallet. Her purse was still at the senator's house. She hollered, "Irwin, can I borrow some money? All I have is plastic!"

"How will I know you'll pay me back?"

The look on her face told him he had better not push her any further. "Oh, okay, I guess I can trust you until we can find an ATM."

He removed his wet wallet from his pocket and gave her a dollar bill. She grabbed it out of his hand and went to the machine and tried to feed it into the slot. The bill was damp and floppy and wasn't cooperating.

"Do you have another dollar? This one isn't working."

"Nope, that's the only single I have. How can you still be thirsty after all that water you drank under the boat?"

He could hear her cursing under her breath. He couldn't resist. "There're probably instructions printed on the front of the machine. Should I read them to you?"

Just then the bill was sucked into the slot. She hit the button, and the bottle of water slid down the chute. She grabbed the bottle and opened it and took a long pull on the cold water. After several swallows, she lowered the bottle and let out a loud sigh.

Then she looked over at him. "Too bad you only had one single and the machine doesn't give change. This water tastes so good. Maybe as you're driving around looking for an ATM for me, you can find a place to get change so you can get a drink too." She took another swallow, followed by an exaggerated sigh. Then she handed him the bottle with a smirk.

They walked around the shed wall and headed for the parking lot where they had left the Explorer the previous night. He unlocked the doors, and they climbed inside. He wondered if he had driven his own automobile, whether it would still be here. He started the engine and they pulled out of the marina heading south. "Where are we headed?" she asked.

"To Fisherman's Village, of course, to find my wife."

Martin peeked in the canvas bag lying in her lap and saw his cell phone. "I doubt this computer we have with us is the only one that's capable of tracking your phone. They'll know you're coming, and we'll be walking into a trap."

"Check the bottom of the bag. You'll find the battery. I removed it from the phone before we left the house on the island."

"Okay, I'm impressed," she said as she nodded with approval.

"How does that computer trace the signals?" he asked.

"The computer runs the software. There's a built-in cellular card that communicates with the network that does the tracking. That means any computer with this program can track us, and that's why I'm sure they knew we were headed for the island last night."

"Yeah, I think you're right about that."

"That's why I think we need to call my office and get some help. We would be crazy to walk into a place like that. I feel bad that I haven't updated my office with the current situation. They're clueless as to what my status is. We've achieved what you set out to do. We have a lead on the location of your wife. Let's get some help now."

"I understand how you feel, Melissa, and I feel terrible about this situation I've put you in. I think you need to do what you think is right, but please don't turn me over to the FBI just yet. Too much time would be wasted trying to convince them I was innocent. It would put Barbara's life in further danger. I'm not sure how I know, but somehow I know she's alive. And we have to move quickly."

She was quiet as she stared out the passenger window. Cole watched her out the corner of his eye. He could see by her expression that she was struggling with her thoughts. He knew he owed her everything; he would be stuck in some FBI jail if she hadn't risked it all for him. He flicked the left turn signal on.

"Why are we turning here?"

"There's a landscape supply store here called Murdock Stones. It's back off the road. I've bought landscaping materials there for my house. I want you to go inside and use their phone to call your office. I've been selfish and I've put you in too much jeopardy already. I'll wait outside in the car because they'll recognize me."

"What should I tell them? What are you planning to do?"

"I'm going to Fisherman's Village for my wife. Get help or do whatever you think is appropriate. If Barbara isn't there, then we are out of clues anyway. Either way, it's over."

She gave him a small smile as they pulled into the parking area. He parked the Explorer out away from the building. "Good luck. Tell them I kidnapped you," he said with a smile.

"Promise me, you'll be here when I come back?"

"I promise."

She began walking toward the building and when she was halfway there she turned and looked at him through the windshield. He waved her on, and she continued toward the building.

The man behind the counter greeted her. "Hi honey, looks like you got caught in that thunderstorm that came through earlier."

She smiled and nodded her head. *You have no idea*, she thought.

"What can I do for you?"

"May I use your telephone? Mine got damaged in the storm."

"Sure thing. It's right over there. Dial a nine for an outside line."

As she picked up the telephone she saw a photograph on a nearby desk. The man and a woman in the picture were facing each other with wide loving smiles. While the couple was unknown to her, the love they felt for each other was obvious.

She paused, staring at the photograph and then dialed the dispatcher's number.

"FBI, how may I direct your call?"

"Yes, would you please connect me to Agent Dodd's mobile number?"

"Please hold one moment while I transfer your call."

She couldn't remember Tim Dodd's number to call him directly. It was programmed into her cell phone which was now useless. She waited while the call was rerouted to Dodd, and she heard several clicks in the background. Finally, there was a ring-back and a familiar voice said, "Agent Dodd."

"Timmy, it's Melissa. I need your help. I'm in serious trouble."

The line was silent for a few seconds. "Melissa, is it really you? Shit, we thought you were dead. They found your bloody clothes, and we've been working under the assumption that you had been killed. Where are you?"

"Listen Timmy, I need a huge favor."

"Anything Mel, you know that."

"I need you to keep this conversation between us for a while."

"Shit Melissa, do you know what you're asking? The Coast Guard has been searching the Gulf for your body for the last sixteen hours. Every cop on the west coast of Florida is checking every ditch and dumpster within fifty miles."

"I can't explain now. I wanted to let you know I'm all right. What's the latest on the Senator Cole case?"

"You're going to get us both fired. That's the latest."

"Timmy, you haven't forgotten last year in Lakeland when I took the rap for you guys, have you?"

There was a long silence. Agent Martin, Agent Dodd, and two other agents had been in Lakeland the previous year working on a case. They stopped at Hooters for dinner, and the three other agents had ordered wings and beer. Officially, they were still on duty and should not have been drinking beer. On the way back to the motel Agent Dodd was driving and a dog ran out in front of the car. He swerved to miss the dog and hit a tree alongside the road. They knew a blood sample would be taken from all of them, and Agent Martin was the only one who hadn't been drinking that night. She agreed to say she was alone in the car, and the others took off on foot for the motel. She had saved their jobs.

"No. Of course I haven't forgotten, and neither have the other guys. All right, the senator is the prime suspect in a homicide at his home. He's also suspected in your murder. The Bureau is still trying to keep it quiet because he's a senator. They have a statewide manhunt going on, but no one knows who they're looking for. You can imagine how that's going. Everybody in the Washington office is running around like chickens with their heads cut off. It's a circle jerk, that's the latest."

"Anything new on that book they found?"

"No, they've fucked that up, too. They had us running in various directions, and finally, Anderson told us to sit tight and wait. The whole episode was embarrassing as hell. They still say the book was definitely written by the senator."

"What about Mrs. Cole, anything new on her disappearance?"

"No, I think they have given up hope of finding her alive."

"Thanks Timmy. Give me your cell phone number, so I can keep in touch with you. My phone bit the big one. Remember, you have to keep this quiet for a little longer. Oh, one more thing, how long would it take to get a backup team in Punta Gorda if I needed it?"

"I'm sure we could have the local sheriff's office there in a few minutes. We're in constant contact with them now. Why, what's up Melissa?"

"Nothing, just in case. You know me, always too cautious. Bye Timmy."

She thanked the clerk and walked outside and headed for the Explorer. As she approached she waved at the car, but couldn't see the senator because the sun had come out and there was glare on the windshield.

She pulled the door open and slid into the seat in one smooth fluid motion. She turned her head with a smile to give him the news. The seat beside her was empty.

"Damn!"

Chapter 14

Tuesday, 4:45 PM

"Damn him, he promised he would be here." Martin sat alone in the front seat of the Explorer, trying to make sense of the situation.

Okay, work the clues. The key was still hanging in the ignition. *Good, at least he wasn't trying to strand me here by myself.*

She looked down at the floor by her feet and the canvas bag with the computer, his cell phone, and her gun, were all still there. *Hmmm.* She got out of the vehicle and opened the rear doors to scan for more clues.

She noticed the driver's side window was down. She remembered that all the windows had been up because of the drizzle, and the engine was running when she left to make the call. Maybe someone approached the vehicle, and he rolled down the window to see what they wanted. She also remembered the air-conditioning was on when she went inside, and the controls were still set for cool.

She bent to look at the ground next to the driver's side of the car. The ground was still wet from the rain and there were several footprints. They mostly pointed toward the car. It looked like at least two people had been there facing the car.

She scanned the area of the landscape supply yard and lot. She waved at a man sitting on a tractor used for loading gravel into truck beds. She approached him and smiled. "How are you doing today?"

"Fine, how can I help you, ma'am?"

"Did you see any other vehicles next to that black Explorer over there?"

"Yep, there was a white utility van parked next to it."

"Did you see what happened?"

"No ma'am, I load the vehicles. The man inside the office takes care of the customers."

"Did you see anyone get out of the van? How many people were there?"

"Oh yeah, two men got out of the van and were talking to their buddy in the Explorer. Then the buddy got out of the Explorer and got in the van with them. Now that I think about it, he might have been their boss."

"Why do you think he might have been their boss?"

"The way they held the door for him and because the one guy helped him climb into the front seat. It reminded me of kissing up to the boss."

"What happened next?"

"They drove out the exit and headed for the highway."

"Did it look as if they were forcing him into van?"

"Can't say, I was working in the lava bin at the time and wasn't paying all that much attention."

"Can you describe the van?"

"White."

"Thank you."

She walked back toward the Explorer and stared down at the dirt again. A few feet to the right there were several footprints facing the other direction as if they were facing another vehicle. And there were two sets of tire tracks in the dirt.

Martin got in the Explorer, started the engine and pulled out of the exit, heading for the highway. She was stopped at the intersection waiting for the traffic to clear when she noticed the top of the dash. The sun was shining through the window, highlighting it. It looked like someone had used their finger to draw a design in the dust collected on the vinyl. She peered at the elementary drawing, and realized it looked like the outline of a fish.

"Fisherman's Village," she said aloud." He's either telling me he was taken there, or he wants me to go there like we had planned."

She pulled out on the highway and headed east toward highway 776. That route would take her to US 41, where she would turn south, toward Punta Gorda and Fisherman's Village. Every time she passed a white utility van, she looked in the windows to see whether the senator was inside. She knew the chances of stumbling on the van were practically nonexistent, but she couldn't help herself.

Thirty minutes later, she was coasting down the far side of the bridge crossing the Peace River. The next right would be the road that would take her to Fisherman's Village. It had been several years since she had been there, but everything seemed to be exactly as she remembered it. She pulled into the parking lot, weaving her way through the aisles, looking for a white utility van.

She drove through the alley that ran between the commercial buildings and the docks to check all the unloading zones. In all, she had seen three white vans parked in various areas, and all were empty. She made a mental note of their locations.

She parked, and began walking through the central retail area, looking for—she wasn't sure what. She noted that there were apartments on the second floor. The retail shops and restaurants were on the first floor on both sides of the open-air promenade.

The area overhead where she was walking was open clear to the roof that spanned between the apartments on the second floor. The roof was broken up by various angles and had open areas to allow the breeze through. Birds were flying through the open rafters of the roof. The area reminded her of the boat shed where they had been earlier. Every six or so apartments there was a catwalk running overhead between the two sides of the apartment buildings. While the area was open, it would be impossible for one person to search the entire complex.

She noticed a boat brokerage office next to the coffee shop and between the two buildings was an ATM. She thought for a moment. If she used her ATM card her location would be given away. On the other hand, if she didn't find Senator Cole, she would have to call in to her office anyway. She withdrew some cash and went inside the brokerage office. A salesman quickly jumped from behind his desk and introduced himself.

Martin reached into her pocket and took out a small piece of folded paper and opened it for the salesman to see. "Can you tell me the exact location of these coordinates?

He smiled. "Yes, those coordinates are right here where we are standing."

"Right here, this exact spot where we're standing?" she asked.

He rolled his eyes and turned pointing to the chart hanging on the wall. "Look I'll show you." He lined up the latitude, then the longitude with his finger, and it was right over Fisherman's Village. He smiled smugly.

She wasn't impressed. "No, you don't understand. I need the exact building that these numbers designate."

The salesman's smile disappeared as he turned and walked to his desk. He opened the drawer, brought out a leather pouch and walked back to her. He opened the pouch, and removed a handheld GPS and powered it on. He stared at the display as he waited for the unit to lock in on the satellites. He tilted the display so she could see the screen working.

"See this little triangle, that's where we are standing. Now look at the latitude and longitude and compare it with your numbers. As you can see they are the same, except this unit's numbers go out one more place. See; the last number is three digits long and that narrows it further, within three meters, they claim. Without that third digit, I can't tell you which building."

She frowned in disappointment. "Thank you for trying. I appreciate it very much."

She walked outside and gazed up toward the overhead apartments and let out a sigh of frustration. She headed for the stairs leading to the second-floor apartments and noticed the sign on the railing, "Guests Only."

She ignored it and walked up the steps and began walking past each room, staring at blank doors. *This is going to be impossible.* She noticed a recessed area off to the one side which had a small table and two chairs set up for the apartment guests to enjoy the view of the marina.

She plopped the canvas bag on the table. She had done everything she could think of, to no avail. Now it was time to call the office and tell them that she was okay, but had lost the senator. As she reached into the bag for the cell phone, she had a sudden thought. She jumped, and rushed down the stairs as she made her way to the entrance in front of the complex.

She looked to where she had seen a taxi when she had first arrived. Fortunately, it was still there waiting as she made her way toward the cab, and the driver hopped out.

"Are you for hire?" she asked with a big smile.

"Yes ma'am, where would you like to go?"

"How much is the fare to the Sheriff's office from here?"

"Probably about eighteen dollars plus tip."

"I'll give you forty dollars to deliver something there for me."

"Listen lady, I don't need any trouble with the cops. I think I'll have to pass on this one."

Martin reached into her pocket and pulled out her FBI badge and showed the driver.

"Okay then. Forty bucks it is, ma'am!"

She reached into the canvas bag and took out the senator's cell phone. She installed the battery and asked the driver for a pen and paper. She wrote on the paper, "Detective Bob Martin. Dad, please keep this for me. I'll explain later. Melissa."

"Deliver this to Detective Martin at the sheriff's office. Ask to give it directly to him, not the front desk. After I walk away from here wait for five minutes, and then I want you to power the phone on. Wait exactly three more minutes after that and head straight for the Sheriff's department. Do you understand?"

"Yes lady, I got it."

She handed him forty dollars and the phone with the note wrapped around it and walked back into the complex. She rushed upstairs and sat in the recessed area at the table. She glanced at her watch while she looked in both directions down the corridor. From this location, she had a good view of all the corridors on the second floor.

Seven minutes and thirty seconds later she saw a door swing open on the left walkway. Two men rushed out, slamming the door and running down the corridor for the stairs. One was carrying a laptop computer and trying to run at the same time.

Yes!

She reached into the bag, removed her gun, placing it in the waist of her jeans. She pulled her shirt over it. She then hid the canvas bag with the computer behind a potted plant next to the wall.

She headed for the door that the men had rushed out of. At this point, she knew the only help her FBI badge would be was to add two ounces of weight to her measly 120 pounds. Wishing she had some backup, she cautiously approached the door.

With one hand on the butt of her gun, she knocked on the door and waited, hoping there wouldn't be an answer. She knocked again louder and still there was no answer. She reached down and tried the knob, and it was locked. Of course, she thought, *why should my luck change now?*

Reaching into her pocket, she pulled out her badge wallet, opened it, and slid out two flat metal picks. Other than at the Academy she had never opened a lock with these picks before, because her male partners were always anxious to show her how adept they were. Picking locks was a "man thing," she supposed.

She inserted the picks in the lock and instantly she could turn the cylinder. She couldn't believe how easy it was. Was it beginners luck or just not as difficult as the guys had made it out to be, she wondered.

She pushed the door and it slowly opened inward, revealing an empty apartment. She removed her gun from her waist and entered the doorway. The kitchen was on her right and a living/dining area beyond that. The only thing in the kitchen was a stack of dirty dishes sitting on the counter. The living area next to the kitchen was empty, and she headed to the door that led to the single bedroom.

In the room was one double bed and it looked like someone had been lying on the bedspread. She scanned the bathroom and there was a toiletry case lying next to the sink. An electric razor was plugged into the outlet, and the bag was full of men's toiletries. In the trash, she noticed an almost new stick of women's deodorant, a toothbrush, and toothpaste.

Leaning over the bed, she put her nose next to the pillow and could smell a faint scent of perfume. She was sure a woman had been lying on the bed. She inspected the surface of the bedspread and found several long brown hairs. Mrs. Cole has long brown hair. Looking around the room, she noticed a single chair sitting in front of the window, like someone had been sitting there staring out. She walked to the window and looked down at the marina below with its slips full of boats.

The small apartment seemed absent of any personal items except what she had found in the bathroom. She went back into the kitchen and began looking in the cabinets and drawers for clues. All she found were the normal kitchen items and piles of junk food.

She slid open the drawer next to the refrigerator and was surprised to find it was full of papers. She scanned the inch-thick stack of papers one at a time. They were all business papers from a company named Gulf-Global Enterprises. The papers were spreadsheets and financial statements for the company's last ten years.

Agent Martin looked up from the papers just in time to see an arm coming straight for her head. A second later she was lying on the floor of the kitchen unconscious.

When she woke she found herself lying on the bed. Her hands and legs were tied up behind her, and she had a cloth gag in her mouth. She could smell the perfume from the pillow of the previous person lying here. Her head was aching from the blow. She was grateful that it was on the opposite side of her head from the cut.

What kind of a mess had she gotten herself into now, she thought glumly. She stared at the closed door. What kind of trouble was on the other side?

A phone rang in the other room. The hollow core door of the bedroom may have provided visual privacy, but it hardly blocked any sound.

"Yes sir, I did call you. We have a situation here . . . Well, we were sitting here when the computer picked up the cell phone signal again . . . No, it was right here in the parking lot at the apartment. We ran down to the parking area, and the signal had already started to move. Juan followed it in the car, and I came back to the apartment. I found the door ajar and found a girl in the kitchen going through the drawers . . . She's an FBI agent, a Melissa Martin . . . No sir; she's fine. I knocked her out, and I have her tied up in the bedroom . . . Yes sir; I understand . . . No, I just talked to him, and he said the cell phone signal is coming from inside the Sheriff's office now . . . Yes sir . . . What should I do with the girl? . . . I understand."

Suddenly the bedroom door opened and a man approached the bed with something in his hand.

Chapter 15

Tuesday, 5:05 PM

Cole's shirt was wet with sweat as he furiously worked the ropes that held his hands tied behind his back. He couldn't believe that he had been way-laid as he waited for Martin at Murdock Stones. But here he was, in the back of a hot, stale-smelling utility van, courtesy of two strangers. He figured they had driven for about ten minutes, and had now been parked for about the same amount of time. He could hear voices talking outside the van, but couldn't make out what they were saying.

He felt dehydrated and faint. If only he could have some fresh air. He leaned back against the side wall of the van and hit it with his fist several times. A moment later the back doors opened.

Two men stared in at him. One was tall, skinny, and had a constant twitch. The other was a short man with a smart-ass grin pasted across his face.

"What the hell do you want?"

"I need some fresh air and something to drink. It's over a hundred degrees in here."

"Excuse us, Mr. Senator," said the short one, "for not making your trip more comfortable. Maybe I could get you a cocktail and a damp cloth?"

"Get him some water before he passes out and we have to carry him," ordered the tall one with the twitch.

He stood looking at Cole contemptuously while his partner went off to get the water. A few minutes later the man returned and tossed a bottle of water into the van.

"Aren't you going to untie my hands, so I can drink?"

The two men exchanged glances, and then Twitch made a gesture with his head. Smart-Ass climbed into the back of the van and untied the ropes. The senator took a long draw of water and then exhaled with relief.

He took another swallow and then addressed his captors. "Where in hell are we, and what do you want with me?"

"If you had done like you were supposed to, we wouldn't be here in this mosquito hole," replied Twitch as he slapped the back of his neck.

"What was I supposed to do?"

"You were supposed to go to the island, alone, and stay there. Not call the FBI yourself, and then go playing detective with Blondie. After all, you wrote a book confessing to a crime—what kind of dumb ass calls the FBI on himself?" He looked at Smart-Ass and they began to laugh.

"Where's my wife? You bastards better not harm her."

Smart-Ass taunted, "Ooh, not only is he a US senator, but he's a tough guy too."

The senator glared at them as he took another swig of water.

Twitch's cell phone rang, and he immediately straightened up his normally slumping posture. They moved away from the rear door of the van while he took the call.

Cole began writing in the dust with his finger on the ceiling of the dirty van.

Smart-Ass came back to the rear of the van. "Come on, tough guy, it's time to get going, and remember, don't try anything unless you want that little wife to get hurt."

Cole climbed out of the van and stretched for the first time in nearly an hour. The air felt cool against his sweaty body, and he breathed in the fresh air. He looked around and realized he was back at the Marina in Cape Haze. They led him down the path toward the boat shed, walking right past Ross's boat tied up in the slip where it was supposed to be. They continued to the other side of the shed and stopped at a boat where the two men directed him to get aboard. He recognized the boat from the night before. It was the same one that almost hit them speeding out of the channel with no running lights.

The boat headed out into the channel and turned south. Cole was sure he knew where they were going. He glanced over at his two captors, thinking. They surely weren't the sharpest guys he had ever met. He was confident he could take care of them with no problem, but he couldn't take the chance of something happening to Barbara because of his actions. He needed to wait and find out more about the situation.

Twitch, who seemed to be in charge, had long hair pulled into a pony tail. He had a narrow pointy face and a bony frame. Although he seemed to have the most sense, his head jerked sideways at regular intervals, which made him seem skittish. Smart-Ass just looked plain dumb. His hair was greasy, and overall he looked as if he hadn't bathed in several days. His fat face with a double chin constantly carried that stupid grin. *What a pair of idiots.*

They made it to the dock on the island without incident. They tied up the boat and left the dock, heading toward the old road. He thought of Melissa, and wondered what she was doing. He thought about the fish he had drawn in the dust on the dash of the Explorer. He hoped she had seen it and was on her way to Fisherman's Village with the help she had called. He knew it was a long shot, but then again, she was an FBI agent, and she was trained to look for clues.

When they arrived at the road, the Jeep was sitting there waiting for them. Someone had repaired the battery cables. It was a short trip to his house from there and they parked the Jeep in its usual place.

As they approached the front door he thought he could see someone moving inside the house. More idiots, he figured. Smart-Ass opened the door and gave Cole a push inside the living room. He stumbled inside and stopped dead in his tracks, his eyes wide. Miles Connor was sitting on the sofa.

"Miles, what are you doing here?"

"Y-Y-You told me to come to Florida r-r-right away."

"I know I told you to come to Florida. I mean what are you doing here on the island?"

"I n-need to t-tt-ell you something I-I know."

"What Miles? What do you need to tell me?"

Smart-Ass turned to Twitch. "What's he doing here?"

"Yeah, what are you doing here?" Twitch demanded.

Miles ignored him. "Senator Cole, I'm so s-s-sorry. I never meant for this t-t-to happen like this."

The senator stared at Miles uncomprehendingly. "Miles you're involved in this?"

"He promised m-m-me no one would get h-h-hurt. I- I didn't want to do it but h-h-he forced m-me t-to help him. He said it would b-be helping y-you."

"Miles, who are you talking about?"

"I'm going t-t-to stand up to h-him and m-m-make him s-stop all of this r-right now. He's not going to b-b-boss me a-a-anymore."

The two guys started to snicker. "Sure you are, Smiley Miley," said Smart-Ass. "I think it's time you shut your trap before you get us all in trouble here."

Miles jumped off the sofa and headed for Smart-ass. "I-I-I told you never to c-c-call me that again!"

Miles was a full foot taller. He grabbed Smart-Ass and shoved him backward across the room into the wall. He jumped back at Miles, and they both landed on the floor.

Cole lunged forward, but Twitch grabbed his arm to stop him. Cole pulled loose and shoved him against the front door. As he came at Twitch with his right arm reared back to punch him in the face the sound of a gunshot rang out.

Cole stopped in mid-swing and turned toward the direction of the shot.

Miles and Smart-Ass both lay on the floor motionless. Then Miles' body began to rise as the other man pushed him off the top. Miles slumped onto the floor, his body covered in blood.

Cole rushed over to him and knelt on the floor. Miles looked up at him, his face distorted with pain. He opened his mouth and tried to speak, but no sound came out.

"It's okay Miles. I'm going to get you some help. Lie still."

Miles opened his mouth again and managed to speak faintly.

"P-P-Please f-f-forgive me S-S-Senator Co—. S-Sulli—v-v-v—S-Sena—t-tor K-Kap—."

"Please Miles, don't try to talk. Lie still while I get you some help. Cole grabbed a throw from the chair, wadded it, and placed it under Miles' head. His voice cracked. "Miles you're the best assistant there is in the Capitol. I'm so fortunate to have you."

Cole saw a faint smile form on Miles' face and watched his eyes flicker as his body went limp. Cole gasped, and pulled Miles' body toward him as he hugged him for the last time. He slowly settled him back down on the floor, and then stood and looked at the man who had killed his assistant and friend.

He started toward the man. "You son-of-a–bitch."

Smart-Ass pointed his gun at Cole. "Hold it right there or you'll be next."

Cole ignored him and walked up to him until the tip of the gun was sticking in his chest. He could feel that Smart-Ass was trembling. He knew from his training this man was no match for him. He could reach down and grab the gun and kill this guy before he knew what happened. Just then he felt another gun being stuck in his back.

"Step back, Senator. Let's not forget your wife," said Twitch. "Go sit down. Now."

Cole slowly turned and went over to the sofa and sat.

Twitch turned to Smart-Ass. "You asshole!" he yelled. "You killed the idiot brother. We're both dead men now."

"I shot him in self-defense. You saw him go berserk and attack me. What else was I supposed to do? We all knew it was just a matter of time before the kid freaked out. He was a nut case; everyone knew it."

Twitch stuck his finger in his chest. "I hope you're right, because I'm not going down for this. It's your screw-up. Take the senator upstairs and cuff him to the hook in the bedroom. I need to make a call and see what to do next."

Smart-Ass turned to Cole. "Get up, let's go." He pushed him toward the stairs from behind.

Cole glanced again at Miles lying on the floor as he climbed the stairs, his anguish turned to rage. He could feel the heat rushing to his face as his contempt for the man behind him boiled inside him.

At the top of the stairs, he was shoved to the right into the master bedroom.

"Stand at the foot of bed."

Smart-Ass removed a pair of handcuffs from his pocket. He hooked the one side of the cuffs to a metal ring that had been installed into the wall behind the bed post. Cole hadn't noticed the hook there earlier in the day when they searched the house. He wondered whether he had missed it or if it was the newest addition to the décor.

He then noticed the picture of him with Barbara on the nightstand. He had removed the red marker from her face. He stared at her picture, and felt her calling for help. He knew he had to do something; he wasn't going to find his wife while handcuffed to the wall.

Smart-Ass left the cuffs hanging on the wall and backed away, motioning to Cole with his gun. Cole approached the head of the bed, while Smart-Ass maintained his distance.

Cole suddenly pointed to the wall next to the man. "What the hell is that?" he exclaimed loudly.

Smart-Ass turned instinctively and Cole swiftly grabbed the man's head from behind with one arm and put his other hand on his face. In one fluid motion, he gave Smart-Ass's head a twist. There was a crunch and instantly Smart-Ass was dead from a broken neck.

Cole lowered the body to the floor. He reached down and removed the gun that was still in his hand and noticed the safety was on. *Not exactly a professional*, he thought.

He stared down at the pitiful excuse for a man sprawled out on the floor. He began to wonder, if Smart-Ass had not killed Miles, would he have still broken his neck? He wasn't sure. It wasn't something he had planned. In fact, it never crossed his mind until a second before he did it.

He was sure he would never forget the sound of the neck bones snapping. He had been trained how to perform that maneuver many years ago in the military. He had never had to use it and when he got out of the service, he had been sure he never would. He had been wrong.

Cole heard footsteps coming up the staircase. He hurried over and stood behind the bedroom door, released the safety on the gun, and took a deep breath.

"What's taking you so long in there?" Twitch breached the doorway. "What the—"

Cole kicked the door mightily, slamming it into Twitch. Twitch fell backwards to the floor with a groan.

Cole came around the door and pointed the gun at Twitch, who was holding the side of his face with his left hand. Blood was pouring from his nose and running through his fingers. The other hand was beginning to rise with a gun pointing toward Cole.

"Drop the gun or you're dead," hollered Cole.

The gun continued to rise and then there was a sudden blast. Twitch's arm dropped and the gun hit the floor with a loud thump. Cole kicked the gun away toward the center of the room.

He bent and grabbed the man's shirt in his fist and pulled him closer. "Tell me where my wife is." Twitch's eyes looked both distant and frightened.

Cole gave him a jerk. "Tell me what's happening here and I will get you an ambulance. Where is my wife?"

Twitch's mouth started to move unintelligibly. Cole leaned in closer. "What did you say? Tell me again."

Twitch's head fell backward, his mouth slack, and Cole released his grip in frustration. "Damn you! Why didn't you listen to me when I told you to drop the gun?"

He took the dead man's cell phone off his belt. Then he rolled him over and removed his wallet from his back pocket. He left both bodies in the bedroom and went downstairs to the living room.

He removed Miles' cell phone from his pocket. It was the same phone as his. He scrolled through the call log until he came to several entries that didn't have a number, or at least not a number he had seen before. It looked just like the scrambled mess that came up on the screen of his black market phone. He scrolled further and stopped on "Senator Cole" and hit the send button. He hoped Agent Martin still had his phone and had it turned on. He waited a few seconds and then heard the ring-back tone. Then a man's voice said, "Hello."

Chapter 16

Tuesday, 8:55 PM

The conference call between the FBI Washington office and the field task team, originally scheduled for 6:00 PM was rescheduled for 9:00 PM, to allow recent events in the case to be included in the discussion.

Bill Hansen and two of his agents were in his room at the motel in Englewood, waiting for the impending call. Mackey was also present.

"It's 8:55. Why don't you go ahead and make the call and get the connection set, Jerry," said Hansen.

Jerry Moore dialed the numbers on the satellite telephone and waited for the response on the other end. He entered an access code and waited while the call was routed to the proper extension. When he heard the ringing on the other end, he hit the speaker button and set the handset in the cradle.

After the third ring, a voice came through the speaker. "William Anderson."

"Hello William. Bill Hansen here, and with me are Agents Moore and Dodd. Also in the room is Doug Mackey with the Capitol Police."

"Good evening everyone. Mackey, how was your flight?"

"Good, William. Thanks again for getting me on that earlier flight."

"You're welcome Mackey, and thank you for finding that neighbor's house. I'm sure it's helping move the investigation along. In the office with me are Tom, Raphael, and Dr. Moiré.

"We'll go first on this end. The reason I delayed our conference call is because we had a setback. I received a call this afternoon from the editor of the Journal wanting to confirm a story they were planning to run in tomorrow's paper. The story is about Senator Cole murdering his wife, including the allegation of the existence of a book confessing to the crime.

"The Director persuaded the editor to postpone releasing the story on the grounds of national security. They agreed to hold the story until tomorrow at 6:00 PM, at which time the Journal plans to run a special edition featuring all the details of the story."

"How the hell did they get the story?" asked Hansen.

"That's what we've been trying to figure out for the last six hours. With the amount of detail they have, it's apparent whoever leaked the story is close to the case. Which side of the case they are on is what we're still trying to determine.

"The reporter is refusing to divulge his source, and the Director is threatening him with prosecution for interfering with a national security concern. The last time I talked with the Director he felt the reporter might be having second thoughts about protecting his source. If we can learn who the source of the story is, we might be able to turn this into a positive lead and figure out who's behind it. Unless the source is on this side, and then we have a new set of problems to confront, and I don't want to have to think about that.

"Anyway, the Director has made the decision that if we don't have the senator in our custody by 6:00 PM tomorrow, he will hold a press conference announcing that the FBI will be issuing an arrest warrant for Senator Cole for suspicion of murder."

Everyone in the motel room turned and looked at Mackey as he stared at the satellite telephone. Hansen put his hand on Mackey's shoulder.

Anderson said, "Tom, why don't you go ahead and bring us up to date on anything new since our last meeting."

"Well, I've been working the telephone concerns. The Coles each have a black market, modified cell phone capable of making calls without sending a traditional telephone number. That's why we were missing the data earlier. The phones run through several layers of companies, and we haven't sorted it out yet. Apparently the CIA was working on a version of this phone a while back but dropped it in favor of a different format.

The Coles have been using those phones to communicate. That's why we couldn't find any record of their calls to each other. At this point, we aren't sure what it means, if anything. The guys in the lab tell me the phones are set up to be untraceable through the cell phone network. Why they needed that I have no idea at this point, although it does seem suspect."

"Tom, Doug Mackey speaking. I know Senator Cole was having problems with his cell phone signal being tracked and sold to reporters. That's probably the reason for these new phones."

"Okay, that makes sense, Mackey. As you know, we have forwarded the Coles' regular phone numbers to my office. Earlier today we received a call on Mrs. Cole's phone from an attorney in Florida. He represented a company called Gulf-Global Enterprises. When he realized he was talking to the FBI, he clammed up big time. All I could get out of him was that he was trying to contact Mrs. Cole about a board meeting she was scheduled to attend. Gulf-Global Enterprises was founded by her late father, Roger Morrison. Bill, I think you should send one of your teams to their office in the morning and see what we can find. They are in Sarasota, and I'll send you the information I have."

"I'll send someone first thing in the morning, Tom."

Hansen's cell phone began to ring. He reached down quickly and checked the display. "Excuse me folks, I need to take this call."

As Hansen listened his expression became alert. "Hold on," he said.

He looked up and around the room and then spoke to the satellite phone. "William, we have a development."

"What do you have Bill?"

"A Detective Charles Martin is on the line with the Tampa office. Detective Martin is Agent Melissa Martin's father."

"Had we notified the family yet?"

"No, we thought it would be better to wait until we had something we could tell them. We didn't want to upset them needlessly. The reason he called is that he received a cell phone in his office this afternoon. It had a note attached to it from his daughter. The note was asking him to hold the phone until she communicated with him."

"Bill, why don't you have your office route his call to our conference link?"

Hansen gave the office the instructions and numbers, and they waited. The speaker clicked and there was a beep.

"Detective Martin?" said Anderson.

"Yeah. Martin here. All I'm trying to do is find out where my daughter Melissa Martin is. I keep getting the runaround from everyone I talk to. What the hell is going on at the FBI? I'm a detective in a small-town operation here with hardly any budget, but we're able to keep track of our people all the time."

Hansen looked around the room at the other men, his face visibly red with embarrassment.

"Detective Martin, my name is William Anderson. I'm with the Washington office of the FBI. Sir, you are on a conference call with the task teams here in Washington and in Florida."

"Sorry, Mr. Anderson. I'm just trying to ascertain whether my daughter Melissa is all right."

"Detective, your daughter is working on a highly sensitive case down in your area. I'm sorry to say she has been out of contact with the team for about twenty-four hours now."

"Out of contact, what the hell does that mean?"

"Sir, we have been unable to locate or communicate with her since about this time last night. Her communication with you is the first indication we have that she may be all right. We need everything you can tell us about the phone and the note."

"Well, the phone is different from any cell phone I have ever seen. I didn't think much about it at the time. You know, with Melissa being FBI, I just assumed it was some fancy new phone she had been issued. Her note attached to the phone said to hold it until she contacted me. So I wasn't that concerned. It wasn't until the damn thing started to ring that I began wondering what the hell was going on."

"Detective, do you have the number that called it?"

"No, that's the crazy thing. No number came up, just a lot of garble on the display. But by God, don't you know I was surprised when I answered the phone and found I was talking to our Senator, Irwin Cole."

That statement created silence on both ends of the conference call. The silence was broken by Hansen's phone ringing again.

Anderson pressed on. "Detective Martin, what did the senator have to say?"

"He said he was trying to contact Melissa. He also said that I had a wonderful daughter, and that I should be proud of her."

"Did he say anything else, Detective?"

"No sir, that's it. I did tell him to give those oil companies hell. Then we hung up."

"Excuse me William, it's Bill. I just received word that the neighbor's Explorer we've been searching for has been found by the local sheriff's office at a place in Punta Gorda called Fisherman's Village. We also received information that Agent Martin's ATM card was used in the same area. We need to head to that location. The local sheriff's department is securing the area until we get there."

"Okay Bill, let me know what happens. Detective Martin . . . Detective Martin are you still on the line?"

Chapter 17

Tuesday, 9:50 PM

Detective Martin was already waiting at the entrance to the Fisherman's Village parking lot when the FBI pulled up. He approached their car and introduced himself to the three FBI agents and Mackey. The parking lot area around the black Explorer had been closed, to preserve it in case the FBI wanted the car examined by their lab people. Roadblocks were on all the approaches and all vehicles were being checked by uniformed officers from the sheriff's department. The four men hurriedly climbed out onto the asphalt parking lot.

Hansen spoke loudly. "If I could have everyone's attention please...I appreciate all the help your group is providing here. We need to find the occupant or occupants of this black Explorer. I need six people to watch the perimeter so no one tries to slip by us. The rest of you can start a room-by-room search of all the buildings. We are looking for a blonde female, twenty-eight, 5'6", and 120 lbs. She is an FBI agent named Melissa Martin, but we are unsure of her status.

"The second person is a male about thirty-nine, six feet tall, approximately 175 lbs. He has light brown hair, and his last name is Cole. We need to check the identification of everyone in this place, no exceptions. If identification can't be verified, please call for one of my agents immediately, and we will make a case-by-case assessment. Are there any questions?"

"Is this Cole considered dangerous?"

"Approach with caution, he is a person in whom we have an interest at this time."

The chatter could be heard as the officers all fanned out in various directions heading for the complex.

Mackey said, "Look at the size of this place, we'll be here searching all night."

"At least all the retail businesses are closed except the bar at the end," replied Hansen.

Mackey smiled. "I like a guy who can see the positive side of everything."

The rental management company manager had been contacted and asked to open the unoccupied units. He was busy opening doors with the master key as the team methodically worked their way through the complex.

An hour later the task force was about two-thirds of the way through the apartments.

Hansen's radio blasted into his earpiece. He missed the first half of the transmission and keyed his microphone. "Negative, please repeat, say again."

A short blast of static came from the speaker, and then a voice. "We have something in unit 226."

Hansen waved to Mackey and the other agents and they made a beeline to the room. They pushed through the small group of uniformed officers gathered at the doorway of the apartment.

"Please, continue your search of the rest of the complex. We will handle this," he ordered.

They were directed into the small apartment's bedroom. On the bed was Agent Martin, tied up, gagged, and unconscious.

"Get the medical team in here now!" yelled Hansen, as Detective Martin began to remove the gag from his daughter's mouth. "We need to make sure this area remains secure. Remember we're still looking for Cole."

Detective Martin cut the plastic ties that held her arms and legs.

The medical team rushed in through the small crowd and began examining Agent Martin.

"She's my daughter, is she going to be all right?" Distress was written all over Detective Martin's face.

One of the paramedics turned to Detective Martin. "She's unresponsive. It appears she's been drugged but her vitals are all good. We're calling an emergency room doctor for authorization to administer Narcan."

Agent Martin was wheeled out of the room on a stretcher and taken to an awaiting ambulance.

"Detective Martin," said Hansen, "Why don't you see to your daughter. We'll handle this."

Hansen and Mackey stood outside the apartment while the search continued for Senator Cole. Hansen dialed Anderson to inform him they had found Agent Martin alive, and he hoped, well.

* * *

Cole stepped out the shower at the island house. After calling his cell phone earlier that night and talking with Melissa's father, he felt sure she was out of harm's way. He felt revitalized by the shower and decided it was time to go on the offensive.

He had been playing this game of being one step behind long enough. Now it was time for him to start kicking some ass. Although, with three down by his count, he was already throwing some shit their way. But now he had two guns and ammunition and no agent to worry about.

It felt good slipping into some semi-fresh clothes he found in the closet. Next, a meal from the stocked refrigerator, and he would be ready for whatever these bastards had planned. He sat on the back porch eating his ham and cheese sandwich, gazing across the moonlit Gulf.

He was sure it would be just a matter of time before one of the cell phones sitting on the table in front him started ringing. He had checked the call log on both phones, and Twitch's phone had a lot of garble instead of numbers, just as his own private phone did. He assumed whoever was behind this would be calling that phone before long, with instructions or to check the status of things. He could hardly wait to give him a status report.

He picked up the other phone, which had belonged to Smart-Ass. He entered a number from memory, hoping it was correct. "Who memorizes numbers nowadays?" He whispered.

A voice said, "Mackey."

"Mackey, it's Irwin."

"Damn, Irwin! Where in the hell are you?"

"I think it's better if I don't tell you where I am, Mackey. I'm trying to figure out who's doing this to me, and at the same time I'm trying to locate Barbara. Are you at home now?"

Mackey spoke in a lower voice. "Hold on one second."

He walked away from Hansen and the other FBI agents until he was outside of hearing distance. "Irwin, no, I'm not at home. I'm at a place called Fisherman's Village in Punta Gorda."

"Punta Gorda—what the hell are you doing down here, Mackey?"

"I flew in today. I'm here with the FBI task force. The car you borrowed from Ross was found here by the locals."

"Have they located Agent Martin and is she okay?"

"Yes, we found her a few minutes ago. She was tied up and unconscious in one of the rooms. I think she is going to be all right, but they think you're a killer. Did you hear me? Irwin, are you still there?"

* * *

Mackey spun around to find Hansen glaring at him.

Mackey glanced back at his phone display. "Call ended."

"Mackey, I need to see your phone."

Mackey slowly held out his hand, and Bill Hansen grabbed it. "Senator Cole?" There was no answer.

He opened the call log and wrote down the most recent number, then handed the phone back to Mackey. "Were you going to tell me he called you?"

"I'm not sure, Bill. I hadn't thought that far ahead yet. I was taken by surprise when he called."

"Did he say where he was?"

"Nope, all he said was he was trying to figure out who was doing this to him while trying to find Barbara. And that's when we were cut off."

Bill looked at Mackey intently, then called Agent Moore over and gave him the slip of paper. "Get me a location trace on this number right away."

Hansen dialed the number on his own phone and was greeted with a recording. "Yeah, you know what to do." Beep.

"Whoever owns that phone sounds like a real sweetheart."

"I'm sorry Bill. Yes, I would have told you he called, even though he didn't say anything that would help locate him. I asked where he was, and he said I was better off not knowing."

"It's all right, Mackey. If I was in your place, I would have done the same thing."

A uniformed sheriff's officer approached Hansen. "We checked all the rooms, including the bar out back, and found nothing of this Cole guy."

"Thanks for your help," Hansen replied. "You can let your people go home now. We will finish in the room where we found Agent Martin."

* * *

"Mackey. Any word on Barbara?"

"Mackey, did you hear me, anything new on Barbara?"

Cole looked at the display on the phone. It was blank.

"Shit, dead battery!" he exclaimed out loud in disgust. He continued in a murmur to himself. "At least I know Melissa is safe and if Mackey had any news about Barbara, I'm sure they would have been the first words out of his mouth."

Cole went into the utility room off the kitchen and opened the huge chest freezer he had plugged in before fixing his sandwich. Putting his hand on the inside liner, he could feel it was ice cold. He retrieved the three bodies and put them inside the freezer, wrapping Mile's body in a blanket first, but not the other two. The freezer would preserve the bodies until he could notify the authorities. He paused and looked inside again before closing the lid. "Miles, I hope you rest in peace now, sweet boy."

He remembered the words Twitch had used earlier, "Idiot brother." Miles had never mentioned that he had a brother. For that matter, he had never mentioned any family at all.

Cole thought back to when Miles was an intern in college. He was sure that the file he had read on Miles indicated he was an orphan, that his parents had been killed when he was a child. He had grown up in several foster homes. Maybe he befriended another boy in one of the homes, and they thought of each other as brothers. Still, it seemed Miles would have mentioned someone that was like a brother.

He leaned back and relaxed on the sofa, ruminating, and in minutes, he was asleep.

He was awakened by one of the phones ringing in the kitchen. He rushed over, and just as he suspected, it was Twitch's phone. The display once again showed the crazy symbols.

He hit the button and waited. After a few seconds of silence he said, "Yes."

A low deep voice said, "Update."

After a short pause Cole replied. "Okay, if you insist. Both of your goons are dead, and I'm free to do as I please."

Another pause, then: "Senator Cole I presume? My, haven't you been a busy man. Maybe I underestimated you."

"Not nearly as busy as I'm going to be when I catch up to you, and yes, you have underestimated me."

"I doubt that. It will only require a small change in my plans, Senator Cole."

"Where's my wife, you bastard?"

"I assure you she is fine, and while you cooperate, she will remain that way."

"Let's hope you take better care of her than you did Miles."

"Miles is fine and of no concern to you."

"You're wrong again. Miles is dead, thanks to you."

After a long pause the low deep voice spoke tersely. "You and your wife are both dead. Hear me? Dead!"

Cole screamed into the phone. "You touch my wife you son-of-a-bitch, and you will be the dead man!" But the connection had already been dropped.

Cole scrolled down and hit the garbled number and tried to call him back, but like his phone, it didn't work, and all he could hear was a ticking noise.

The low deep voice he had listened to was no brother of Miles, he was sure of that. The voice was too raspy; it was the voice of a much older man. But it had a familiarity, as if he had heard it before. He packed the backpack he had found in the closet with the guns and a few bottles of water. He headed for the front door. It was time to get off this island and find his wife.

Chapter 18

Wednesday, 7:15 am

Agent Martin was sound asleep in her hospital room bed when the telephone on the stand next to the bed began ringing. It rang a few times before she stirred. Disoriented, she reached over and picked up the receiver. "Hello," she said sleepily.

"Hello Melissa, it's Bill Hansen. How're you feeling this morning?"

"Uh . . . just woke."

"I apologize for calling you so early, but I had a few questions to ask you and the hospital said it would be all right. They also said you might be able to go home today if the doctor clears you during his morning rounds."

"I-I don't—"

"It's all right Melissa. They said it would take some time for your head to clear from the drug given to you. But I wanted to know whether you have any idea where we might find Senator Cole."

She wasn't prepared to answer questions, and lay speechless for a moment. She thought she would have some time to think about what she was going to say. Finally, she spoke haltingly, her voice still thick with sleep. "No sir, I have no idea where he is. The last time I saw him was at a landscape supply in Cape Haze. I went inside to use the phone. When I returned, a witness said he had been taken by two men in a white utility van. Sir, the Coles own a beach house on Little Gasparilla Island and I think it is the key to discovering what's going on here."

"Okay Melissa, I'll get someone to investigate. Don't worry about it. You need to get some rest. You gave us all a big scare."

"Sir, I don't believe the senator is guilty of any of this. And there's one more thing. Somehow, I think the security of the Capitol's computer system has been compromised. I'm not sure why."

"If that's the case, I need to notify Washington right away. Okay Melissa, this information gives us plenty to work with. You did a good job, get some rest, and you can put it in your report when you get to work. I'm sending Agent Dodd down to the hospital later this morning, and if you're released, he'll drive you back home to Tampa. Melissa, I'm glad you're all right."

"Thank you, bye sir."

Agent Martin lay in the bed, still clouded in fog, trying to gather her thoughts further. Everything she said had been the truth, and he didn't care about all the details. Maybe she had made this out in her mind to be worse than it actually was. She thought about Senator Cole. Where was he, was he all right? Her job had been to protect him and not to let him out of her sight. She had failed dismally at that, but her boss hadn't even mentioned that either.

Her head throbbed as if she had been out on an all-night drinking binge. She closed her eyes and tried to remember how she had ended up lying in a hospital bed.

The last thing she remembered was entering the apartment at Fisherman's Village and then nothing.

"Hello sweetheart."

She opened her eyes to see her father standing next to the bed.

"Daddy. It's so good to see you."

"How are you feeling, pumpkin?"

"Groggy, my head feels as if it's in a vise."

"I talked to the nurse, and she said you're going to be fine. In fact, she said the doctor may release you after he checks you out this morning." He leaned over and gave her a hug. "I was so worried about you last night when I was on that conference call with all those FBI agents."

"What conference call? You were talking to the FBI? Why?"

"That phone you had delivered to me yesterday started ringing last night, and you'll never guess who called."

"Senator Cole?"

"Yeah, how did you know?"

"It's part of the case I was working on and Daddy, I think I may have screwed up big time."

"Well, I didn't get that impression from Bill Hansen or William Anderson."

"You talked to William Anderson in Washington?"

"Yeah, he's a hell of a guy. He was concerned about your welfare, and I shouldn't have yelled at him like I did."

"Oh my God, I'm dead."

"Sweetie, you worry too much, like your mother, always worrying about something."

"I know you're right Daddy. But remember after the graduation ceremony you told me my greatest asset as an agent would be to follow my instincts?"

"Yeah, I remember our little talk; you inherited your instincts from me. That's what has made me such a good cop all these years. I was never much into that crime scene studying and profiling crap. Good police work comes from the gut; either you got it, or you don't. If you followed your instincts on this case, then you'll be fine, you didn't do anything wrong. You can tell those pencil pushers to go to hell."

She smiled widely and reached out her arms for another hug. It seemed his bear hugs always had a way of making her feel better, no matter what she had done.

"Thank you Daddy."

* * *

Hansen dialed his contact at the local sheriff's office.

"Frank? Bill Hansen. I need your help checking out a house on Little Gasparilla Island that has to do with the case. There's a house out there reportedly owned by the Coles, but it wasn't listed in their name when we reviewed the records. Would you do a property check under Roger Morrison for a home on the island?"

"Sure Bill, I'm typing in the computer now. Here we are, number six, Little Gasparilla."

"Do you have a boat or helicopter that can get to the island right away?"

"Yes Bill, I have both. I'll dispatch them immediately."

"Thanks Frank. I have an agent on the way to the marina, and he should arrive in about twenty minutes. If you could pick him up I would appreciate it."

Hansen's next call was to William Anderson.

"William, I just got off the phone with Agent Martin at the hospital."

"How's she doing, Bill?"

The Cole Hard Truth

"Good. According to the nurse she will probably be released later today. She's still groggy, and she doesn't know the whereabouts of Senator Cole. She believes he was grabbed by some unknown assailants in a white utility van yesterday afternoon."

"What the hell do you make of that, Bill?"

"I don't know William. She's still confused, and recovering from the effects of the drugs and the hit on the head. She claimed the senator was innocent of everything."

"I see."

"She did give me some information about where the senator had been staying. We've discovered his wife's family owns a beach house on an island south of here, and I have the Sheriff's office sending a boat and helicopter as we speak. Also William, she claims the Capitol's computer system security has been compromised."

"How would she know that?"

"She didn't know, and as I said, she is still very groggy, but I think we should investigate just in case."

"I'll get on it right away. By the way, the reporter from the Journal is coming in this morning. The Director wants us to lean on him until he gives us his source. I'll let you know what happens. Talk to you later."

Bill Hansen dialed Agent Dodd's room next door. "Tim, I need you in my room right away."

Tim Dodd slammed the phone down. "Oh shit. They probably discovered that I spoke to Martin yesterday."

He left his room and went to Hansen's to face the music.

"Yeah boss, what did you need?"

"I need you to drive to the hospital in Punta Gorda. They may be releasing Melissa today and if so, I want her driven to her home in Tampa."

"Okay sure, I'll leave right away."

"Tim, she has been through a lot, but I need to try to find out what she knows about this case. Don't push her; just learn what you can about the case. Got it?" "Yes sir."

Chapter 19

Wednesday, 8:00 AM

Senator Cole sped across the water in the same boat that he had come across in with the two thugs the evening before. The morning was still early, but the sun shone brightly in his eyes as he headed east toward the mainland. It was Wednesday, the day the book said his wife would die, and his stomach was full of acid.

Just as he turned the boat north in the channel, he saw a Sheriff's Department boat heading south with its lights flashing. He slumped slightly in the seat as they passed him going in the opposite direction. Since there were several other boats on the water around him, he wasn't too concerned. Once they were far enough past him, he straightened back up and peered behind him to make sure the sheriff's boat hadn't stopped.

As he pulled into the marina, he heard a helicopter flying overhead. It was flying low, as if hovering and searching, and he knew he'd been caught. But then the chopper gained altitude and flew toward the south. It looked like it was headed for the island. *Got out of there just in time,* he thought.

He tied the boat to the dock and ran down the pier to the parking lot, before anyone else showed up. He scanned for the white utility van as he reached down in his pocket and removed the keys he had taken from Twitch.

He found the van parked two rows down. He inserted the key into the door lock, but it didn't want to turn at first. He wiggled around until finally it turned and he pulled open the driver's door. Throwing his backpack inside, he lifted his leg to slide in when he heard a voice. "Senator Cole, hold it right there."

He froze. Slowly, he tilted his head back out to look at a man standing about three feet away. The man opened a wallet, displaying an FBI badge and identification. "My name is Agent Garrett, sir."

Cole looked at the clean-cut young man standing in front of him wearing a dark-gray suit and sunglasses. He looked as young as Melissa. He thought, *either I'm just getting old or the world is getting a lot younger.*

Cole instinctively raised his hands, but he didn't see a gun aimed at him. He asked the agent, "Am I under arrest?"

"No sir, I'm here to place you in protective custody."

Cole lowered his hands. "Protective custody, what do you mean by that?"

"Sir, it is the belief of the FBI that your life is in danger." *No shit, Sherlock.*

"I have *instructions* to take you to a safe house until the threat has been diminished. Senator, please follow me to the car."

"Is it alright if I grab my bag from the van?"

"I'll get it for you, sir."

Cole and Garrett walked to the black Ford Crown Victoria. Garrett opened the trunk and threw the bag inside. It landed on the floor of the trunk with a metallic clanking sound. Cole watched for a reaction from the agent, but there wasn't one.

The two men were silent as the Crown Vic pulled out of the marina parking lot. The mood felt awkward as the car headed down the highway. Finally, Cole asked, "Where is this safe house?"

Garrett said, "Sir, I'm not allowed to divulge that information. The location of safe houses is a closely guarded secret."

Cole nodded his head. "Has the FBI located my wife yet?"

"Sir, I've been instructed not to discuss any details of the case."

"Listen to me Agent Garrett, she is my wife. I deserve to know what her status is right now.

"Sir, I'm not—."

"I know, you're not allowed to discuss that information. What can you tell me, Agent Garrett? Why does the FBI suddenly believe my life is in danger?"

Garrett shifted in his seat. "Well sir, I can tell you that the book is an obvious hoax to discredit you. We believe they are a well-organized group attempting to remove you from your leadership role as an opponent of offshore drilling. If they don't succeed with discrediting you, we have credible information that your life may be in extreme danger."

Cole regarded Garrett with a look of surprise. "That's sure a change from yesterday when they thought I was a cold-blooded killer. I would have never thought the FBI would change their position so quickly. Don't get me wrong Agent Garrett, I'm not complaining."

"Yes sir. While you understand I can't discuss any details of the case, we've been known in the past to leak, shall we say, misinformation, to advance the progress of a case."

"You don't say. I know you can't tell me where we are going, but if we don't get there in the next fifteen minutes, I'm going to need a relief break, if you know what I mean."

"Yes sir, I understand."

They progressed slowly toward the northeast as Garrett navigated the heavy traffic of the business district. Cole noticed he had turned on the right turn signal as they passed a "To I-75" sign. He knew if they got on the interstate in this section, there would be no rest stops.

Fortunately, he saw a gas station sign ahead on the right. "Agent Garrett, do you think we could stop here for that restroom break?"

Garrett turned in the parking lot and pulled in next to the store. He turned the engine off and sat silently in his seat. Cole popped his door open and wasted no time stepping out of the car and heading straight for the facilities inside the store.

He was surprised that Garrett didn't follow him into the restroom, assuming he had explicit instructions not to let the senator out of his sight. He tried to think of a way that he could get hold of the backpack in the trunk. It looked as if he wasn't going to need the guns, but he sure would like to have Miles's special phone

Then he had an idea. He washed his hands and as he emerged from the restroom he saw Garrett standing next to the car. *This guy is as stiff as they come,* he thought.

He came out the exit door and smiled across the roof of the Ford at Garrett. "I need to get a bottle of water out of my backpack, if that's all right."

Garrett wordlessly held up two bottles of water. Cole's stomach did a flip flop. If Garrett had been in his bag, he had surely seen the guns. He wondered if that would put him back on the FBI's suspect list. And how was this going to affect the disposition of this young agent.

Cole opened his door and slid into the passenger seat. "You read my mind."

It wasn't until he took the bottle of water from Garrett that he could relax again. The bottle was ice cold, just bought inside the store.

Garrett opened his bottle and took a long draw of water and made a small sigh. The mannerism and sound of him drinking the water seemed so familiar. Instantly, Cole had a feeling of déjà vu. The way he held his mouth as he swallowed seemed familiar. He watched him with curiosity as his pale skin and slight New York accent seemed out of place here in Florida.

Finally, Cole opened his bottle and took a small swig of water, but he wasn't thirsty.

As they drove north on I-75 Cole noticed that Garrett was constantly glancing in his rearview mirror. His eyes flicked from his side mirror, down at the dash, then back to the rearview mirror. His hands were fidgeting on the steering wheel. "Is there anything wrong, Agent Garrett?"

"No sir."

Cole observed the routine for the next few miles out of the corner of his eye. At one point, Garrett suddenly stopped his eye-flicking routine and simply stared straight ahead. Cole stretched his right arm behind his head as he glanced over his shoulder.

There was a sheriff's cruiser passing in the left lane. He found it kind of comical that an FBI agent would be concerned about being pulled over by a local cop. He wondered if maybe the bureau frowned on traffic tickets received by their agents while on duty. They were both silent as the cruiser moved past them and began pulling away.

As they approached the Laurel Road exit, Garret flicked the turn signal and began slowing down. Just before reaching the light at the intersection, he pulled the Ford off the edge of the pavement, and stopped.

Garrett lowered his sun visor and removed a clear cellophane bag from under the elastic strap. Inside the bag was a black cloth band. He handed it to Cole.

"Sir, I need you to put this on."

"What's this, Agent Garrett?"

Garrett spoke apologetically. "It a blind, sir. It's policy. Anyone approaching the safe house compound has to wear one."

"My God, I'm a United States senator, son."

"Yes sir, Senator, but that makes it more imperative that you don't know the location of a government safe house. Knowing could endanger your life and others."

Cole shook his head. "This is crazy. I hope you people know what you're doing."

He tore open the cellophane wrapper and removed the black latex blind. It had a stretchy cloth material attached to one side of it. Using both hands, he stretched the band around his head and lowered it over his eyes. Now his world was dark and he immediately felt disoriented.

"Thank you, Senator."

Cole pondered his situation. The cellophane wrapper had a company logo on it. Who was the company's biggest customer—the good guys, or the bad guys, or was there a difference? He began to feel uneasy.

He thought it would be easy to tell what direction they were going. But at the first turn he was already finding it difficult to determine which way the car was heading. The darkness was playing tricks on his mind. At one point, it felt like the car was moving sideways. Within minutes, his orientation was completely lost.

He felt the car slowing, and his upper body moved to the left from the centrifugal force as it turned. He felt the suspension in the car begin to bounce, and the sound of the tires changed also. They were no longer on a paved road. The car was moving slowly, and it felt as if he was riding on a horse rather than in a modern luxury car. Finally, the car picked up speed again, and then made several more turns. They came to a stop and the engine was turned off.

"Agent Garrett, I would like to speak to your supervisor immediately."

"Yes sir. Please keep the blind on until you are instructed to remove it."

He heard the driver's door open and a few seconds later the passenger door on his side opened. He felt a hand grab his arm. "This way sir, be careful of your head getting out."

He was led a short way across a smooth concrete surface. The strong smell of recently cut grass was heavy in the air. He could feel the sun shining bright and hot on his face. He was already beginning to sweat uncomfortably.

He heard a door being opened, and the cool dry air from the interior of the building hit his face.

The floor seemed uneven, a brick or scalloped tile, he supposed. The strong smell of cut grass disappeared and was replaced by several odors. A sweet citrus smell was what he noticed first, then a faint odor from a recent meal that had been prepared. As he was directed forward, the next thing that his senses picked up was the ticking of a clock, and the stale smell of cigarette smoke.

His navigator stopped him and held his arm in place. Garrett said, "Please sir, wait here and someone will be with you shortly."

A second later he heard the sound of a door closing, followed by the sound of a dead bolt sliding into the locked position.

Cole pulled the blind off his head. His eyes were assaulted by the light rushing into his dilated pupils and he instinctively squeezed them shut. He squinted and slowly opened his eyes as he turned his head in a 360-degree sweep of the room.

He was standing in the middle of a windowless room with one door, obviously the one he had heard the dead bolt lock from the outside. A single light bulb hung from the ceiling by a wire, and the floors were bare concrete. The walls were covered in unpainted plywood. He was in some sort of makeshift jail cell

He raised his hand to his forehead and combed it back over his head as he murmured under his breath. "Shit."

Chapter 20

Wednesday, 9:00 AM

Barbara Cole paced in frustration. The room at the marina had been small, but at least it had a window with a view of the boats. Her new room didn't have a window; it was more like a prison cell. The worst part was that she couldn't even remember being brought to a new location. All she knew was that she'd been there for nearly a full twenty-four hours.

She feared something was wrong. She should have been informed by now, and it had been hours since anyone had been in the room. Her stomach was aching with hunger, and she had finished the last bottle of water in the room.

Had she made a terrible mistake? Everything seemed so plausible at the time, and she had gone along with the plan willingly. She thought back on her visit to her mother's.

Other than the funeral she hadn't seen her in eight years, and she'd been leery about trying to patch things up. But, this was her mother, after all, so she had steeled herself and gone for the visit. That first evening her mother had been determined to engage only in light small talk, though Barbara noticed that she was drinking quite a few glasses of wine during dinner. After they finished the meal, Barbara had offered to clean up the dishes and the kitchen and sent her mother to relax in the living room.

Her mother had acquiesced, armed with yet another glass of wine and the remainder of the bottle. About forty-five minutes later, she had found her mother fast asleep on the sofa. She'd lifted her mother's legs onto the sofa and covered her with a throw, and then retreated to the guest bedroom.

The next morning, after her shower, she'd found her mother already sitting at the small table in the kitchen in front of the window. Barbara had noticed from her inscrutable expression that something wasn't right. Their conversation still haunted her.

"Good morning dear, I hope you slept well."

"Yes Mother, I slept soundly. But now I need you to tell me why I am here."

Her mother had hesitated, then let out a big sigh and began. "A few days ago I received an unusual visit from a man who introduced himself as Agent Garrett with the FBI. He showed me his badge, and I invited him in. He was professional and businesslike, and he showed me some pictures he had in an envelope. He told me, 'Your daughter's life is in danger.' I thought I was going to faint right there on the sofa."

"What pictures did he show you, Mother?"

"They were pictures of a book, of the front cover, the back cover, and the first few pages. He said the book was scheduled to print next week. Barbara, it was a book about murdering you!"

"What? Who would write such a terrible book?"

"I'm sorry Barbara, but it was written by Irwin."

At that, Barbara had jumped up in anger and shouted at her mother. "Mother, how could you? You ruined your own marriage, and I'm not going to let you ruin mine."

In spite of the tears sliding down her mother's face, she'd stormed out of the kitchen and out the front door, slamming it shut. She'd paced aimlessly down the sidewalk of the tree-lined street, thinking she'd been crazy to come visit her mother in the first place.

Eventually she'd noticed a small coffee shop ahead and had gone in and planted herself at a booth to gather her thoughts. As she was sipping her coffee she'd become aware of someone approaching her. She looked up, thinking it was the waitress, but instead she saw a man in a dark gray suit.

"Mrs. Cole?"

"Yes, I'm Barbara Cole," she'd replied with surprise.

"Mrs. Cole, I'm Special Agent Garrett with the FBI." He opened his jacket and removed a small wallet revealing a badge and photo identification.

"May I sit down Mrs. Cole?"

She'd been momentarily speechless as her mind spun. "Then my mother was telling the truth?" she'd asked flatly.

He removed a hardcover book with a bright red dust jacket from his leather pouch and laid it on the table in front of her. *The Cole Hard Truth.* Below the title was the author: "Irwin S. Cole."

She flipped the book over and saw the worst picture she had ever seen of her husband. Then she skimmed the first few pages. Then she'd slammed the book shut and slid it back at Garrett.

"I don't know what kind a sick joke you're playing, but I'm not laughing, Agent Garrett."

"Mrs. Cole, I can assure you it's no joke. When we discovered the book we didn't know what to think. Now we believe that both you and your husband are in danger. Mrs. Cole, we are convinced that someone is trying to set up your husband. From what we have discovered thus far, we believe the threat is coming from a high-level source. We believe some influential people, perhaps within the government as well as the private sector, are plotting this attempt to discredit your husband."

"Does Irwin know about this?"

"No ma'am, we couldn't take the chance at this point of informing the senator. We were afraid that even the slightest change in his routine might spook them and endanger him. We are working on the assumption that as long as they believe their plan is still a secret, they won't do any harm to your husband.

"The other problem is that we are not sure who we can trust. There could be a mole working in his office. We're not sure, but we believe our Washington office may be compromised. We have a small group in our New York office that is aware of what's going on. That's why we are communicating with you in this manner. We hope, with your help, we can catch these people before their plan succeeds."

"What can I do to help?"

"We were hoping you would ask that question. We have you scheduled on a flight to Florida today, instead of Tuesday as you originally planned. We will have a car at the airport to pick you up. Don't let anyone know you're leaving early, especially your husband. We know he's being watched, so it's important that he doesn't do anything unusual."

"How did you know I was leaving on Tuesday for Florida?"

"It's part of our job, Mrs. Cole. Now, I need you to go back to your mother's apartment and remind her of the importance of keeping all this quiet. I will call you shortly with more specifics."

It had all seemed so plausible, she thought, as she paced between the windowless walls in her new quarters. Could she have missed something? She tried to remember anything that seemed amiss in retrospect. But Agent Garrett had been very professional and seemed so concerned about Irwin's welfare.

She'd gone back to her mother's and apologized, and she'd noted that her mother had already started her very early cocktail hour. While she'd been packing up Agent Garrett had called, as he'd said he would.

She also hadn't noticed anything unusual on the flight or at the airport.

Then she stopped in her tracks.

"Oh my God!" she exclaimed aloud. "Agent Garrett called me on my private cell phone that morning. But only Irwin and Miles have that number."

Chapter 21

Wednesday, 10:00 AM

Agent Moore and Mackey were exhausted as they pulled into the small parking area of the corporate offices of Gulf-Global Enterprises in Sarasota. The night before, they had left Fisherman's Village and stopped at a sports bar in Englewood to look for two guys reported to hang out with the man found dead at Senator Cole's house. One of them was Juan Esposito, and supposedly he and his partner frequented the bar just about every night. His partner was reported to be short and stocky with a cocky attitude. It had been a waste of time. They never showed up. The next morning, on only a few hours' sleep, they'd headed for Sarasota, following the suggestion that Tom had made from Washington last night to check out Gulf-Global.

"Swanky place here," said Mackey. "What do they do, again?"

"It's in the file folder there on the console."

Mackey picked up the folder and scanned the two short pages. "What the hell are absorbent booms? Anyway, there's not much information here."

"Privately held company, not much reporting is required."

"White-collar crime. That's your specialty, isn't it, Jerry?"

"Yeah, these crime scenes with bodies lying about are new to me. Give me a computer spreadsheet or a stack of files and I'm happy."

They entered the lobby of the huge glass tower and studied the directory on the wall. Mackey noticed a glass elevator across the lobby from the primary elevators.

Mackey said, "Come on. Let's take the scenic route. I'm buying," They stepped inside, and Agent Moore hit the button for the twelfth floor. They turned and regarded the stunning view of Sarasota Bay as the elevator moved upward. They stared at the turquoise water of the bay, and the keys in the distance. After they passed the eighth floor, they could see the Gulf of Mexico stretching out behind the keys.

Mackey said, "I think we're both in the wrong kind of work."

Moore replied, "Yeah, but with that view, I don't think I would get much work done."

The elevator chimed, and the doors opened onto the twelfth floor, revealing a long narrow reception area. As they approached the reception desk, Moore opened the file and glanced at the papers for a moment. "We would like to see Mr. Hank Carlson, please."

The woman behind the desk looked up. "Do you have an appointment?" she asked stuffily.

Moore opened his jacket and took out his badge. "Special Agent Moore, FBI."

"One moment, Agent Moore. Would you care to take a seat over there while I see whether Mr. Carlson can see you?"

* * *

Hank Carlson had been acting CEO of Gulf-Global Enterprises for the last three months, ever since the death of its founder and former CEO Roger Morrison. Up until then, Carlson had been the CFO, second-in-command, and a friend of Morrison's since before the company was started twenty-seven years earlier. As he sat in his chair behind the huge desk and looked around the office, he recalled what Roger Morrison used to say about this office.

"This room is too damn big. It makes me feel isolated from the rest of the company."

Carlson had never understood how he could think that way about this superlative office. Deep down, he had been jealous and wished his office was half this size. But now that he had been in here for a while he could understand what Roger had been saying. The view from his office window in this downtown Sarasota building was spectacular. He could see Sarasota Bay and the Gulf of Mexico in the distance. But the room was too big; it wasn't personal. It wasn't a place he felt secure in. It was beautifully decorated, but it did have a cold impersonal feel about it, like a lobby instead of a person's office. Nevertheless, he wouldn't trade it for anything.

Roger had been against the idea of moving the corporate offices to this expensive downtown location. Their offices had always been in the manufacturing plant in an industrial park on the east side of town. A few years ago Carlson had talked Roger into contracting a consulting firm to help improve their business model, and relocating the office was one of the suggestions that had been made. Roger hated the idea of being away from the heart of the business but agreed that it would be foolish to pay the consulting company all of that money and not follow their recommendations. The move was to improve the corporate image and make them a more significant player in the new worldwide market.

Carlson leaned back in his chair as he looked through the huge glass windows at the world surrounding him. The intercom on his phone buzzed, and his secretary informed him that two men from the FBI were there to see him.

Carlson bolted upright in his chair and touched the speaker button. "I will be with them in a moment." He picked up his phone and dialed a number from memory.

"The FBI is here to talk to me."

Carlson listened a few minutes, then responded, "I hope you're right," and hung up.

He buzzed his secretary. "Please send in the gentlemen from the FBI."

The receptionist smiled at Mackey and Moore. "Mr. Carlson will see you now; please follow me."

She knocked and then opened a huge oak door and directed the two men into the office. A man stood and began to approach them from behind a desk. "Gentlemen, I'm Hank Carlson. Please come in."

"I'm Special Agent Moore with the FBI and this is Lieutenant Doug Mackey with the Capitol Police."

They shook hands and Carlson pointed to two chairs in front of his desk. "Please sit down, gentlemen. What can I do for the FBI today?"

"Mr. Carlson, do you know Mrs. Barbara Cole?" asked Moore.

Carlson smiled. "I was at the hospital the day she was born. I drove her mother, Helen, to the emergency room because Roger was out of town that day. She's the daughter I never had."

"So you've been a friend of the family for a long time now?"

Carlson chuckled. "Roger and I grew up together in the same neighborhood. We've been best friends since we were kids."

"So from childhood friends to owning a large corporation together…that's quite an achievement, Mr. Carlson. Do you mind me asking how you got started?"

"Not at all. The short of it is that I had my degree in accounting, and Roger was a heck of a salesman and had an all-around good head for business. With the product knowledge of our other partner, Mark Kraus, and Roger's small inheritance, we started the company from scratch, and here it is today." He smiled.

"Obviously, it took a little more than that. Mark Kraus had been Roger's roommate in college. He was a chemist, and considered brilliant by all his peers, I might add. Roger and Mark always talked about starting their own business someday. They were inseparable back in those days, destined to be lifelong friends. I was the baby of the group, three years behind them.

"Mark had finished his Ph.D. and was working for a chemical company at the time. One day Roger, Mark, and I were having lunch together, talking about the old days at school. Roger asked him where he was with his college project he had been working on for years. Roger told him he had been thinking about it often lately and thought he had the perfect application for his process. Roger always said he had no clue how someone could spend so much time developing a process for which he had no application."

Mackey and Agent Moore glanced at each other as the soliloquy grew more confusing.

"So, with my accounting background, Roger's money and ideas, and Mark's breakthrough technology, together we formed Gulf-Global Enterprises, manufacturer of absorbent oil booms and pads using materials free of fossil fuels and twice the performance of any current product on the market.

"Yeah, Roger was quite the businessman; he had the Midas touch. I feel sad that Roger isn't here to see the huge growth the company has experienced. The business over the last few months has grown a hundredfold because of that unfortunate oil spill in the Gulf. Although the company has always achieved steady growth through the years, nothing like this could have ever been imagined."

Mackey asked, "I would suppose that if offshore drilling in the Gulf was banned it would affect your company considerably, would it not, Mr. Carlson?"

Carlson leaned forward in his chair. "Yes Mr. Mackey, that has become an important part of our business. If that happened, it would change our approach, but handling drilling accidents is just one part of our business. Transportation and processing are also areas where accidents can and do happen.

"When Roger started the company after college, it was more a dream of saving the environment than making money. He felt as if he was nature's last chance against the greed and gluttony of humanity. Look around the room at the pictures and plaques on the walls. Roger was an avid big game fisherman. He was all his life, and that's what he was trying to protect through his work."

Moore and Mackey glanced around the room at the pictures of Roger Morrison landing game fish on a huge sport fisher.

"Business was much simpler back then. We had a small office in the corner of the manufacturing plant. The office was a 20' x 20' space shared by Roger, Mark, and myself."

"What can you tell us about Barbara Cole's husband, Senator Irwin Cole?" asked Moore.

Carlson's expression changed. "I'm afraid I don't know the senator that well. I did attend their wedding, but when Barbara became involved with him, we didn't see much of her after that. It was quite a disappointment for Roger, as he was grooming her to take over the company someday."

"So you're not aware of any family problems with the Coles?" pressed Agent Moore. "By the way, did she inherit her father's portion of the company?"

Carlson was silent for a few moments before he responded. "I don't believe that it is my place to discuss Barbara's personal or financial situation. What I can tell you is that when Roger initially set up the stock ownership, it was done so that the three principles couldn't sell or give away any portion of their stock. When any of the three of us passed on, their stock would be redistributed to the remaining principles. He wanted to be sure that he never lost control of the company.

"I can tell you, Roger had become a wealthy man aside from this business. He had the knack for knowing a good business investment. He never removed any money from the company in all the years since it was formed. The three of us have simply drawn salaries through the years." Carlson paused. "In all that time not a single bonus has been issued to any of us. So yes, Barbara inherited a large estate, but it was from her father's other business interests. As far as family problems, I'm not aware of any."

"Mr. Carlson, does Senator Cole know his wife will not be inheriting any of this company?"

"I don't know the answer to that, Agent Moore. Why are you asking me so many questions about Barbara? Is everything all right with her?"

"That's what we are trying to determine, Mr. Carlson. A Mr. Philip Hoffheimer from this office tried communicating with Mrs. Cole yesterday. Do know anything about that?"

Carlson swallowed. "Yes, he's our corporate attorney and was contacting her about a meeting this evening. She is scheduled to attend so she can sign some legal documents. Roger had given her power of attorney several years ago because he was away so much on business."

"If Mrs. Cole cannot attend your meeting, what kind of problems does that create for your company?"

"No big deal, we'll have the attorney drop by at her convenience."

Moore stood and extended his hand. "Thank you, Mr. Carlson, for taking the time to answer our questions."

Moore and Mackey walked out of the office and headed for the elevators. When the doors closed Mackey said, "If you ask me, he's hiding something."

Moore said, "I tend to agree with you, I just don't know what it is. I do know he's not happy about not receiving any bonus. Did you notice how his expression changed when he talked about that?"

Mackey smiled. "Like day and night."

* * *

Carlson let out a sigh as the door closed behind the agents. A few seconds later a wood panel in the wall slid open and a man stepped into the room. Carlson looked at the man with concern. "I think they know something."

"They know what I've allowed them to know and that's it."

"I think we need to postpone this," Carlson said nervously. "The timing isn't right."

The man regarded Carlson and said gruffly. "That's why I do all the thinking around here. Just do as you're told and everything will work out just as I planned it."

He left Hank Carlson's office through the same hidden panel as he had entered and made a call on his cell phone. "It's time. Make it happen, bring her now, and be sure to call me when you're on the road."

Chapter 22

Wednesday, 11:15 AM

By the time Agent Dodd reached the hospital in Punta Gorda, Agent Martin was being discharged. He met her in her room on the third floor as she was preparing to leave.

"Timmy, it's so good to see you."

He gave her a big hug. "You had us worried, Mel. How are you feeling today?"

"Not bad, considering everything that's happened, but I have to tell you, getting hit on the head is no fun."

"I always suspected that's the one place where you could take a hit and not get hurt, Miss Hard Head! Man, I sure thought I was busted this morning when Hansen called me to his room. I thought he found out you had called me. I was shitting bricks the whole way, but instead, he was sending me here to take you home."

"I'm glad I didn't get you in trouble, Timmy."

"You and me both. Come on, let's get out of here. I hate hospitals."

Dodd teased her about having to be discharged from the hospital in a wheelchair. He made engine and skidding sounds as he pushed her around the corner on one wheel. She wasn't laughing.

"Don't you boys ever grow up?"

He took her to the car, and they were silent for the first fifteen minutes or so of the drive, as each was lost in thought.

Dodd was thinking about what Bill Hansen had said to him about trying to get some information out of her. He certainly wasn't planning to rat her out, but it couldn't hurt to have some extra points scored with the boss, in case he needed them. Nothing that could get her in trouble, he promised himself.

"So Melissa, can you tell me about what had happened with you and Senator Cole?" He supposed the more direct approach was the best.

They were crossing the northbound bridge of US 41 across the Peace River. On the left, in the distance, was the Fisherman's Village complex.

Instead of answering his question, Martin screamed. "Shit!"

Dodd slammed on the brakes, unsure of what was happening, and the car behind them also screeched to a stop, barely missing them.

"Timmy, quick, turn the car around, we're going back to Punta Gorda."

He looked at her incredulously. "I can't do that! Hansen would have my ass for not following a direct order to take you to Tampa."

"Timmy, please don't argue with me now. I know what I'm doing. We have to go back to Fisherman's Village. I can't believe I forgot. I hid the computer there."

"What computer are you talking about?"

"The one we found over on the island at the senator's place. I think it's going to be the key to us solving this case and finding the senator and his wife."

"I'll call Hansen, and he can send someone else to pick it up."

"No, that would make me look worse, leaving a key piece of evidence behind. Not just behind, but in a public place. Please Timmy, we have to hurry."

The car behind them was laying on the horn. Dodd looked in the rearview mirror then eased the car forward and slowly worked his way into the left lane, so he could make a U-turn when they got off the bridge.

The car whipped around at the first intersection and headed south for Punta Gorda. "I can't believe I'm doing this," Dodd muttered. "Fortunately, I can still play the guitar. Maybe I can get a job playing music somewhere when I get out of prison."

She leaned across the front seat and gave him a kiss on his cheek. "Thank you, Timmy."

About ten minutes later they pulled into the parking lot at Fisherman's Village. She jumped out the door before the car had completely stopped. Dodd parked the car and ran to catch up to her as they entered the complex.

Martin hopped up the stairs jumping two steps at a time. Rushing to the small table and chair area, she reached behind the potted plant where she had hidden the bag. She turned back to Dodd, and the expression on her face revealed it all.

"It's gone. Either the guy that tied me up and drugged me found it or the local police stumbled across it."

She frowned as she thought aloud. "If the locals found it, then my dad would have said something about it. If the FBI found it, you would know about it. So I don't think it was found by law enforcement. Someone else must have stumbled onto it."

They headed back down the stairs. As they reached the bottom, Martin suddenly pointed at a sign on the wall. "Yes! The Property Management Office!" She headed inside with Dodd close behind.

"Hello," she said loudly.

A man stepped out of the back room. "May I help you?"

"Yes, I lost a canvas bag with some personal items in it yesterday, and I was wondering whether anyone turned it in?"

"Just a moment."

He bent behind the counter and did some shuffling through a plastic bin. Standing up with a red face from bending, he asked, "Is this it, Miss?"

She beamed. "Yes, thank you so much."

She opened the bag and peered inside, and the computer was still there. As they left, Dodd said, "Before we go anywhere, I want you to buy me a Lotto ticket. Do you know how lucky it is to have a computer turned in?"

"I know. Can you believe how fortunate I am?"

Once they were back on the road heading north again, Martin slipped the computer out of the bag and opened it on her lap. It made all the usual noises as it booted up to the logon screen. She did her bypass again on the password screen. She reached the second password screen that required the sixteen characters. "Damn, Senator Cole entered the password last time. I have no idea what it was."

"How did Cole know the password? I thought you said this computer belonged to the people supposedly behind this."

"His password from the Capitol computer system has been hacked. I told Hansen, and I think he has already notified Washington."

Dodd bit his lips. "Well, maybe, maybe not. What if this computer belongs to the senator?"

"Stop it! Why is everyone so convinced he's guilty?"

"The question is, why are you so convinced he's not guilty?"

Just then Dodd's cell phone rang, and he looked at the display. "Shit, it's Hansen. He's probably tracking us on satellite and wants to know what the hell we're doing."

"Just answer it, Timmy."

He pushed the talk button. "Yes sir."

He listened, nodding in agreement. Finally, he said, "Yes sir, I understand. She's doing fine. Yes sir."

"Well, what did he have to say?" asked Martin.

"Um, that was Hansen."

"I know it was Hansen. What did he say?"

"Um, he didn't say it was okay to tell you."

"Timmy!"

"Okay, he said he received a call from the sheriff's deputy sent to that island house. They found three more bodies stuffed in a deep freezer in the utility room. They also think that Senator Cole spent the night there last night."

She turned away from Dodd and stared out her side window. Then she resumed her typing on the computer, and in a few minutes she was back to the log screens she had used before to trace the programs that had been accessed on the computer. "I think I can find the password in the keystroke log if it hasn't been written over." She tapped a few more keys and then scrolled through the log.

"Here it is." She entered the password, and the S and D program started. The three names and numbers came up on the screen, just as before.

Her dad had told her he had given Irwin Cole's phone to the FBI, so it was probably on its way to the Tampa lab to be analyzed. Barbara Cole's phone was turned off last time, so she decided to try Miles Connor's since he was supposed to be in Florida by now. Maybe he spoke to the senator and might have an idea where he was.

Agent Dodd broke into her thoughts. "You know the Bureau is sure that Barbara Cole is dead. They say that the statistics are against her being alive after this amount of time."

"Irwin told me he could feel she was alive."

"Oh, it's Irwin now. I suppose you two are pretty tight after spending the night together."

She gave him a look of disgust. "I'm not even going to answer that, Timmy."

She clicked the cursor next to Miles Connor's name, and the screen started the spiral spinning. She stared at it intently.

"What's wrong?" asked Dodd. "I can see it in your face."

"I don't know exactly. Something about this screen seems so familiar to me. I don't know what it is. I've had that feeling from the first time I saw it."

"Yeah, it looks like that old television show *Secret Agent Man*."

"That's what I thought the first time I saw it. But it's something else. I just can't pin it down."

The spiraling screen finally collapsed, and a map of Southwest Florida appeared with a blinking star. The star was located off Laurel Road in Nokomis.

She looked over at Dodd, surprised. "I know the senator told Miles to come down to Florida right away. But what the hell is he doing in Nokomis? Timmy, we have to go there now. It's on our way to Tampa."

"No you don't. I'm in enough trouble as it is. Call it in and let the team investigate it."

"I can't. Hansen would want to know how I knew he was there."

"Yeah, I'd like to know that one myself? What kind of program is that on the computer?"

She turned the screen so he could see it. "Look, it's a short distance off the interstate. We'll get off, check it out, and be back on the highway before anyone knows the difference."

Dodd stared straight ahead. They were still about twenty minutes away from the turnoff on Laurel Rd. She placed the cursor next to Barbara Cole's name, and the spiraling began again. The screen flashed a dialogue box advising that no signal could be found. Last known location was 26 55.70 n. 82 3.85 w. at 15:43 8/07/10. The same location as before... Fisherman's Village.

"Melissa, you know we shouldn't go there without backup."

"Timmy, what if it turns out to be nothing? Then Hansen will know about me screwing up with the computer. We'll both be in trouble needlessly."

"We?" he said under his breath.

Martin watched the star flash at the location a few miles ahead. She turned to Dodd. "Turn off at this exit and make a right at the light."

"Oh no!" she cried out suddenly.

"Now what...do I even want to know?"

"The low battery warning, it's dying, and I don't have a charger with me."

Chapter 23

Wednesday, 1:05 PM

Barbara Cole was growing more concerned as every minute passed. It was as if her mind was clearing after awaking from a deep sleep. She turned toward the door when she heard it unlock, and watched it swing open. She was shocked to see Agent Garrett step into the room.

"Agent Garrett! What are you doing down here, and why am I being locked in this room?"

He gave her a small smile. "Mrs. Cole, please accept my apology for the way you have been treated during this operation. Trust me; it wasn't our intent that you be held in these various rooms, day after day. As I explained in the beginning, we've been unsure who could be trusted, even within our own organization. We ran into a few problems, but I now believe that in a matter of hours we will have this all behind us, and you and Senator Cole will be safe to go back to your lives. I'm having some food and fresh clothes brought in for you. Please have something to eat, and then get dressed. In an hour we will be leaving."

The Cole Hard Truth   225

"Agent Garrett, I appreciate your situation, but I want to know where my husband is. Now," Barbara said sternly. "If I had known I would be locked away from him for days, I never would have agreed to do this. And how did you know my private cell phone number when you called me in New York, when only my husband and his assistant know that number?"

"Your cell phone is FBI-issued, like mine." He removed his phone from his pocket and showed her that it was identical to the phone she had been given by Miles.

She gave him a piercing glare.

"It's illegal for you to have that phone, but I won't tell on you," Garrett said with a guarded smile. "I understand your concern, Mrs. Cole. As we speak, Senator Cole is at a safe house under protective guard. When the time is right, in a few hours, he will be transported to your new location and the two of you will be reunited."

"I still want it on record with the FBI, Agent Garrett, how I have been treated. I feel as if I'm a prisoner, not a wife trying to help protect her husband."

Garrett stepped closer to her and spoke in a low voice. "I didn't want to frighten you, Mrs. Cole, but we had reason to believe that you were going to be their next target."

"What kind of target?"

"If their original plan to disgrace the senator didn't work, we felt they might try to force the senator to meet their demands by threatening your life. Because of that development, we felt it necessary to keep you hidden, out of harm's way. That's why we kept you isolated in these various rooms."

"I wish you would have been more forthcoming in the beginning, Agent Garrett. Then I wouldn't have had all of these misgivings about what's occurring. When I was at Fisherman's Village, if I'd had a chance, I would have given those men to the local authorities."

"Yes ma'am. Please, enjoy your meal and get dressed, and I will be back in a little less than an hour, at 2:00 PM sharp."

"Can you at least tell me where we're going, Agent Garrett?"

Garrett shook his head as he walked out of the room.

He passed a man in the hall carrying a tray of food toward her room. He stopped the man and silently raised his head with an inquiring look. The man nodded in affirmation and then continued to Barbara Cole's room.

Barbara was finishing her dessert when there was another knock at the door. It was the same man, this time holding a garment bag. He hung it on the bathroom door. "Your clothes," he said simply, and left the room, locking the door behind him.

She showered and put on her new outfit. It was an attractive business suit and it fit her perfectly. Standing in front of the mirror, she used the rudimentary makeup provided for her in the bathroom cabinet. She thought about what Agent Garrett had told her earlier and suddenly it all seemed to make perfect sense.

As she sat on the bed putting her shoes on, again there was a knock on the door as it opened part way. A voice asked, "Are you ready, Mrs. Cole?"

"Why am I still being locked in this room, Agent Garrett?"

"Please don't think of it as being locked in the room, Mrs. Cole. Rather, the door is locked to keep others out for your protection. The door is reinforced steel, and it will stop a bullet, or even a small explosion."

They walked through the hallway toward the front room of the mostly empty house. When they reached the end of the hallway, she stopped and braced herself against the wall.

"Is everything all right, Mrs. Cole?"

"Yes, I'm fine, just a little light-headed. Probably from being locked in those rooms," she said with a raised eyebrow.

They continued through the front door to an awaiting black Ford. Garrett opened the rear door of the vehicle as Mrs. Cole climbed into the space behind the tinted windows.

Garrett slid into the driver's seat and started the engine to cool the car with the air-conditioning.

After waiting for Mrs. Cole to get settled, he put the gearshift in reverse and backed out on the dirt road, glancing in the rearview mirror.

"Are you sure everything is all right, Mrs. Cole?"

"Yes, I'm fine, but I feel as if I drank one of my mother's homemade martinis."

"There are bottles of water in the seat pocket in front of you, if you would like one."

"Thank you. Where are we going, Agent Garrett?"

"To Sarasota, so you can attend your meeting at Gulf-Global Enterprises."

"How did you know about my meeting? I forgot about it with everything going on."

"It's my job to know everything," he said, smiling, as he looked back over his shoulder.

She laughed aloud. "I'm sorry Agent Garrett. I have no idea what has gotten into me. I suppose finally getting out of those cramped rooms after all these days is making me giddy. By the way, Mr. Garrett, what is your first name? Is it 'Agent'?" She giggled like a teenager as she rocked forward in the seat with her hand over her mouth.

Garrett was running late, and he knew tardiness wasn't tolerated. He sped out of the drive, creating a cloud of dust as the car fishtailed around the first curve. He flew down the dirt road as fast as the bumps would allow. The dust was swirling and covering the windshield, and he strained to see as the car swerved from side to side as it bounced on the dirt road. Garrett glanced in the rearview mirror and saw her swaying loosely with the car's movement. He took out his cell phone and dialed.

"We just left; we should be there in thirty minutes."

"Very good," was the gruff response.

* * *

The gruff man immediately dialed another number and waited. It rang twice, and then there were a series of beeps, followed by a long tone. The sixty-minute timer had been remotely activated.

Chapter 24

Wednesday, 2:15 PM

Senator Cole sat on a wooden chair, the only piece of furniture in the locked room. It had been three hours since Agent Garrett had left him in the room. He jumped up angrily and strode over to the door and kicked it in frustration. The door was solid, and hurt his foot. *That was stupid,* he thought. He beat on the door and hollered. "Let me out of here!" He shook his head. "I've been had," he muttered under his breath. "How could I have let this happen? I knew something wasn't right."

He glanced at his watch. 2:16 PM. According to that damn book, he had less than four hours to find Barbara. He had to do something.

He hadn't heard any sounds from outside so he supposed the room was soundproof. He stepped up on the chair, and on his tiptoes he could just touch the ceiling with his fingertips, enough to discern that the drywall flexed slightly to the pressure.

He jumped, hitting the ceiling with his fist, and he came down on the edge of the chair, tipping it over and landing on the floor. He got back to his feet and grabbed the chair by the rungs and jammed it at the ceiling. The leg made a small hole. He repeated the action several times, until there was a good-sized hole in the ceiling. He stood on the chair again and pushed his hand through the hole and grabbed a 2 x 4 truss. He tried to find something to grab onto with his other hand, finding only the edge of the hole. It gave way, and a piece of the ceiling fell and hit him in the head as he hung from the truss with one hand.

He heard a noise coming from the door lock. It was now or never, he decided. He readied himself as the door began to swing inward.

* * *

Agent Dodd turned the car into the deceleration lane and slowly approached the intersection of Laurel Road. "Look Timmy, there's a drugstore in that strip mall. Pull in there so I can buy a charger for the computer. "If it dies, we are going to lose a lot of time."

He pulled up in front of the store and parked. She gave him a big smile. "Would you be a darling and get one for me? She pointed to the power pin on the back edge of the computer so he would know what it looked like.

He grimaced. "Can I get you anything else while I'm shopping, some water or a soda, perhaps?"

"A bottle of water would taste good, Timmy ol' buddy."

She tapped her hand anxiously on the seat as she waited for Dodd to return. The computer began beeping a warning.

A few minutes later Dodd emerged from the store with a full bag of supplies. Melissa reached in and pulled out a bag of potato chips, a bag of pretzels, four bottles of water, and a twelve-volt charger.

The computer was making its final squeal when she pushed the cord into the power outlet. She let out a huge puff of air. "That was close." She didn't want to go through all the booting and logs to get back into the program again. "Okay, go down to the next road and make a left turn."

They had gone about a mile when she looked up. "Turn right on this dirt road."

They sped down the bumpy, single-width dirt drive. Agent Dodd was eating potato chips with one hand, maneuvering the wheel with the other, and holding a bottle of water between his legs.

"Be careful, Timmy. Do you have to eat that junk now?"

"I'm starving. I haven't eaten anything all day, thanks to you."

Glancing back down at the screen, she noticed the star for Miles' cell phone was moving their way.

Just as they were going around a sharp curve to the left, a black Ford appeared, speeding from the opposite direction and headed straight-on. She screamed, and Dodd dropped the bag of chips and swerved to the right as hard as he could. The black Ford sped past as their car careened sideways, sliding in the grass. They rammed into a tree, which jammed against the driver's door and Dodd.

There was a moment of stunned silence. "Timmy, are you okay? Are you hurt?"

"I think my leg . . . it feels as if it's broken. I need to sit here for a minute."

A huge clump of dirt and debris fell on her as she opened the door to get out. She went around to the driver's side, and saw that the tree was pretty well embedded into the door. There would be no getting out from that side. She walked back around and stuck her head in the passenger side.

"Timmy, how are you doing?"

"I'm pretty sure my leg is broken. It's starting to really hurt now."

She thought for a moment. "Timmy, hand me your cell phone and gun."

"I'm dreading to ask, but what do you need my gun for, Melissa? You're not going to put me out of my misery are you?"

"No silly, I'm going to call in and get you some help, and then I'm going to walk the dirt road to see where that damn black car came from. Don't worry, I'll be right back."

"Me, worry? Why would I worry, I'm stuck in a wrecked car with a broken leg, and I know there's no sense trying to talk you out of this."

"I'll be back before you know it. Try to sit still, Timmy, so you don't hurt your leg further. Since there isn't much I can do for you, I may as well take the time to check this out while we wait for your medical help."

As she walked down the dirt road she opened Timmy's phone and explained their situation to the FBI dispatcher and requested medical help, instructing the dispatcher to use the cell phone signal to locate them because she wasn't sure of their exact location.

She saw a house about a hundred yards in the distance. As she neared it, it looked to be deserted. Then she saw the sign in the front yard. "Foreclosure."

She looked in the windows next to the front door, and the house seemed empty. The road was a dead end so the people in the black car had to have come from this house. She tried the doorknob, and it was locked. She reached into her pocket and removed her wallet with her credentials and picks. She inserted the picks into the cylinder and gave it a twist, and it turned easily. She smiled. *Damn, I'm good.*

She entered the house and walked across the tile floor with the gun extended in front of her. The house was empty of furniture. She searched the kitchen and dining room, finding nothing. Then she heard a noise coming from down the hall and stealthily headed that way. The first door had a huge deadbolt mounted on the outside. Strange, she thought, as she noted that the oversized lock was on the outside of the door.

She slowly slid the dead bolt, and then pushed the door open cautiously with her gun in front of her in the opening.

Instantly she was met by a flying body kicking her arm, sending her gun flying. In the next instant she was slammed to the floor, with a knee in her lower back.

Martin hardly knew what hit her. But before she could regain herself, she was suddenly spun over onto her back and was face to face with her attacker. Neither said a word.

"Of all the rooms in all the world, and you had to come into mine," said Senator Cole.

Martin stared dumbly, frozen.

"Melissa? Are you okay? Did I hurt you?"

Then she snapped to. "Senator, what are you doing here? What is this place? And most important," she demanded, "Why did you leave me at the landscape supply?"

The senator smiled at her sudden repossession of herself. He explained that he was grabbed from the landscape supply and taken to the island and then brought here by Agent Garrett.

"We don't have an Agent Garrett working in this area," she interrupted.

"Well, he showed me his badge and identification. Could he have been brought in from another area? His complexion was pale, and he had a faint New York accent. He told me I was being taken to a safe house because my life was in danger, and that they knew the book was a setup. I was blindfolded and brought to this room and locked inside."

Martin stared at him with disgust.

"Please, Melissa. Tell me nothing bad has happened to Barbara."

"There's no new information about Mrs. Cole. Unlike the other three people you killed on the island."

"Melissa, listen to me, I did not kill Miles. He was killed during an argument with one of the other men and later I was forced to kill them both in self-defense. Well, at least one of them was definitely self-defense. I just lost it with the other one when he shot poor Miles."

She pulled herself up from the floor. "I need to check on Agent Dodd."

"Where is he?"

"I left him in the wrecked car. He has a broken leg. I wanted to check this place out while we waited for help to come. I'll explain while we walk back to the car."

As they walked back down the dirt road she pulled out Agent Dodd's cell phone.

"Yes, Agent Martin again, would you please forward this message to Bill Hansen. Tell him I have Senator Cole in custody at the accident scene." She turned her head and stared back at his already surprised face.

"What's going to happen now?" he asked.

"I don't know yet. First we need to check and make sure Agent Dodd is doing all right. Then I'll decide."

"What happened?"

"A black Ford Crown Vic ran us off the road into the tree."

"I'll bet that's the same car that brought me to this place. Was Agent Garrett driving?

"I told you we don't have an Agent Garrett working with us down here."

"What did he look like? Did you get a look at him? He's about your age and was wearing a gray suit. He has short black hair, 5'10", about 160 lbs."

She tried to recall the few seconds before the cars almost hit. It happened so quickly, but now she wondered if there had been a flash of something familiar. As they approached the car she said, "No, I didn't get a good look at the driver." She leaned into the wrecked car.

"Timmy, how are you doing?"

"I'm good; the pain in my leg is much better. You found Senator Cole?"

"Yep, here he is, in person. I got hold of the office, and they said help will be here in twenty-five to thirty minutes. That was twenty minutes ago. I also informed them we had the senator in custody. With any luck, that will save our asses because the director said if we didn't have the senator in custody by 6:00 PM today he was holding a press conference announcing that Senator Cole was being sought for suspicion of murder."

"Maybe my luck is beginning to change," said Dodd. "I also didn't spill the water bottle between my legs when we hit the tree."

She reached in and put her hand on Dodd's shoulder. "Will you be all right here by yourself until help arrives?"

"Yes, I'll be fine. Where are you going now?"

"Back to that house to look for some clues. EMS should be here in a few minutes. Or would you rather I stay until they get here?"

"No, get going, time is running out."

"Here, take your phone and gun just in case."

"Just in case what?"

Chapter 25

Wednesday, 2:30 Pm

Mackey and Agent Moore walked into Bill Hansen's motel room, which had become the local center of operations.

Hansen greeted them. "You're just in time for the conference call with Washington."

The speakerphone made its usual series of beeps, and a voice spoke.

"William Anderson here, is Florida on the line?"

"Yes William, it's Bill Hansen. We're all here, including Doug Mackey."

"Hello to all. We've also got Raphael on the line. He's been up in New York investigating the role of Barbara Cole's mother in all this. I know you've been working horrendous hours the last few days, but it's the consensus up here that it's going to be over in the next few hours, one way or another.

"The reporter from the Journal finally broke down this morning and gave us the source of his story. His name is Allan Sullivan, a political lobbyist here in Washington. We sent agents to his home and office, but he wasn't at either location, so we're searching the entire city for him. We already had a file on him, and based on his history, I'm not surprised he's somehow involved.

"Bill, you've had some recent developments, so why don't you fill us in."

"Okay. I'm sure you know that we discovered three bodies in a deep freeze at the Coles' island house. We've made a positive identification of one of the bodies as Miles Conner, the senator's aide."

Raphael spoke up. "That must be why he didn't make it to the meeting we had scheduled yesterday. We've been searching for him all morning."

"Bill, you have any thoughts on his involvement in this case?" asked Anderson.

"We found his rental car on the mainland at the marina with his luggage in the trunk and his flight information in the console. He flew in on the same flight as Mackey yesterday. In his suitcase, we found several pieces of electronics used for surveillance. That got us thinking so we went to Senator Cole's house and found it was bugged in every room. The same was found at the beach house on the island. I would be willing to bet if you sweep their home in Washington you will find the identical situation. This could change our perspective about the case if the senator and his wife have been under constant surveillance."

Hansen looked over at Mackey and gave him a nod.

"I'll send over a team right away," replied Anderson. "I agree that it sheds a new light, Bill, unless of course this turns out to be another decoy and this Miles kid was working with the senator and helping him set up this whole complex scheme."

"Well, that's the first thing that ran through my mind also. Then one of our agents spotted a white utility van in the same marina parking area as Miles Conner's car. Agent Martin informed me that prior to that, a witness had seen the senator being taken into a white van by two men.

"We checked out the van and fortunately it was unlocked. The van was registered to a Juan Esposito. His name had previously come up as a known acquaintance of Billy Parker, the man found dead at the Coles' home. I'm willing to bet one of the fellows in the deep freeze will turn out to be Esposito. The other will probably be his sidekick Jasper Allen, as he fits the description."

Agent Moore and Mackey exchanged glances. That explained why the two men hadn't been at the bar the night before.

"Also in the back of the van we found a note written in the dust on the metal ceiling. It said, 'Irwin Cole kidnapped Tuesday PM two men Cape Haze,' and his signature was next to it. The van was covered with fingerprints, including Senator Cole's in the back."

Hansen's phone rang, and he looked down with disgust. "Sorry, I need to take this call, it's from the office."

"No problem, Bill. In the meantime, Raphael, why don't you bring us up to date with the New York situation."

"Yes sir. We've just returned from Helen Morrison's place; that's Barbara Cole's mother. We had too many inconsistencies in her last interview, so we paid her another visit with a voice stress analyzer. What a difference just the presence of that equipment makes. We didn't even have it turned on.

"She told us she had been visited last week by an FBI agent named Garrett from the New York office. There is no agent by that name at the New York office. She also told us the agent showed her pictures of the book supposedly written by Senator Cole. He told her that her daughter's life was in danger, and she needed to bring her to New York right away.

"When her daughter arrived, she told her about the FBI agent and the book. She said her daughter became extremely angry and left the apartment. She came back an hour later and apologized and said that Agent Garrett had met with her. Her daughter told her not to say a word about this to anyone, because both she and Senator Cole's life depended on it.

We're arranging for a sketch artist to go see Helen Morrison, and we're also sending pictures of all the agents working out of the New York office just in case."

Bill Hansen strode back into the room. "I just found out we have Senator Cole in our custody as of thirty minutes ago. I don't have the details, but the office received a call from Agent Martin. She was being transported home from the hospital by Agent Dodd. They were involved in an automobile accident and requested medical help. They also informed the dispatcher they had Senator Cole in custody. When I can get the details, I'll let you know immediately, William."

"Ok Bill. Gentlemen, things are happening quickly. If we can just get a lead on the senator's wife, maybe we can make it through this with our jobs. That's all for now."

The conference call was disconnected, and Mackey immediately approached Bill Hansen. "Where is the senator, Bill? I'd like to go to see him, if you don't mind."

"I don't have the exact location. It's out in the boonies east of Venice, and the office is using Dodd's cell signal to find the location. Why don't you and Agent Moore head in that direction and I'll call you with the location when I have it."

"Thanks Bill."

Hansen nodded. "By the way, how did you guys make out at Gulf-Global Enterprises?"

"Hank Carlson, the CEO, I think he's hiding something. We're just not sure whether it's anything that has to do with this case."

"What's your gut telling you?"

"My gut says it has to do with this case."

"Okay then, after talking to the senator, if you don't have any new leads, head back to Gulf-Global and lean on Carlson."

Chapter 26

Wednesday, 3:00 PM

"I'm not letting you out of my sight this time, Senator," said Agent Martin as they headed toward the abandoned house. "And I mean it." She rubbed her arm. "Did you have to kick me so hard?"

"My first thought was to snap the neck of the person coming through the door. I changed my mind at the last second."

"Thank God for small favors."

They reached the house and entered through the front door into the living room and proceeded cautiously through to the rear, passing the room he'd been kept in earlier. The only furniture in the back room was a bed, dresser, and an upholstered chair. There were no windows. The room had a feel as if someone had been there recently.

They went into the adjoining bathroom and there were toiletries on the vanity and the shower walls were wet. A stack of woman's clothes sat on the floor next to the tub.

Cole picked up the clothes and stared at them. Then he smelled them. He turned to Martin. "They're Barbara's." He went through all the pockets but found nothing.

"I knew you were alive, baby," he murmured. "I could feel you."

The drawers of the vanity were all empty. He was fingering the makeup on its surface when he saw it. Under the compact was a bracelet. He picked it up, and it was the same as the one he had given her for her birthday. He reached into his pocket for the bracelet he had found on the island. They were identical.

He examined the underside of each. The one from the vanity had an inscription: "I love you always. Irwin." The other one had nothing.

"The one on the island must have been placed there as a diversion," said Martin. "Once again, Irwin, I'm sorry for the things I said about Mrs. Cole."

"Don't be. I was having the same doubts, but didn't want to admit it."

Cole looked down at the tile floor in the living room as they headed for the front door. He remembered feeling it under his feet when he was brought in blindfolded. He opened the front door and saw a car pulling up in front of the house.

"Melissa, we've got company."

Martin instinctively reached behind her back for the gun in the waist of her jeans and remembered leaving it with Dodd. "Hurry, get back inside the house."

Both doors of the car opened at the same time, and two men stepped out. Cole pushed by Martin and rushed out the door.

"Mackey!"

Mackey broke into a full grin. They met halfway and gave each other a hug and a slap on the back.

"God damn it, Irwin. I'm going to send you my doctor's bill for treatment of my ulcer when this is over. This is Agent Jerry Moore."

Cole shook hands and then turned back to Mackey. "Is there any news on Barbara?"

Mackey shook his head silently. As they went back inside Cole filled them in on how he came to be in the deserted house and that they believed Barbara had been kept there recently. Agent Moore's cell phone rang, and the display indicated it was Bill Hansen. He opened his phone.

"Agent Moore."

"Where are you guys now?"

"We are in an abandoned house with Agent Martin and Senator Cole. It's the house in which Senator Cole and his wife were both held captive."

"We searched the house of Juan Esposito," said Hansen. "He's one of the dead men from the island. We found a large quantity of materials for making explosives, including remote detonators. I would get away from that house, right now."

Agent Moore looked up at the others and said, "Come on, get out of the house fast, RUN!"

They charged out the front door and continued past the car. When they were about a hundred feet from the house, they stopped to catch their breath.

"What's wrong?" asked Martin.

"Hansen thinks there may be explosives in the house."

They looked at one another.

"We've already done a thorough search of the house, said Martin. "I don't think we need to go back in there until the bomb squad checks it out. Let's go see Timmy."

They climbed inside the car with Moore in the driver's seat. The four doors all closed in unison, and a second later they heard the explosion. The windows were blown out of the house, and a fireball rose from the exploding roof.

The four of them leaned over as the car rocked from the shock wave of the explosion.

"God damn, they're really pissing me off now," said Mackey.

Moore headed the car down the dirt road. When they pulled up to the wreck, the fire department had already arrived and had gotten Dodd out of the car and onto a stretcher in the back of the ambulance. Mackey stepped out of the car and spoke to the firemen.

"I hope you didn't have plans. The house down the street exploded and is engulfed in flames."

"Yea, we heard it." One of the firemen called in the explosion and asked for backup. Martin walked to the back door of the ambulance. "Timmy, how's it going?"

"Well, the leg is broken, but it's not a bad break, they tell me. You know me, tough as they come."

"Good. I'll let the paramedics know that you won't require any pain medication." They gave each other a quick smile.

She headed for the wrecked car and retrieved the computer lying on the floor. She opened the top panel and found a small crack in the upper left corner of the screen. She pushed the power button and heard the hard drive begin to spin. "Yes," she said triumphantly, as she waited for the display to come to life.

Senator Cole and Mackey stood next to Moore's car, sharing and discussing the facts of the kidnapping. Moore stood to the side talking to Bill Hansen again on his cell phone.

"You know Mackey," said Cole, "Miles would have been one of the last people in the world that I would have ever suspected of being involved in something like this. He was such a good kid and seemed so dedicated to me and Barbara."

"I know, Irwin. I know how much you thought of him. I would have never suspected anything either."

"I had a bad feeling from the beginning about that FBI Agent Garrett who brought me here. I'm not sure what it was exactly, but something about his mannerisms weren't right, or maybe it was too right. I don't know."

Mackey blinked. "Did you say Agent Garrett?"

"Yeah, why?"

"That's the name of the agent who communicated with Barbara's mother in New York. He said he worked out of the New York office, but according to the FBI they don't have anyone by that name. He showed her pictures of the book and talked her into bringing Barbara to New York."

"That son-of-a-bitch."

Moore approached them. "Excuse me. Bill Hansen would like to talk to both of you. I'll put him on the speaker phone."

"Okay boss, we're all here on the speaker except Martin."

"Hello Senator Cole, my name is Bill Hansen with the Tampa office of the FBI. Mackey, glad to hear you're all safe."

Mackey said, "Thanks to your quick phone call, Bill. I owe you one."

"I'll let you buy me a cold beer when this is over."

"You got it."

"I wanted to let you know we discovered that the personnel records of your aide, Miles Connor, have been altered. The IT people have determined that his file had been tampered with about eight years ago. They say whoever broke into the system was way before their time. The security software installed last month was finally able to detect the breach, but only because they were looking for it. Whoever we're dealing with here has immense resources, so everyone stay sharp."

Cole said, "Yeah, when I talked to him, he said I was a dead man, and he came close to making that happen. I assume he believes I am dead now."

"Senator, let me get this right. You talked to the person behind all of this?"

"Yes, I believe I did. He called the cell phone of the guy in charge on the island, looking for a status report. I informed him his two goons were dead and he didn't seem to have any kind of a reaction. When I told him that Miles had been killed, it sent him into a rage. That's when he said both Barbara and I were dead."

"Senator, were you able to get anything else out of the conversation?"

"No, it was short, and he made his point. But I remember that when Miles was shot, the goon in charge had said to the other that he had — and I quote — killed the idiot brother — but the man's voice on the other end of the phone line was too old to be a brother of Miles."

"Mackey, at this point I don't think we have any other choice except to go ahead with what we planned earlier. Keep in touch, gentlemen."

Agent Martin walked up to the group carrying the computer under her arm. "It's fried."

"What computer is that?" asked Mackey.

"This is the computer they were using to track the senator's and his wife's movements using their super-duper cell phones." She smirked at Cole.

Moore interrupted. "We should get out of here and head for Sarasota."

They climbed in the car with Moore and Mackey in the front, Martin and Cole in the back. Cole checked his watch. It was 3:45 PM and he thought sure he could hear his watch ticking the seconds away.

Chapter 27

Wednesday, 3:10 PM

Raphael drummed his fingers on the table at Helen Morrison's apartment as the sketch artist from the New York office worked with her on producing a likeness of Agent Garrett. It took more than an hour to refine the drawing to match Helen's mental picture, but it was finally starting to come together.

"What do you think?" The artist held up her sketch with the latest changes. Helen nodded decisively. "Yes, that's Agent Garrett."

Tears suddenly welled up in her eyes. "It's my fault," she whimpered. "I should have told you everything I knew from the beginning."

Raphael handed her his handkerchief. "It's okay Mrs. Morrison, why don't you start from the beginning now and tell us everything that happened."

At that moment the telephone in her bedroom rang. She wiped her eyes and got up. "Please excuse me while I answer the telephone."

She walked into her bedroom, and they could hear her say, "Hello."

Raphael quickly got out his cell phone and called Anderson.

"The mother hasn't been forthcoming about everything she knows about this case. Now she's ready to talk and tell us what she knows."

Suddenly, a loud gunshot rang out from the bedroom.

"Oh shit. Hang on a second boss, something has happened."

Raphael drew his gun in one hand and held his cell phone in the other as he walked toward the bedroom. Helen Morrison lay on the floor next to the bed with large blossom of blood spreading in the center of her chest.

Raphael spoke into the phone. "Mrs. Morrison has apparently shot herself in the head. She's dead, boss."

* * *

The black Ford Crown Vic with Barbara Cole inside pulled into a parking garage and parked in a reserved spot next to the building. Barbara Cole hadn't spoken a word for the last thirty minutes, and just stared dully out the window. She was awake but unfocused and lethargic.

Agent Garrett turned off the engine and glanced in the mirror at his passenger before getting out of the car. He opened the rear door and held out his hand. "We're here, Mrs. Cole. It's time to go inside."

She slowly turned her head and looked at him vacantly. Then she slid across the seat and got out of the car in a mechanical fashion.

"This way, Mrs. Cole." He led her by the arm to a blank steel door, with a sign next to it that read "Authorized Personnel Only." He pushed the buttons on the key pad below the doorknob, then turned the knob and pulled the door open. They walked down a long concrete corridor to a large room that looked like a warehouse with a loading dock. The room had overhead doors on one side and a service elevator on the other side.

Garrett punched the button next to the elevator door, and the huge doors split open as they stepped inside. Barbara Cole had no idea where she was and didn't seem to care. He hit the button for the twelfth floor as the doors slammed closed and the elevator box lifted upward with a jerk.

A few seconds later the doors opened, revealing a staging room not much larger than the elevator itself. They stepped out, and he closed the doors behind them as he directed Barbara Cole through the small steel door into a carpeted hallway. Walking a short distance to the left, he opened a darkly stained wood door and placed her in a chair at a table in the conference room.

"I'll be right back, Mrs. Cole. Relax here for a few minutes."

She looked up at him as if she understood and maintained a smile as he walked across the room and left through a different door.

Garrett walked down the hall into another office and approached the desk where a man was sitting. He was about sixty, with graying hair and a goatee, and he looked tired, as though he hadn't slept in some time. His eyes darted back and forth as he watched the monitor for a camera in the conference room.

Garrett took a deep swallow as he knew the lack of acknowledgment meant he wasn't happy about something. After waiting awhile, he finally cleared his throat.

The man looked up. "How much of that shit did you give her? She looks like a goddamn zombie."

"I . . . I'm not sure. I gave the vial to Karl to put it in her food before we left."

"I told you to use half the vial, no more. That fool probably dumped the entire thing in her food. This will never work; we have to have her acting alert and normal when she signs those papers. That sleaze ball lawyer and Hank Carlson will know she's in la-la-land if we leave her in this condition. You should have handled something this important yourself."

"Sorry, I didn't realize how strong the stuff was. Her other medication was wearing off, and she was getting suspicious toward the end."

The man's expression suddenly relaxed, and he smiled slightly. "Like everything else, it's something that can be fixed. It helps to keep it exciting when things don't go as planned, especially when you're dealing with a group of fools like these people are. Constantly changing the plan helps keep me sharp when I'm dealing with inferior intelligence."

He reached under his desk and brought out a briefcase. He set it on the desk and opened it. The case was full of bottles and vials of pills.

He pulled out a small bottle containing a clear liquid, and a hypodermic syringe. He pried the plastic end off the needle and stuck it through the lid of the bottle into the liquid, pulled back on the plunger and withdrew the liquid into the syringe. Holding the needle into the air he pushed on the plunger until liquid shot out of the tip. He reached into the case and grabbed a packet containing an alcohol wipe.

"Here, give this to her right away and by the time of the signing she should be right where we want her."

Agent Garrett took the items and put them in his pocket.

"I hate the sight of these needles."

"Do it as I showed you. By the way, we are going to have to change our plans for tonight."

"Change how?"

"Senator Cole will not be here to fire the blank at his wife as we had originally planned."

"Why won't he be here? You promised that no one would get hurt."

"Situations change, so plans have to change accordingly. When it's all over later tonight you will understand the reason."

He opened his desk drawer, pulled out a pistol stored inside a Ziploc bag, and held it up to Garrett, his eyes shining. "Here's the gun that will seem to kill Barbara Cole instead of the one you retrieved from the senator's house with his prints on it."

"Who does that gun belong to?"

"The person who will be blamed for her death, that's who."

"Her death? The gun was supposed to be filled with blanks and fired by the senator to look as if he was acting out the story in his book. You said it would be enough to ensure he was locked away, and no one would be hurt."

"Yes, that's what I meant, her apparent death. Now, do what I told you and everything will go exactly as planned."

Garrett's face was pale. He hesitated a moment, then left the office to inject Barbara Cole with her new drug.

The man behind the desk watched him on the monitor with approval. He then put on a pair of latex gloves and removed the gun from the plastic bag. Removing the clip, he verified that it was full of bullets and smiled as he pushed the clip back inside the weapon.

He picked up his phone and dialed a number from a paper on his desk and waited while it rang on the other end.

"Hello?"

"Helen Morrison, please."

"This is she. Who's calling?"

"Helen, I wanted to be the first to tell you, that because of your actions, your daughter Barbara and her husband Irwin are both dead. With Susan, that makes three deaths you're responsible for. Have a wonderful evening, Helen." He hung up the phone. "Bitch."

Chapter 28

Wednesday, 4:00 pm

Agent Martin determinedly punched the keys on the computer in her lap as the car headed north on I-75. Senator Cole watched her as she made several more keystrokes and then stopped and stared at the blank screen. He stretched in the seat and let out an exaggerated sigh.

"The computer is working fine," she announced. "It's the display that's out." Then she whispered to him. "If I can hook this up to a separate monitor, I could see whether it's still tracing a signal from the phone."

"Which phone…Barbara's?"

"No, Miles's phone. That's how I found you out in the wilderness. As we turned on the dirt road, the signal started moving, and then we had that accident."

"Yes, I forgot. I put Miles's phone in a bag in the trunk of Agent Garrett's car."

Moore turned off the interstate on Fruitville Road in Sarasota, and headed west toward the downtown area. Martin leaned forward and pointed. "There in that strip mall, there's a computer store. Pull in so I can hook this computer up to a separate monitor."

"We don't have the time to do this; it's already past 4:00 PM."

"We have to stop. It's the only way we'll know where they may have taken Mrs. Cole."

They looked at one another and Mackey said, "Irwin, it's your call."

Cole looked at Martin for a moment and made his decision. "I think we need to take the time to do this."

"Okay then, let's do it," said Mackey.

They pulled up in front of the computer store and she hopped out with the computer under her arm.

"I sure hope she's right because we're running out of time," said Mackey.

Cole thought about the clock on the wall in his kitchen. If only he and Barbara could listen to the ticking sound together, he would never complain about it again. Hell, if Barbara was safe, he would leave that damn doorbell alone.

After several minutes, Moore said, "What is she doing in there? We can't waste any more time. I'm going to have to go in and get her if she doesn't come out in the next couple of minutes."

Martin had successfully hooked the laptop to a monitor, and the program was running. The screen was doing its rotation, then a map flashed on the screen, and a star appeared where Miles' cell was located. She asked the computer technician for a screen print, and he went to get a cable. Agent Dodd's cell phone in her pocket began to ring.

"Melissa Martin."

"Agent Martin, this is dispatch. I have a call re-route request for you. May I put it through on this phone?"

"Yes, that's fine, send it through."

She heard a click.

"Agent Martin, I'm glad to hear you are out of the hospital. I hope all is well?"

"Who is this?"

"Let's just say, we have a mutual interest in Barbara Cole."

"What do you want, and where is she?"

"Relax, Agent Martin. That's why I'm calling you, so you can come pick her up. The address is 16305 Tamiami Trail in Sarasota, the office of Argosy Travel on the eleventh floor. At 5:30 PM sharp."

"Why, after all of this time, is she being released, and why are you calling me?"

"She has served her usefulness, and I know I can trust you to come alone and not say a word about this to a soul."

"I think you're giving me too much credit."

"Not at all, Agent Martin, because as we speak I have a man with a gun aimed at Detective Martin's forehead. We all know what kind of mess that can make, and I'm sure it would ruin both your day and his."

"Let me speak to my father."

"That won't be possible. Detective Martin is in Punta Gorda with one of my associates. If I don't place a call to him at exactly 5:35 PM he has instructions to put a bullet through the detective's head."

"Please leave my father out of this. I'll be there."

"I knew you would. That's why I chose you. And remember, Agent Martin, if I see any other face beside yours, Daddy's head will be missing seconds later. Have a good day."

She ended the call and dialed the dispatcher to get the caller's number. "That's strange," said the dispatcher. "There's no number, just a group of odd symbols."

"Thank you." Martin grabbed the printout and charged out the door.

"Damn Melissa, about time," Moore complained.

"I got it." She held out the printout which showed the location of Miles' phone in Sarasota. Mackey and Moore looked at the map, and then looked at each other. Martin looked questioningly at Cole, who hunched his shoulders in ignorance. "What's going on?" she asked.

"That's the exact location we were headed, Gulf-Global Enterprises," Mackey replied.

"That's Barbara's father's company," said Cole.

"Wait a minute," said Martin. "That's the name on all those documents I found at that apartment in Fisherman's Village before I got hit on the head. I forgot about it. I'll bet that's why they gave me those drugs, so I wouldn't have any memories of finding those documents."

They looked around the car at one another and no one spoke.

Martin asked, "Do you know the address?"

"Yeah, it's here on these papers." Mackey opened the folder on the console next to him. "16305 Tamiami Trail."

"What floor is it on?"

"The twelfth floor. Why, are you afraid of heights or something?"

"No."

"The only thing agent Martin is frightened of is boats," said Cole.

She gave him a measured look, then turned and stared out the window so no one would see the concern etched across her face.

Moore pressed the accelerator pedal to the floor, and the car picked up speed with a roar from the engine. His cell phone rang. It was Bill Hansen.

"Yes boss."

"Jerry, would you please hand the phone to Senator Cole?"

Moore handed the phone over his shoulder. "It's for you, Senator."

"Irwin Cole here."

"Senator Cole, I'm sorry to inform you that your mother-in-law, Helen Morrison, committed suicide about ten minutes ago. We had a team at her apartment with a sketch artist trying to get a likeness of this Agent Garrett that contacted her and your wife. Her telephone rang, and she went to answer it in another room. A few minutes later they heard a gunshot. They found her dead on the floor and there was a note on the nightstand that said, 'Barbara, please forgive me.' I'm sorry Senator; the team at her apartment never suspected she was in that state of mind."

"I understand, Mr. Hansen. Helen had a lot of problems in her life. Maybe now she has found peace. The same Agent Garrett who visited her is the one who brought me to this place and locked me away. I could give you a detailed description of him, but at this point I think it's too late. Time has all but run out."

"We're not giving up yet, Senator. Let me speak with Agent Moore."

He handed the phone back to Moore, who spoke first. "Boss, the consensus here in the car is that Mrs. Cole is at Gulf-Global Enterprises. We believe they are involved somehow. We are about ten minutes from that location. I'm requesting backup, but we need to go inside first to see whether we can locate Mrs. Cole. I don't want a swat team to bust in there until we've had a chance to assess the situation."

"I understand. I'll have officers from the Sarasota Police and the Sheriff's department standing by. Also, I want to say, you've done a good job, Jerry. I'm on my way and should arrive shortly."

"Thanks boss."

Mackey said, "I don't get it. What could that company possibly have to do with all of this? I was sure Hank Carlson was hiding something this morning when we talked to him, but not all of this. I mean, kidnapping Barbara, murder, and that damn book. None of this makes any sense to me."

"Lieutenant Mackey, you and Jerry visited this location earlier?" asked Martin.

"Yes, we interviewed the CEO."

"What made you think he was hiding something?"

"He seemed to get nervous when we asked him about Barbara's finances and her future involvement with the company. He said there was no inheritance of Roger Morrison's stock ownership. The way the stock was set up, it would automatically be redistributed to the remaining principles. And—he smiled too much."

"That's my understanding of how the company stock was set up," said Cole. "Barbara's father had a hang-up about losing control of the company."

"That would kind of eliminate financial gain from the puzzle," added Martin.

"I'm not so sure about that," said Mackey. "When Jerry and I asked Carlson about Roger Morrison's finances, his demeanor changed. He seemed to me to be jealous of Roger Morrison's business success outside the company. He also made a point to mention that he and this Kraus fellow had never received any kind of bonus from the company in all the years they had worked there."

Cole spoke up. "I didn't know Roger Morrison that well, but I do know he treated Barbara like a princess. I also got the impression that he could be a son-of-a-bitch if he wanted to be. Hank Carlson seemed like a great guy. He adored Barbara. I met Mark Kraus once at our wedding and all I can say is that he was odd for a man with his intelligence."

Moore pointed. "There's the building ahead. And that looks like the local police over there."

Martin quickly sat up in her seat and looked out the window grimly. Mackey rolled down his window. "Pull up alongside their car."

Mackey introduced himself and everyone in the car to the two Sarasota police detectives. He explained what they wanted to do and the two detectives said they would coordinate with the Sarasota County Sheriff's officers on the other side of the building. One of the detectives handed Mackey a portable radio. "Call us when you need our help."

"Thanks, I'll keep you updated."

Moore pulled out and headed toward the front of the building.

"Jerry, why don't you drive around the building once so we can get the layout," said Mackey. "Maybe there's a better way in than the front door."

They drove around the block and found an entrance to a parking garage and entered the narrow drive. They noticed several Sheriff's cars parked down the road. When they rounded the corner of the first-level, Martin said, "Look, that's the car that ran us into the tree. See, it's covered with dust from that dirt road."

They stopped next to the car, and Martin jumped out and looked in the tinted windows. She turned back around. "There's a purse on the back seat."

Cole got out of the car and bent over next to the glass window. "I'm not sure, but I think that's Barbara's purse."

They parked the car a few spaces away and got out. "Let's do this," Mackey said.

Martin grabbed Cole's arm. "I can't let you go in there, Senator. The situation could be dangerous."

Mackey nodded. "Irwin, she's right. You two stay here. Jerry and I will investigate, and call you when we know what's happening inside."

The two men started toward the building.

Then Martin suddenly cried out, "Stop! Don't go in there."

Chapter 29

Wednesday, 4:45 PM

Barbara Cole was seated at the conference room table when the door opened and three people walked into the room. Her eyes widened with recognition.

"Uncle Hank, it's you." She stood up and went to him and they exchanged a hug.

"Barbara sweetie, it's so good to see you again. I'm sorry I haven't called you since the funeral. It's been so hectic around here and, well, I miss Roger not being here keeping things going."

"I miss him too, Uncle Hank."

Barbara was smiling oddly. He grabbed her hand and held it in his, and he felt it trembling.

"Barbara, is everything okay? I didn't think you were going to make it in today. Some men from the FBI were here asking questions about you. Be sure and let me know if there is anything I can do for you."

* * *

Agent Garrett and the gruff man were watching and listening on the monitor from the office down the hall.

"That idiot Carlson, he needs to shut that big mouth of his before he blows this deal."

Garrett said, "He seems nervous. I've never seen him look so jumpy before."

* * *

Carlson noticed Barbara's strange demeanor. She seemed both preoccupied and subdued. He glanced at the two others who had accompanied him into the room. "Barbara, this is Ethel Snyder, my assistant, and our corporate attorney, Philip Hoffheimer. They will be joining us today."

They shook hands, and Barbara's smile returned. They all sat down at the conference table.

Hoffheimer opened a folder and removed a stack of papers. He looked at Carlson. "Will Mr. Kraus be joining us this evening?"

"No, he had a problem at the plant that required his attention."

"Okay, we can get started then. Mrs. Cole, as power of attorney for Roger Morrison I will need your signature at each of the little sticky arrows on these six pages. I believe there are three lines. Your signatures will install Mr. Carlson as CEO of Gulf-Global Enterprises with authority to execute all responsibilities of that position. Mr. Carlson, I'll need you to sign at all the same spots and Mrs. Snyder, I need you to witness their signatures."

Mrs. Snyder said, "I'm sorry Mrs. Cole, but I don't know you personally. I will need to see your identification."

Barbara Cole looked up blankly. "I don't have my purse with me. I never go anywhere without my purse. Has anyone seen my purse?"

* * *

"Where the hell is her purse?" asked the gruff man.

"I don't know. She had it with her when we left the house. It must still be in the car."

"I can't believe this is going to get screwed up by a missing purse." He swung back his arm, ready to knock the monitor off his desk, when he heard Hank Carlson say, "It's okay Mrs. Snyder, I will vouch for Barbara."

His calm instantly returned. "Yes, Hankster. Way to go."

* * *

They signed the papers and handed them back to Hoffheimer. He took out his pen and signed his name also.

"Okay we're done here; that's all we needed, Mrs. Cole. Thank you for taking the time to come down this evening."

Hank Carlson cleared his throat. "I have one more document I need you to sign, Barbara, before you leave."

"Oh, I wasn't aware of any other documents," said Hoffheimer.

Carlson gave him a quick glare. "Barbara, I need your signature here for the stock transfer."

Barbara signed where she was instructed without questioning and pushed the papers to Mrs. Snyder to witness.

"Philip, if you'll sign at the bottom as legal counsel, we can all go home." Carlson slid the papers across the polished surface of the table in front of Hoffheimer, keeping his hand on top of the papers.

Hoffheimer looked at Carlson. "I'm an attorney. I never sign anything without reading it first."

Carlson forced a smile. "An attorney employed by me, I might add."

Hoffheimer picked up his pen and paused as he looked at Carlson once again. With a small frown he leaned down and signed the papers. Carlson said, "I'll see that you get a copy of this after Mark signs it, tomorrow."

Carlson's cell phone rang and he looked at the screen, and took the call. "Yes?"

"Get the goddamn folder out of the room now."

Carlson closed his phone. "I'm sorry, but I'm needed in my office right away. Barbara, it was wonderful to see you again and please, we must stay in touch."

He bent over and kissed her cheek and walked out of the room.

* * *

"Get Barbara Cole and take her downstairs to the room as we planned," the gruff man instructed Garrett.

"Everything went smoothly, so nothing will happen to her, right?"

"Right, give her one of these pills before you take her down. It will help her relax some."

"But, the papers are all signed and Senator Cole isn't here to pretend to kill his wife, so we don't need to take her down there any longer. I can drive her back to the abandoned house where Senator Cole is held and leave her there."

The man looked down at this desk and rubbed his temples in an exaggerated gesture of patience. Then he looked back up at Garrett with barely concealed rage. He spoke slowly, punctuating his words. "We don't have time for this now. Do as I say now. I will explain everything to you later. Then you will understand."

Garrett took in a deep breath and let it out again. "What about Miles? Have you heard from him lately? I'm getting worried about him. He never showed up at the house as he was supposed to. You know how nervous he gets when things around him get tense."

The man slammed his fist down on the desk. "Go now, son."

Garrett jumped, and quickly turned and left the room. A few moments later there was a knock at the same door, and the man yelled, "What?"

Hank Carlson opened the door with a big smile and a stack of papers in his hand.

"With your signature here, Mark, you're looking at the new CEO of Gulf-Global-Enterprises."

Carlson laid the papers on the desk, and Mark Kraus signed the last open spaces on the documents. He handed the papers back to Hank and then opened his desk drawer. He brought out a stack of his own papers and laid them on the desk in front of Carlson.

"And your first duty as the new CEO of Gulf-Global Enterprises is to sign these papers making it legal for us to sell or distribute our stock shares as we see fit."

Carlson registered a look of surprise.

Kraus pressed. "Right here, Mr. CEO," he said, pointing to the blank line. When Carlson didn't move, he asked, "Is there a problem, Hank?"

"No, not at all," Carlson said slowly as he bent over and signed the papers. Kraus immediately grabbed the papers and put them back in his desk.

Carlson asked, "Have you run those by Philip yet to make sure everything is legal?"

"I will tomorrow, but I think they're fine. Now let's have a drink to celebrate our new partnership." Behind him on the credenza were two glasses already filled with scotch. He grabbed the glasses and handed one to Carlson.

"To our new partnership, may it be profitable and all get what we deserve."

The two men raised their glasses in a toast and drank the scotch.

"Now, if you will excuse me, Hank, I have some additional business I need to take care of before the night is over."

As the door closed, Kraus reached for his phone and dialed.

He got a voice recording and began to speak. "Mr. Sullivan, Kraus here. I now own a hundred percent of Gulf-Global Enterprises. I want to meet tonight at the plant as we had planned. Let's say 9:30 PM. Make sure your clients are there with the money, and I will have all the necessary documents for the purchase of the company."

Chapter 30

Wednesday, 5:15 PM

Mackey and Agent Moore had spun in their tracks upon hearing Agent Martin cry out. Senator Cole was also taken aback.

"Melissa, what's going on?" asked Moore. "What do you mean you can't let us go in there?"

"Uh, you were in there this morning. They probably have surveillance and they will recognize you coming and it could put Mrs. Cole in danger. Let me go in first. With these clothes they will never suspect me as an agent. I'll take a radio and as soon I assess the situation I'll call you on the radio."

Cole turned to Mackey. "She makes a good point, guys. After all, Barbara's safety is our primary concern."

"Melissa, it could be dangerous in there," said Agent Moore. "We have no idea what the situation is. I'm not comfortable with you going in there alone."

"I'll be careful Jerry, I promise."

Cole studied her for a moment. "Gentlemen, I think we should wait here while Agent Martin assesses the situation."

Moore reached into the trunk and grabbed a radio with the wires. Martin ran the wires under her shirt and tested the reception with Moore. Everything was working fine.

She reached in the back seat of the car and picked up Agent Dodd's gun and stuffed it in the waistband of her jeans. She entered the lobby and ran across the shiny marble floors to the elevators and mashed the up button. The doors didn't open.

"Come on," she muttered impatiently under her breath. Finally, there was a ding and the far left door opened. She hurried inside and pushed the button for the eleventh floor. She watched the lights count off as she passed each floor on her rise, until she felt the jerk and a moment later the door opened. She removed the earpiece from her ears and the radio from her waist as she pulled the wires from under her shirt. She hid the radio and gob of wires behind the trash receptacle next to the elevator door.

The place looked deserted. The only sounds were her shoes hitting the floor and her heart beating in her ears. She walked slowly toward the entrance of what seemed to be the only office on the floor. The name over the small storefront was Argosy Travel, just as the caller had said. The office looked empty as she approached the glass door. She twisted the doorknob, and it was unlocked. She went in and found herself in a furnished office with awful wallpaper that had welcome signs printed on it from cities all over the world. "Welcome to New York . . . Welcome to Paris."

Past the reception area was a hallway with several doors on both sides. She stared down the hall, and her instinct was telling her it was a trap, but she didn't have a choice. If she had to give her life to save her father's, she would.

She crept silently down the carpeted hallway toward the first door, and peered in cautiously. It was empty. She let out a small sigh. Her pace hastened as she headed for the next room, which was also empty. She quickly glanced at her watch and it was 5:30 PM. She quickened her pace and found the next room empty. Her stomach began to churn. She ran to the next door and swung it open. Empty.

"Shit."

Martin ran back down the hall toward the reception area and headed for the exit. As she approached she noticed the wall to her right. It looked like a temporary wall erected across the reception area. It had the same ridiculous wallpaper as the rest of the office. There was a door in the middle of the wall which she hadn't noticed earlier because it was also covered with the wallpaper.

She pushed the door open and stepped out onto a small inside balcony, like a mezzanine. Standing against the balcony railing was Barbara Cole. Martin gasped and froze for a second as she tried to assess the situation.

A voice from behind echoed through the empty room. "Good evening, Agent Martin. I'm so glad you could join us. I was beginning to worry that you may not show."

Martin turned and found a man standing with a gun pointed at her. She flinched. "Easy Agent Martin...I don't see a holster, so I'm guessing you have a gun at your waist in the back. Why don't you be a good girl and remove the gun. Set it on the floor in front of you and kick it this way."

Martin had no choice. She removed the gun and set it on the floor. With her left foot, she slid the gun across the floor to the man.

"Very good Agent Martin."

He appeared to be in his late fifties or early sixties, and his hair was starting to turn gray on the sides. His goatee was completely gray. He was calm and relaxed, as if he was enjoying himself, but she also saw that his piercing gaze was menacing.

Martin looked back at Barbara Cole. She was leaning with her back against the rail, staring vacantly into the unfinished room. She seemed emotionless. On the other side of the rail behind her, was a space about ten feet wide that was open to the floor below. The wall beyond the open space was covered with the same wallpaper.

The man approached Martin and ran his hand down her back and around her waist.

"Very good Agent Martin, no communications."

"I'm here. Now make your call to the person with my father."

"I do like a person who gets straight to the point. I'm sure under other circumstances, we could have been friends. That call won't be necessary, Agent Martin, as your father is safe at his office. I had to bluff you into coming here tonight. I asked you here so you can shoot and kill Mrs. Cole."

"I don't know who you are, or who you think you are, but that's not going to happen."

"I'm sorry, but it will, whether you pull the trigger or not."

He was already wearing tight-fitting clear plastic gloves. He was holding the gun gingerly, as if he didn't want to disturb any fingerprints.

"Do you recognize this weapon, Agent Martin?"

She did, but replied, "No, should I?"

"Well, of course you should. It's your service weapon. I checked the serial number for you. And of course it's also covered with your fingerprints."

"How did you get my gun?"

"Are you having memory problems, Agent Martin? You should be careful what substances you put into your body. They can cause side effects."

Barbara Cole seemed oblivious of the spectacle occurring around her. The man looked at his watch and said, "It's time to get started."

He reached into his pocket and pulled out a second gun. "This is Senator Cole's personal weapon."

He held Martin's gun in his right hand and Cole's in his left hand as he walked closer to her. He stopped about five feet away from Martin, raised and pointed the gun in his right hand at Barbara Cole while the gun in his left hand was aimed at Martin.

"Don't!"

Her shout caused Barbara Cole to turn her attention to the man pointing the gun at her. For the first time the situation registered and she let out a scream.

* * *

Ten minutes had passed since Agent Martin had gone inside the building alone. "I have a bad feeling about letting her go in by herself," said Moore. "I can't wait here any longer."

"Call her on the radio, she has an earpiece. It won't put her in danger," said Mackey.

Moore put the radio to his mouth. "Martin, what's your status? Martin, do you copy? Martin?"

There was no response. "Shit, I knew it was a bad idea." Moore grabbed his FBI blazer.

"I'm going with you," said Mackey.

Agent Moore looked at Senator Cole. "Senator, I'm going to have to ask you to stay at the car."

"Irwin, he's right. We can't take a chance on anything happening to you."

"I can't just sit here and wait for you guys," Cole protested. "I need to do something."

"Irwin, the way you can help is to stay here and be safe. You do your job in Washington; let us do ours here. We can handle what's inside, and I have the radio if we need backup."

Cole nodded his head reluctantly as the two men rushed toward the building wearing blue FBI blazers over their bullet-proof vests. They found a glass door on the back side of the first-floor lobby. They entered the same lobby they had been in earlier that day. This time they didn't care to take the scenic route up to the twelfth floor. Mackey pointed to a different elevator on the other side of the lobby.

The two men entered and Agent Moore reached to hit the button for the twelfth floor when Mackey suddenly grabbed his arm. "Wait."

* * *

The man moved his glove-covered finger to the tip of the trigger. Agent Martin prepared to dive for him. But her one second of hesitation was enough for him to squeeze the trigger. The scream coming from Barbara Cole stopped instantly.

Martin saw Barbara Cole's body jerk violently backwards, sending her over the railing. Her legs were the last thing Martin saw before she disappeared below the bottom of the railing, and there was a crash on the tenth floor below.

"You bastard!" she yelled, as she dove at him. He twisted and jumped backward and she hit the floor in front of him. He pointed the other gun at her. "That will be quite enough of that, Agent Martin. Now, unfortunately, you must die of a bullet wound from Senator Cole's gun."

He tossed the gun he had used to kill Barbara against the wall. He looked at his watch and smiled. "I love it when things go as planned. 6:00 PM sharp."

"You're going to burn in hell, you son-of-a-bitch."

Suddenly a door she hadn't noticed on the other wall popped open and a man stepped through. At first, she didn't recognize him. Then he stepped into the light. "Melissa?"

Instantly, her mind went back to the spinning screen on the computer program. Now she remembered where she had seen it before. Her eyes widened. He had been working on designing a program while they were in law school together. She never knew what the program was going to be used for. ..until now. "Josh?"

"Melissa, what are you doing here?"

"Why don't you ask this bastard?"

Josh turned to the man pointing his gun at Martin. "Father, what's going on here? Why is Melissa here and what are you doing with that gun?"

"Josh, this bastard is your father?"

"Josh, I told you to go to the car and wait for me there," said Kraus angrily.

"No, we can't leave without Miles; he was supposed to meet us here hours ago."

Martin spoke up. "Miles is dead. He was killed by one of the guys working for your father."

"Josh, I'm sorry," said Kraus. "Miles is gone. Senator Cole murdered him. That's the reason he and his wife both had to die."

Josh looked disoriented as he glanced around the balcony where he had left Barbara thirty minutes earlier. He sniffed the lingering odor of gunpowder. "No!" he yelled. "She didn't do anything wrong!"

Martin saw her opportunity. "Senator Cole didn't do anything either, and your father blew him to pieces in that abandoned house this afternoon."

Kraus nodded. "Very good Agent Martin. I thought it would be weeks before his DNA was identified."

"Josh, can't you see your father's insane? We have to do something to stop him now. I missed you Josh. I tried to locate you three years ago with the FBI database, but it came back empty. It was like you no longer existed. I wanted to stay friends."

Josh was glaring back at his father angrily. "I did too, but he wouldn't let me contact you. He says the FBI is evil and inferior, and they need to be punished for not allowing me be an agent like you."

Kraus said, "I underestimated you, Agent Martin." He raised the gun again and pointed it at her.

"No!" Josh screamed as he rushed for his father's arm to knock the gun away. The gun fired with a loud blast and another cloud of smoke.

* * *

"I noticed before we got on the elevator that there's a stairwell next to us," Mackey said to Moore as he pressed the button for the eleventh floor. "We can take the stairs up to the twelfth floor. That way, we won't be walking into their front door blindly."

Moore nodded. "Good thinking. That's why I'm an analyst and not a field agent."

The elevator stopped and they stepped out into the headquarters for Argosy Travel Agency which was plastered with tacky wallpaper.

Mackey said, "I'd go crazy if I had to work in this place all day."

"You and me both," agreed Moore.

The area inside the lobby was empty, so they walked toward the stairwell door next to the elevator and climbed the single flight of stairs to the twelfth floor, coming out in a lobby at the opposite side of the building from where they had entered earlier in the morning. Mackey held the door so it wouldn't make any noise as it closed behind them. They walked toward the reception area.

Moore's cell phone rang, sounding like a siren in the quiet lobby. He quickly fumbled for the phone, saw that it was Bill Hansen, and quietly answered.

"Jerry, it's me. I'm here in the parking garage now. What's your status?"

"Mackey and I have entered the twelfth floor lobby, and it's deserted. We're going to check the offices next."

"Okay, I'll head into the building and meet you at your location on twelve."

"Before you enter the building, can you check on Senator Cole? We left him at the car."

"I'm standing next to your car right now, and the senator is not here. I'm heading for the front door. I'll see you guys in a few minutes."

Moore turned to Mackey. "The senator isn't at the car."

"Christ!" Mackey swore. "I knew I should have cuffed him."

They headed past the reception desk where "Ms. Stuffy" had been seated earlier, to the huge oak doors of Hank Carlson's office. Mackey turned the knob and slowly pushed the door open. They entered with guns extended.

Hank Carlson sat frozen behind his desk, staring at the two guns aimed at his face.

"Where're Agent Martin and Barbara Cole?" Moore demanded.

"I don't know any Agent Martin, but Barbara Cole was here earlier to sign papers, then she left."

"Left?" Mackey blurted. "Where did she go?"

"I don't know. I assume she went home. I wasn't in the conference room when she left."

A small noise behind them caused both men to spin around and aim their guns at the door.

Chapter 31

Wednesday, 6:05 PM

"Easy guys…" Bill Hansen entered Carlson's office and joined Mackey and Moore in front of the desk. "What's the situation?"

"According to Mr. Carlson, Barbara Cole was here earlier to attend a meeting, and left."

"Mr. Carlson, my name is Bill Hansen, supervisor of the Tampa office of the FBI. How did Barbara Cole arrive for her meeting?"

"I don't know. She was already sitting in the conference room when I arrived."

"Was there anyone else with her, and how did she leave after the meeting?"

"She was by herself. Our attorney and a witness were the only other people at the meeting. I left the conference room before her, so I didn't see her leave."

"What was Mrs. Cole's demeanor during the meeting? Did she seem normal to you?"

Carlson paused. "Now that you mention it, she didn't seem herself."

"In what way did she seem different, Mr. Carlson?"

"She seemed distant, spacey, not the sharp wit I'm used to."

Hansen pursed his lips. He turned to Moore. "Where's Agent Martin?"

"We don't know. She wanted to come in by herself first."

Hansen's voice raised a notch. "You let her enter the building alone? Why would you allow a fellow agent to enter a potentially hostile environment unaccompanied? I don't understand."

Mackey spoke up. "Bill, she persuaded us to let her come in first to assess the situation since both of us had been here earlier. She was afraid they would recognize us and it would put Barbara in jeopardy."

Hansen sighed. "I can't believe this. Martin is going to give me an ulcer before this is over."

Mackey reached into his pocket and took out the radio the Sarasota detective had given him. He apprised him of the situation and requested assistance. The local officers would start at the bottom floors and work their way up. The FBI would work their way down, and they would meet somewhere in the middle.

"Mr. Carlson, I want you to stay here in your office," said Hansen. "We'll have more questions for you shortly."

They split and began the search on the twelfth floor. A few minutes later they were back in the lobby, not finding anyone.

Mackey said, "I found a service entrance in one of the back offices. I'll go that way and meet you two on eleven."

Hansen and Moore headed for the passenger elevator. Mackey returned to the office with the service elevator. The light indicated that the elevator was in use, so he was forced to use the adjacent stairwell.

The Cole Hard Truth   277

He stepped out into the eleventh floor lobby, and he was assaulted again by the garish travel wallpaper. The door to Argosy Travel was unlocked, so he entered and searched the rooms, finding nothing. Then he noticed the temporary wall with the camouflaged door, and his alert level rose. He opened the door and found the makeshift room with the balcony.

A 9mm FBI- issued service weapon lay on the floor next to the wall. "Damn it!" He knew it was the service weapon Agent Martin had taken with her.

His mind raced as he took in a deep breath, smelling the faint scent of burned gunpowder. He noticed something else on the floor, and bent down. "Shit...blood."

He felt his stomach lurch as he looked up at the wall beyond the railing. At that moment the words on the wall registered. *"Welcome to Naples."* Dr. Moiré's words from the meeting in Washington flashed through his mind as if he had just heard them.

He ran to the railing and looked down to the floor below. Barbara Cole lay in the middle of a stack of cardboard boxes.

Hansen and Moore entered the room at the same time Mackey shouted. "No God, please!" He turned around, stricken, as the two men approached him.

* * *

Senator Cole paced back and forth next to the car. Five minutes had passed, but it felt like an eternity. Though he understood what Mackey had said, he just couldn't wait any longer. His wife was in that building.

He opened the trunk and searched through the plastic tubs of FBI gear. He found what he needed and shrugged on a dark-blue FBI blazer as he had seen Mackey and Moore do earlier.

As he approached the building a blank steel door swung open. A delivery man with a hand trunk was struggling through the doorway. The senator grabbed the door and held it for the man.

"Thank you, sir."

"My pleasure." Now he was inside without going in the front entrance.

He entered the concrete hallway and walked to a room with a loading dock on one side and a service elevator on the other. He studied the directory next to the elevator door, found "Gulf-Global Enterprises", then entered the elevator and hit the button for the twelfth floor. He watched the lights for each floor blink on and off as he rose. When the light for the eleventh floor came on the elevator stopped, and the doors began to open. *What the hell?*

Agent Martin and Agent Garrett stood at the opening, and with them was Mark Kraus, a partner at Gulf-Global Enterprises, whom he had met before.

Only Martin had known that he survived the explosion at the abandoned house. As he stared at Garrett and Kraus, they stared back, equally shocked. Then he noticed that Garrett was bleeding, and was being partially supported by Martin. More importantly, Kraus was pointing a gun at him. Cole thought, *I have a gun just like that.*

"Senator Cole, I see you are as full of surprises as your FBI friend Agent Martin. That's all right, because things always have a way of working out for the best. I can use your help with my son."

"Mr. Kraus, what's going on here? Why are you pointing a gun at me and what's wrong with Agent Garrett?"

"His name is Josh Kraus, not Agent Garrett," Martin announced, "and this is his father, the man who shot him in the chest."

Cole stared at Josh and his mind flashed with images. The expression of pain that Miles had had before he died in his arms was the same as this man's. Earlier in the day when he was in the car with Agent Garrett . . . he remembered the image of him drinking the bottle of water. The mannerisms were the same as Miles'.

"Are you saying this is your friend Josh from school?"

"Yes, this is Josh." Martin answered.

"This is touching," said Kraus, "but I'm afraid I'm on a time schedule. Senator Cole, help Agent Martin bring my son into the elevator."

They rode down to the first floor and headed to the steel door through which Cole had come in.

"Wait here while I check the area outside," said Kraus.

He surveyed the adjacent parking area and signaled with the flipping of the gun for them to come outside. They had to practically carry Josh to the car, where they were instructed to put him in the back seat.

"Agent Martin, you're in the back with Josh. Senator, you're in the front with me. You're driving."

They were in the same Ford the senator had ridden in earlier that day, the same one that had run Agents Martin and Dodd off the road. Cole eased the car out of the parking garage and headed for the exit. As they entered the street several Sarasota police and sheriff's cars were converging on the parking garage with their lights flashing.

Kraus shoved the gun into the Senator's side. "No one move." The cars flew past them in the opposite direction.

"We have to get Josh to a hospital," said Martin. "He's losing a lot of blood."

"Just let me worry about my son, Agent Martin."

"You didn't seem worried a few minutes ago when you shot him in the chest."

There was silence in the car as Kraus used hand signals to direct the senator toward the east side of town. They entered an industrial park and headed down a narrow alley, stopping in front of a large steel building with a "Gulf-Global Enterprises" sign.

Kraus removed a pair of handcuffs from the glove box. "Turn off the engine and hand me the keys. Then help Agent Martin get my son out of the back seat and take him inside the building."

Cole had to practically carry the fading Josh into the industrial building. Kraus locked the door behind them and directed them to place Josh on the stainless steel table in a small room at the far right wall. The room was full of cabinets stocked with first aid supplies. Kraus swung a hinged arm with a bright light down over Josh.

"Sit in those chairs over there while I attend to my son's wounds."

Martin and Cole sat down next to each other silently. Kraus opened Josh's shirt, and rolled a cabinet over next to the table and opened a drawer that was full of medical supplies.

Cole whispered to Martin. "What about Barbara? Did you see her inside? Was she all right?"

Martin closed her eyes briefly then spoke quietly. "Irwin, I'm so sorry. She's . . . she's been shot."

His jaw quivered.

"Is she going to be all right? Melissa, is she going to be all right?"

She slowly shook her head and spoke falteringly. "I don't think so. I'm so sorry, Irwin."

Cole turned away, as his eyes welled. Then he covered his face with his hands and wept. Martin put one hand on his arm and the other across his back to try to comfort him. She was grieving too.

Suddenly, he pulled back from her hold, and looked at her wildly. "Who did it?"

The Cole Hard Truth

281

She swallowed, but said nothing. He grabbed her by the shoulders. "Melissa! Who did it? I want to know, now."

She silently turned her head toward Kraus. "You son-of-bitch!" Cole yelled, and started toward Kraus. Kraus quickly picked up the gun on the table next to Josh and squeezed off a shot at point-blank range into Cole's chest.

Agent Martin screamed as she watched him fall to the floor.

* * *

Hansen and Moore looked down over the railing. "Oh Mackey, I'm so sorry," said Hansen quietly. "If only we'd gotten here sooner."

Mackey radioed the Sarasota detective that they needed paramedics on the tenth floor. He then handed Moore the radio as he pushed past them and went down the stairwell to Barbara.

The two men looked over the railing at Barbara Cole's body. She lay twisted on her back, her white business suit showed a bullet hole in the chest. "Jerry, there's really nothing else we can do here," said Hansen. "Let's give Mackey a few minutes alone with Mrs. Cole. The locals can finish searching the remaining floors, but I have a feeling Martin's not here. Let's go back and talk to Carlson, I think he knows where she is. I now agree with Mackey; he knows more than he's saying. Did you notice the sweat on his forehead when we were talking to him earlier?"

The two men rode up the elevator and entered Hank's office. He was still sitting behind his desk, just as they had left him earlier. He was still sweating profusely, and looked pale and tired.

Hansen said, "Mr. Carlson, we found Barbara Cole two floors below."

Carlson's uneasy expression turned into a small smile. "How is she?" he asked weakly.

"What do you think? She has a gunshot wound to the chest and fell fifteen feet off a balcony."

Hank leaned back in his executive chair, tilting his head all the way back. He dragged his hand across his face and hair and locked it behind his neck as he stared upward.

"Mr. Carlson, do you know anything about Mrs. Cole's death?"

"No. Barbara was like my own daughter. I can't believe this is happening, first Roger and now Barbara. It's not fair."

"Mr. Carlson, while you may not have been directly involved in Mrs. Cole's death, accessory to murder is still a serious charge. I need for you to start leveling with us right away."

Carlson leaned forward in his chair and his eyes searched the two men's faces.

"I'm afraid I don't know what you're talking about, Mr. Hansen."

A bead of sweat trickled down his forehead, and he reached up to loosen the collar of his shirt.

"I mean, Mr. Carlson, I'm sure you're not telling us everything you know. Either you begin talking now or face the consequences later."

Carlson was silent for a few moments as he shifted uncomfortably in his chair. Finally, he said, "It wasn't my idea. It was his, and I tried to tell him it wasn't necessary."

"Who is he, and what idea are you talking about?"

"Mark Kraus, my business partner. He wanted me to have Barbara sign the stock certificates without explaining to her what they were. I told him it wasn't necessary to do it that way. Barbara would gladly sign them if I explained everything to her."

"Mr. Carlson," said Moore, "slipping a fast one over a business partner is unethical, but it wouldn't require murder. I think there's more to—"

Carlson's eyes began to roll back in their sockets, and he reached for his chest and tried to draw a breath.

The two men glanced at one another as froth began to ooze from Carlson's mouth. He fell forward in his chair and slumped over his desk.

"Jerry, call the paramedics, quick."

Moore made the call on the radio. "Heart attack?" he asked Hansen.

"I'm no doctor, but I don't think so. Did you see how he was frothing before he collapsed?"

They moved Carlson to the floor in front of his desk and further loosened his shirt. Hansen leaned down with his ear to Carlson's chest. "His heart sounds like it's going to beat out of his chest."

Hank's body began to twitch and convulse. The two men were trying to hold him still when the paramedics rushed into the room and took over.

They moved over near the door of the office and stood next to Detective Marsh of the Sarasota police.

Hansen said, "You sure arrived quickly."

"We had a spare team on-site because we had no idea what we were going to run into here," replied Marsh.

"I'm Bill Hansen, with the FBI, any signs of Agent Martin or Senator Cole in the building?"

"Sorry, no. We've completed a search of every floor. I can assure you they're not in this building."

Hansen's cell phone rang. It was William Anderson. "Hello William."

"How's it going down there, Bill? 6:00 PM has come and gone."

"You can tell Dr. Moiré he was right about Mrs. Cole not being killed in Naples. It appeared that she died here in Sarasota at 6:00 PM. We were too late by just minutes."

"Damn. I'm sorry, Bill. How's Mackey taking it?"

"Not well. He was the one who found her body. I'm quite sure the principals of Gulf-Global Enterprises are somehow behind all of this, though we don't know the actual reason. We were interviewing the CEO when he went into a seizure. I suspect poisoning."

"Well, keep at it. And for what it's worth, you were right. The Coles' residence here in D.C. was full of surveillance bugs. We also checked Miles Connor's residence and it's a gold mine of evidence. His computer had a link to a remote server that had copies of Senator Cole's original papers that we used as the basis for determining the author of the book. Apparently the senator never read the final drafts of the papers that were submitted to the Senate, because they were different than his original versions. That's why the book and the papers were determined to be written by the same person. We also found several pictures of Senator Cole on the server that had been altered in Photoshop. The IT people did find a breach in the Capitol computer system, but they are still assessing to what extent. Bill, we learned a great deal from this one."

"Yeah, unfortunately, we learned it the hard way, and I don't think it's over yet. William, I'm not sure we have Senator Cole in our custody any longer. He and Agent Martin have been missing for the last thirty minutes or so."

"Christ. Any ideas about where they might be?"

"None, but I suggest changing any codes or security protocols the senator may be forced into divulging. I have a feeling this thing is much bigger than the senator and his wife."

"I understand. Oh, by the way, we also found some e-mail references to Alan Sullivan on that same server. He's the political lobbyist we've been looking for concerning the leak to the press. His specialty is clients in the oil industry. We're still trying to track him down, and I think he's going to figure prominently in the middle of all of this."

"Yes," agreed Hansen. "There's definitely more to this than we first thought. I'll let you know as soon as we find any new information on Senator Cole and Agent Martin."

Bill Hansen ended his call. The paramedics had Carlson on the stretcher and were rolling him into the service elevator. He and Moore followed. Hansen looked down and noticed blood on the floor of the elevator. He motioned to Moore and they bent to inspect it. It was still wet.

"I suspect it's either Agent Martin's or Senator Cole's blood," Hansen said. "We need to get the lab boys down here right away."

They followed the path of blood through the loading dock and out the steel service door. The trail of blood continued to the parking garage and then stopped.

Moore said, "The car we think that brought Mrs. Cole was parked here when we arrived."

"How did you know that was the car?"

"Martin recognized it. Plus she had been tracking—"

Moore took off toward his Ford with Bill Hansen a few steps behind. The laptop was still on the seat.

"With this computer, we can track that car. The display is broken, but if we hook it up to another monitor, we will know where Agent Martin and Senator Cole have been taken."

"Let's do it, Jerry."

They grabbed the computer and headed back toward the first floor lobby where the local Sheriff's office had set up a command post. They disconnected a monitor at the reception desk and plugged it into the laptop. Moore opened the lid, and the computer began to whir.

"Good," said Moore. "It was in sleep mode and should open into the program that Martin was running when she closed the lid."

The two men watched as the monitor came alive with a program called Search & Discover. Then a password window popped up in the center of the screen, and the two men looked at each other with blank expressions.

Moore said, "Shit, I'm no good at password breaking. We're going to need help with this."

"Get Morgan on the line and see whether he can talk you through trying to get past the password."

They both knew it would be a long shot at best.

Chapter 32

Wednesday, 9:10 PM

Senator Cole lifted his head and opened his eyes to the realization that he was sitting on a concrete floor, leaning against a railing, with his right arm pulled behind him. The back of his head hurt, and the right side of his chest felt like it had been crushed. His neck was sore too, because he had been sitting with his head hanging. Then he realized that Martin was sitting next to him with her arm handcuffed to his. She had her legs pulled up to her chest, and her head was resting on her right arm, supported by her knees. Her eyes were closed.

He fidgeted in discomfort, causing Martin to open her eyes.

"Thank God you're awake," she said. "How are you feeling?"

"Like someone hit me in the back of the head with a baseball bat, then used it on my chest."

"Fortunately, you were wearing that Kevlar vest, or you would be dead instead of having a broken rib."

He raised his left hand to the back of his head. "And what happened to my head?"

"When you were shot you fell backward and hit your head on the concrete floor."

"How long have I been out?"

"Almost two hours."

His head was still fuzzy as he processed the information. With a sharp pang he remembered Barbara. He closed his eyes again and they both sat silently for a few minutes.

Martin spoke softly. "Irwin, I am so, so sorry about all this."

"Thanks Melissa. It still doesn't seem real to me." He rubbed his temples. "Right now, what we need to do is focus on getting ourselves out of here. Where's Kraus?"

"He removed the bullet from Josh's chest and dressed the wound. He had me help him load Josh into the car before he cuffed us to this railing and left. His phone rang as we carried Josh out, and I heard him say he was going to meet somebody here at 9:30 PM."

Cole looked at his watch. It was 9:15. He grabbed the railing and shook it, but it was secured solidly to the floor. "We have to get out of here before he gets back."

"I've spent the last two hours trying to think of a way out of here," replied Martin. "Short of cutting off one of our arms, there isn't one. In any case, we don't have a knife or a saw."

He studied the railing, then looked at her. "I think you can fit through the opening between these two cross rails."

She regarded the space between the round metal rails. "I'm flattered you think I can fit through there, but there's no way."

"Sure you can. Turn your head sideways and slip it through between the two bars. The rest of your body will go through with no problem."

"Are you saying I have a big head?"

"No, that's not what I meant. Come on, I'll help."

"Well, I guess it can't hurt to try. "She turned her head sideways and carefully slid it between the bars, stopping when the bars met her ears. "I don't think I can go any further. I don't want to mangle myself," she protested.

"You're almost through. I'll give it a little push."

"No!" She yelped as her head popped through the bars.

"See, that was easy, I told you that you could do it."

She touched one ear then the other with her free hand. "I guess I'm all right."

"Now move the rest of your body through," he said briskly.

She put her right arm and shoulder through the narrow opening and wiggled her torso as she continued to slide her chest forward in a seesaw motion. She had to stop again when she was through up to her butt.

Cole said, "Here, I'll give you another little push."

"Wait—" she began, but in another moment she fell to the floor on the other side.

"Now, all you have to do is squeeze back through on this side of the post, and we're out of here. Trust me. It will seem easier this time."

They heard a car outside the building. "We have to move fast. Sorry about this, but…" Before she could protest, Cole pulled her over to him and licked each of her ears. "Hurry and slip through as fast as you can."

She leaned down to the rail and they manipulated her through much more quickly the second time. He grabbed her hand and began to lead her through the warehouse. He walked stiffly, as the movement aggravated his painful rib, and Martin tried to give him some support.

They left the warehouse section and entered the production area, which still felt hot from some previous activity of the giant, ominous-looking machines, and smelled of resins, lubricating oils, and cardboard.

They saw a doorway on the far wall, and had to squeeze through an area that had no aisles in order to reach it. Cole stopped and leaned against the wall. The pain in his chest was unbearable from twisting his way through the machinery.

"Just a little further," coaxed Martin. She opened the door to reveal a dark office full of desks and filing cabinets. A streetlight was shining through the glass door on the other side of the room.

"There's an outside door. You can do it," she said. Their progress had slowed to one step at a time as she tried to support his weight.

They were about halfway across the room when they saw a shadow on the outside of the glass door. "Quick! Over here." Martin helped him through a narrow opening to a small area behind the filing cabinets. They collapsed to the floor and Cole stifled a grunt of pain.

They heard voices, then the sound of a deadbolt retracting into the door. A hinge squeaked as the door swung open and some people entered and flicked on the lights.

Mark Kraus asked, "Did you tell your clients I want cash, no check bullshit?"

"Yes, Mr. Kraus, they understand. And have you taken care of all the details of your part of the bargain?"

Cole was sure he recognized the familiar twang of the second voice, but couldn't quite place it.

Kraus said, "I wouldn't have called you for the transaction if I hadn't fulfilled my part of the deal. There's one small final loose end, and it will be handled shortly, I assure you."

"The reason I'm asking is because I think we both know my oil clients have little tolerance for incompetence," said the second man.

"You can assure them that Irwin Cole will be out of their way for good."

"And you're sure it can't be linked back to me or my clients?"

"Positive. It will be a miracle if they find his body, much less identify his remains. Besides, the FBI is going to be so busy covering their asses and pointing fingers they won't have time to do any investigating."

Kraus asked, "Where the hell are those Chinese buyers of yours, Sullivan? They were supposed to be here by 9:30 PM."

Now Cole could put a face to the voice. Sullivan was a lobbyist well known among the Washington political community as "Sleazy Sullivan."

"They'll be here any moment. We both know that without me, you would have never found anyone willing to pay this kind of money for the business, much less a cash deal. So don't get too cocky with me."

"And let's not forget, Sullivan, you're going to be a legend among your oil clients thanks to me. Ah, here they are."

There was a noise at the door as some additional men entered the room.

"Come in, gentlemen, and make yourself at home. After all, you will be the new owners in just a few minutes," crooned Sullivan. "Mr. Kraus, I'd like to introduce Mr. Feng and his three associates."

The two men shook hands and exchanged brief pleasantries. It was enough for Cole and Martin to hear their Chinese accents. "I'm in somewhat of a hurry," said Kraus. "I need to check on my son, so if you don't mind I would like to proceed with the transaction. This folder contains the completed paperwork for the sale of Gulf-Global Enterprises. I believe you will find everything in order."

There were several minutes of silence save for the rustling of papers as Mr. Feng distributed them to the other three men and they read through them. Eventually Mr. Feng said, "We are ready."

Cole and Martin heard the sound of a briefcase being plopped on the table and opened. "I think you will find that the currency is all there, Mr. Kraus," said Mr. Feng.

"Indeed," replied Kraus, as he snapped the case shut again.

"Mr. Feng, you've made one heck of a deal here," said Sullivan.

Mr. Feng chuckled. "Yes, my people tell me that by reducing quality twenty-five percent, we will increase profits by seventy-five percent in less than a year's time."

Kraus tossed a ring of keys on the desk. "An old friend named Roger Morrison always said, 'If it's too good to be true, it probably is.'" Kraus walked briskly to the outside door and disappeared.

"Don't be puzzled by him, Mr. Feng," said Sullivan. "Eccentric. Shall we go in and look at your new factory, gentlemen? After you..." The door leading back into the factory slammed shut.

"This is our chance," whispered Cole. "These are the men who want me out of the way. When they see that we're not handcuffed in the warehouse, they will come searching. Let's get out of here now."

He started to rise, but a surge of pain stopped him. At that moment the building shook with the deafening sound of an enormous explosion. He fell on top of Martin.

* * *

It had taken Agent Moore two hours to bypass the computer password with the help of Agent Morgan at the office. The program showed the Ford was on the east side of town at an industrial park. Moore and Hansen took off to the location while they called for backup from the Sheriff's office. On the way they saw a fireball light up the sky and the sound of an explosion hit their ears. They turned and looked at each other. They both knew where the explosion came from.

Chapter 33

Thursday, 11:20 AM

Cole was caught under the huge machine and the gears were spinning above his head. They were coming closer and closer to his body, and the heat from the machine was becoming unbearable. He could feel his skin starting to singe.

The machine was going to win. He was pinned in the tiny space and couldn't move his body at all. He was ready to give up when he saw Kraus's face high above the machine. "Kraus, you son-of-a-bitch!"

He was determined not to let Kraus win. He made one final attempt at summoning his remaining strength as he heard a distant voice say, "It's only a dream."

He opened his eyes. The bright lights blinded his vision and everything was blurry. Then he realized the machine pinning him down was gone. As his eyes began to focus, he saw a woman standing over him. She said, "It's okay, Irwin, you must have been dreaming."

Still foggy, and with a ringing in his ears, he looked around the room. He recognized the woman but couldn't remember her name. He noticed that he could still hear the beeping noise and he turned his head sideways. The sound was coming from the monitor next to him. He realized he was lying in a hospital bed with several leads attached to his body. His brain engaged, and the events began flooding back. He was looking at Agent Martin.

"The explosion. We made it? We're alive?"

"Thanks to you, we made it," she said with a smile.

"What about the others in the building? Sullivan and the Chinese men?"

She shook her head. "No; they were at the center of the explosion. The building was completely destroyed. The Fire Department squad said it was a miracle that we survived. We wouldn't have made it if we hadn't been on the opposite side of the building behind the double rows of concrete-lined fireproof file cabinets."

"What about that bastard Kraus? Did he survive?"

"He got away. They think he remotely detonated the explosion once he was at a safe distance."

With a weak smile, "I'd love to see the expression on his face when he discovers he failed to blow me up again."

"The FBI is conducting a nationwide search for him. He'll crawl out of a hole somewhere, and we'll be there to nab him."

"Do you think they'll catch him? You have to admit he's clever. I'm sure he had an escape plan all thought out."

"It doesn't matter how clever a person is. Things go wrong, and that's when we catch them. It'll happen to him too. You'll see."

Cole looked down at his arms which were wrapped in gauze.

"You were singed by the heat," explained Martin. "It burned your skin. They put an antiseptic cream on them to stop any infection, but they said there shouldn't be any scarring. The back of your head and neck were singed also."

Martin took out her new cell phone and dialed a number. "He's awake." She closed the phone and put it back in her jacket.

"That sleaze ball Sullivan," said Cole. "Is that what this mess was all about, him working for those Chinese guys who wanted me out of the way?"

"No, that was only a small part of the plan. It's very complicated, and we're still trying to sort through all of it. First it was about revenge for Josh and his father. More precisely, I think it was Mark Kraus trying to inflict revenge on William Anderson for removing Josh from the Academy. He wanted the FBI to look like a bunch of idiots, especially Anderson. He used the book to provide us with disinformation and confusion, to keep us looking in all the wrong places, at the wrong people, and it worked. Basically, through the book he was controlling our every move.

"According to Dr. Moiré, it was an elaborate scheme to show his superiority to the rest of the world. The doctor admitted that he had been fooled himself into thinking it was a case of multiple personality.

"Mark Kraus wanted to prove he was smarter than the FBI, and everyone else, for that matter. I think Kraus took his son's rejection from the FBI harder than Josh did. Probably because he knew he had screwed up Josh's mind as a child, causing him to fail the FBI psychological review. Dr. Moiré thinks he has been grooming Josh for this since he was a child. We reviewed old medical records that indicated several incidents of possible childhood abuse.

"Miles Conner was actually Miles Kraus, Josh's brother. As children they witnessed their mother commit suicide. Obviously, they were both affected by the traumatic event. I think we can also assume that if Kraus wasn't already crazy, his wife's death pushed him the rest of the way.

"We don't think Miles understood what was occurring with his family. He was used by his father to plot his revenge. We think he changed Miles' identity and planted him in your office long ago, so he could be in place when he needed him."

Cole asked, "How could they have known way back then how things were going to play out? It doesn't seem possible."

"I know, for someone to carry that kind of anger and need for revenge for so long seems incredible. We're still speculating at this point, but somehow Kraus found out about the stock arrangement many years ago and decided to get back at Roger Morrison. Unfortunately, you were the vehicle that he used to exact his revenge against Morrison and the FBI.

"When Roger Morrison set up the stock ownership of Gulf-Global Enterprises, he must have had some concerns about his partners, or at least Kraus. Hank Carlson didn't know this and assumed all those years that the stock had been evenly distributed among them. But Kraus knew better.

"After Morrison's death, his safe was opened, and that's when Carlson discovered he and Kraus had only been given 20% each. Roger had retained 60% ownership of the company for himself. The other caveat was that their shares of stock were non-transferable. They couldn't sell or assign their shares. At their death, their stock would be redistributed to the remaining principles. Kraus used that point to recruit Carlson into his plan. They were both upset after learning that Roger Morrison's shares *were* assignable. He assigned them to Barbara, so she would become the owner of 60% of the company.

"Roger Morrison had supposedly died of a heart attack. But now they think he might have been poisoned by Kraus and it was made to look like a heart attack. We won't know until we exhume Morrison's body.

"Kraus then tricked your wife into helping with this elaborate scheme, thinking she was helping you. He drugged her and got her to sign over her share of the company, having never realized she was the rightful owner.

"Kraus made Carlson's first task as the new CEO to rescind the stock restriction on the forty percent of the shares that they owned. With 100% of the company stock now transferable and in their control, Kraus had more plans.

"Kraus tricked Carlson into signing the sale of the company documents, and then poisoned him. He sold the company to those Chinese investors for a cash deal through Alan Sullivan. The Chinese investors weren't the ones interested in getting rid of you. They were only interested in acquiring the company.

"Sullivan had other clients willing to pay him to get you out of the picture so that offshore drilling could continue. Sullivan was playing both sides. He was paid by both Kraus and his oil clients.

"Kraus wanted the money, but he never intended to let them take over the company. We discovered through talking to other employees that Kraus had always thought he was the rightful owner of Gulf-Global Enterprises. So rather than letting someone else have it, he destroyed it and them with it."

Martin stopped speaking. Cole was staring across the room, the anguish plain on his face. "Why Barbara?" he asked. "She never harmed anyone."

"Senator Cole, I need to tell you —."

"Please," he interrupted. "I just want to be left alone for a while."

The door to the room popped open and Mackey stepped in and latched the door in the open position. "Irwin, you look like hell. You should take better care of yourself, especially when you're on vacation."

"I appreciate your concern," Cole replied dully.

Mackey stepped back out of the room and re-entered, walking backwards and pulling a wheelchair. He stopped and spun the chair toward the bed.

Cole gasped. "Barbara! You're alive!"

"I was trying to tell you," said Martin.

Barbara Cole's leg was in a cast, and her arm in a sling. She smiled broadly. "Irwin honey, I've missed you so much. I was so afraid I would never see you again."

They both began weeping openly. Agent Martin and Mackey were visibly moved as well. Mackey turned away to wipe his eyes.

Cole threw his covers aside and slung his legs off the bed, but was stopped by the monitor leads and IV line. The monitor let out a squelching alarm from a disconnected lead.

Mackey moved the wheelchair as close to the bed as he could, while trying to conceal his damp face.

Cole hugged Barbara gingerly with his gauze-covered arms. "My God, I thought you had been shot and killed."

Mackey jumped in. "She was shot, but Josh Kraus had put a Kevlar vest on her before he took her downstairs. Apparently, he had a suspicion about what his father was going to do. Barbara's one tough lady, though. She fell fifteen feet over a railing onto a stack of cardboard. She has a broken leg, a sprained arm, and I'm told a heck of a bruise on her chest."

"Irwin, I'm so sorry," wept Barbara. "I thought I was helping you."

"It's all right, baby. We were all tricked."

Martin's cell phone rang and she walked to the other side of the room to take the call.

The Coles continued their embrace, murmuring to each other.

"I'll be waiting out in the hall if you need anything," said Mackey.

A nurse rushed into the room. "There you are, Mrs. Cole. I couldn't find you anywhere. You're late for a test downstairs."

She started to move Barbara Cole toward the door. As she passed Mackey, she said, "Sir, we have rules around here that need to be followed."

Barbara Cole smiled tenderly at her husband. "Love you, Irwin."

"I love you too Barbara. Hurry back."

As the nurse exited with Barbara, Cole said, "I hope you don't land in the hospital, Mackey. That nurse would make your stay here a little difficult, I think."

"Nah, not at all, she likes me, I can tell." Mackey winked.

Martin came back across the room with a triumphant look. "You're not going to believe this. I just spoke with Agent Moore. He's at the headquarters of Gulf-Global Enterprises with the State Attorney's office, going through their files. He said he was in Hank Carlson's office, and he noticed an envelope in the incoming mail basket.

The packet was postmarked last week, but had never been opened. He opened the envelope and inside there were papers from Roger Morrison's personal attorney. This attorney, a Shawn Rizzo, was the executor of Roger's will and a good friend. He was instructed through the will, to verify sixty days after his death, that there weren't any concerns with the remaining partners. If the business was operating normally, he was to process the paperwork that would lift the transfer restriction on the 40% of the shares held by Carlson and Kraus. Also the remaining 60% of the shares originally held by Roger were to be split between the other two partners. The company would be 100% theirs to do with as they wished. I guess Mark Kraus wasn't as clever as he thought after all."

They were all quiet for a moment, digesting the new information.

Martin's phone rang again. "I'm beginning to realize how nice it actually could be to not have a phone for awhile."

She looked at the display. Cole recognized her expression. He had seen it several times, and it never brought good news. Martin glanced at Cole and then at Mackey, her face tense. She raised the phone to her ear. "Agent Martin."

"Agent Martin, it's so good to hear your voice. I hope I'm not catching you at a bad time."

"We were just talking about you, Mr. Kraus. We found it amusing to discover that Roger Morrison had left instructions with his attorney to transfer the company stock to you and Hank Carlson sixty days following his death. It kind of makes you look a bit foolish, don't you think?"

The line was silent and she winked at Cole and Mackey. "By the way, I'm sorry to disappoint you that your plan didn't work and we survived."

"To the contrary, Agent Martin, I would have been more disappointed had Senator Cole and yourself not made it out of that small predicament. Just to show there are no hard feelings, in the cabinet next to Senator Cole you'll find a small gift for the two of you. Have a good day, Agent Martin."

She shut her phone. "Kraus said he sent us a gift."

She went to the cabinet and pulled the drawer open, revealing a gift-wrapped package. As she reached in to take it out, Mackey shouted.

"Wait, don't touch that! Knowing Kraus it's probably an explosive of some sort."

"No, I don't think so this time," replied Martin. "Not this time. If he really wanted us dead he could have done it at any time. I think he enjoys having us around to show his superiority."

She looked over at Cole, who said, "I agree."

"Apparently you two know Kraus better than me," Mackey said.

She looked at Cole again, and he nodded. She lifted the package from the drawer, her hands quivering slightly. A single strip of tape held the colorful paper in place. Sliding her finger under the seam, she slid the paper off in one continuous move and it fell to the floor. She turned to Cole, her eyes wide. In her hands she was holding a brand new shiny book, with a dark-blue dust jacket.

###

Coming novel by Eric Dwyer

Timeless Pursuits

David Dawson was stuck in a dead-end career with a boss he hated. Following a flash of insight, he makes drastic changes bringing him one step closer to his life long dream of cruising the Caribbean aboard his own boat.

Just as everything seems to be going his way, including a new romance in his life, he finds himself unwittingly caught up in the pursuit of a mysterious object with the potential of bringing ultimate power and wealth to its owner.

The violent death of a friend and the threat of losing his newfound love compel him to engage in a battle against time itself. On the run, with both reality and his identity a distant memory, Dawson desperately tries to return to the cruising life he once knew.

His only hope of survival lies with a strange new acquaintance. . . Howard.

Timeless Pursuits is the first book of a mystery-thriller Trilogy.

Coming in the fall of 2012

For more information visit *www.ericdwyer.com*

About the author

Eric Dwyer grew up in Southwest Florida. As a child, he spent time fishing with his stepfather in Matlache and around Charlotte Harbor developing a great love of Gulf Coast life.

He spent most of his adult years working for a large corporation in Sarasota, Florida until opening his own corporate sponsored store in North Carolina. Wanting to return to his beloved Florida, he sold the store after 8 years and came home. He now now resides in Port Charlotte with his wife Marell, together cruising aboard their boat *Admarell* as often as possible.

www.ericdwyer.com

Made in the USA
Charleston, SC
16 April 2016